Riggs, Cynthia

The cranefly or-
chid murders

THE
CRANEFLY
ORCHID
MURDERS

———

ALSO BY CYNTHIA RIGGS

Deadly Nightshade

THE
CRANEFLY
ORCHID
MURDERS

CYNTHIA RIGGS

THOMAS DUNNE BOOKS
ST. MARTIN'S MINOTAUR
NEW YORK

THOMAS DUNNE BOOKS.
An imprint of St. Martin's Press.

www.minotaurbooks.com

Library of Congress Cataloging-in-Publication Data

Riggs, Cynthia.
    The cranefly orchid murders : a Martha's Vineyard mystery / Cynthia Riggs.
      p. cm.
  ISBN 0-312-30145-6
    1. Women detectives—Massachusetts—Martha's Vineyard—Fiction.
2. Martha's Vineyard (Mass.)—Fiction.   3. Aged women—Fiction.
I. Title.

PS3618.1394 C73 2002
813'.6—dc21

                                      2001058553

First Edition: May 2002

10 9 8 7 6 5 4 3 2 1

FOR

DIONIS COFFIN RIGGS
POET

1898–1997 = 99

ACKNOWLEDGMENTS

Many thanks to the same patient members of my writers' group, friends, associates, teachers, bed-and-breakfast guests, and relatives who read and critiqued both *Deadly Nightshade* and *The Cranefly Orchid Murders*. Arlene Silva, an expert nudger, deserves repeated thanks for urging me to go back to school for my MFA at Vermont College.

I'm not sure I can ever express enough gratitude to my plot doctor, Jonathan Revere, who nurses me through bouts of temper, tears, and writer's block, tosses weird plot twists to me, minds Britty every time I take off, fixes my computer when it gets temperamental, keeps my guests returning for his breakfast repartee, and keeps me more or less sane.

Kevin and Duncan Green not only decoded my cryptic letters, but read and corrected the parts involving Victoria's eleven-year-old assistant. Forgive me, Brendan O'Neill, director of the Vineyard Conservation Society, if I got the cranefly orchid spiraling the wrong way.

Again, thanks to my agent, Nancy Love, and my St. Martin's Press editor, Ruth Cavin. Thank you to assistant editor Julie Sullivan and to copyeditor Edwin Chapman.

I hope Police Chief Beth Toomey, West Tisbury's real police chief, will forgive me again for the liberties I have taken with our town's police procedures. My fictional Casey, like Chief Toomey, is an off-Islander working in a traditionally male job on a fairly small island. That's as far as the resemblance is meant to go.

—CYNTHIA RIGGS

THE
CRANEFLY
ORCHID
MURDERS

———

CHAPTER 1

When she heard a knock on her door right after Christmas, Phoebe Eldredge was ready to invite the missionaries in for tea and cookies. The only people who called on her without telephoning first, especially this time of year, were Jehovah's Witnesses or the Mormons. They usually were young, usually came in pairs, and usually were dressed nicely, not in Vineyard chic of torn jeans and ratty sweaters that Islanders, young and old, favored.

Phoebe lived alone at the end of a dirt road off Tea Lane. Her house was on the bare rock-strewn top of a wooded hill, surrounded by two hundred acres of woods, fields, marshes, and hills. Her property included the great Sachem's Rock.

She was disappointed when the caller turned out to be a slim, small woman, much too stylishly dressed in a dark red coat, matching hat, and black high-heeled boots, and carrying a briefcase. The woman had parked her large gray car in front of Phoebe's herb garden, blocking the view from the parlor windows of the ice pond at the foot of the hill.

"Yes?" Phoebe's voice didn't hold the warmth she would have used for young missionaries.

"Phoebe Eldredge?" The woman held out her black-gloved hand.

Phoebe put hers under the apron she was wearing and the woman withdrew her hand and clutched the briefcase instead.

"Yes, I'm Mrs. Eldredge." Phoebe waited.

"My name is Karen Underwood, and I'm from CARP." She smiled, showing small white teeth with a smear of lipstick on them.

Phoebe waited, her hands still clasped under the apron, a frilly thing her daughter Janice had given her years ago when they were still on speaking terms.

"Have you heard of CARP, Phoebe?"

"I'm Mrs. Eldredge."

"I'm sorry. Mrs. Eldredge." The woman had the grace to blush. "Have you heard of CARP, Mrs. Eldredge?" She remained standing on the granite step at Phoebe's front door.

Phoebe stared at the woman without answering, pale eyes squinting in the sunshine, white hair wispy around her face.

"CARP is 'Conservation Acres Real Property,' a new concept in land preservation," Karen said.

Phoebe waited. She had a hunch this was another slick real estate person trying to buy her land. She had already talked with Josiah Coffin about a conservation restriction on the property, and Josiah and his assistant, Zachariah West, were working on it.

Taxes had gone up so high she could no longer afford to keep the old place. Thirteen generations on this land and it looked as if she would be the unlucky one who would lose it.

"I'd like to talk with you, Mrs. Eldredge."

"May I ask what about?" Phoebe stood in her doorway.

"CARP would like to make a presentation to you on innovative ways to preserve your land. May I come in?"

"I'm not interested," Phoebe said.

"You're not interested in preserving your land?" The woman looked and sounded appalled.

Phoebe was silent.

"There's no obligation." Karen shifted her briefcase in front of her and held it with both gloved hands.

"I said, I'm not interested."

"It will take only about fifteen minutes of your time, and it's really quite a fascinating presentation." The woman's voice quavered slightly.

"I don't have fifteen minutes to spare."

"I've come all the way from Boston today to see you."

Phoebe started to close her door, right in the face of Karen Underwood. "Next time call first."

As the door closed, Phoebe saw with astonishment that Karen's chin was trembling, and realized she was about to cry.

Phoebe opened the door again. "Come in," she said gruffly.

"Thank you." Karen stepped over the front doorsill into Phoebe's parlor, pulled off her black gloves, drew a white hanky out of her coat pocket, and dabbed carefully at her eyes, patting around the dark eyeliner.

"What's this presentation you have?" Phoebe muttered.

"Let me show you," Karen said more brightly than Phoebe had expected, and set her briefcase on Phoebe's mahogany table.

"Not there. Not on my table."

"I'm so sorry." Karen looked around the small parlor and finally laid the briefcase on the ancient carpet, its Oriental nap worn through to burlap backing.

Phoebe wiped the tabletop with her apron. This Boston woman was too stylish, too rapidly recovered. Phoebe remained standing and clasped her hands underneath her apron again. "Get on with it. I don't have all day."

Karen Underwood perched on the couch and bent over her open briefcase, angling her booted feet away from her body as if she were posing for some fashion magazine. Her hair, too black and too curly and too long, fell in front of her face. She brushed it back behind her shoulders.

"It's so kind of you to let me intrude like this." Karen looked up, brown eyes bright. "It was rude of me not to call first. I'm so sorry."

"Yes. Well."

Karen brought out glossy colored brochures and laid them

on the couch next to her. She brought out a plastic-covered report with a title in large letters that Phoebe could read from this distance, "Sachem's Rock Property," and her name, "Phoebe Eldredge" underneath.

Phoebe felt as if she had let a skunk into her hen house. This slick presentation with her name on it must have cost a pretty penny. "Look, Miz Underwood, I'm not interested after all." Phoebe went to the door and opened it. "Please leave."

Karen looked up in apparent consternation. "But Mrs. Eldredge, I've come all this way."

"Next time call first. I'm in the phone book." Phoebe held the door open.

"Won't you even listen to me?" The woman was beginning to look and sound more and more like Phoebe's daughter, and Phoebe had wanted nothing to do with Janice for the past twelve years.

"Please leave. You're letting cold air in."

Karen Underwood carefully placed her brochures back in her briefcase and got to her feet. "I'm so sorry, Mrs. Eldredge. Apparently I've offended you in some way."

Phoebe remained silent, remained by the open door.

Karen crossed the room, stepped down onto the large granite entrance stone, got into the big gray car, started it up with a puff of transparent blue vapor, and drove away. The car bounced over rocks in the rutted road. Phoebe watched it disappear into the trees below the crest of the hill.

Then she called Josiah Coffin's number at the Conservation Trust. She got the answering machine, and hung up.

In Santa Barbara several weeks later Phoebe Eldredge's granddaughter Melissa learned through an item in the weekly *Island Enquirer*, to which she subscribed, that her grandmother was negotiating with a conservation group to sell the family land. Melissa's first thought was to call an

4

attorney, since she and her grandmother weren't on the best of terms. The only Island attorney whose name she could remember was a Montgomery Mausz. She debated with herself for a couple of hours before she finally called the long distance operator and got the number. When Mr. Mausz turned out to be a sympathetic listener, Melissa talked to him for almost an hour.

She was sitting on the unmade futon on the floor of the room she shared with Butch on East Victoria Street, her legs crossed under her, the receiver tucked against her shoulder. She played with the silver rings on her bare toes, twisting them around and around as she talked.

Mr. Mausz murmured understandingly when she told him her father and aunt were estranged from her grandmother and that she was probably the only one in the family on speaking terms with the old lady, and just barely. She was probably her grandmother's heir, she told Mr. Mausz.

She got up from the futon, the cordless telephone still held against her shoulder, took a bottle of nail polish from the bathroom cabinet, and sat at the spindly table she'd bought at the flea market. She opened the bottle and put her foot up on the other chair. She stuffed cotton between her toes and began to paint her nails, a nice glittery dark blue.

Mr. Mausz was such a sensitive listener, she found herself telling him family stuff, like how her grandmother and Aunt Janice had quarreled over her aunt's third marriage to a Nigerian taxi driver, and how weird her father was after Vietnam.

She finished painting the toes of one foot, set that foot on the floor, and started on the toes of the other foot.

She found herself telling Mr. Mausz something she had never told anyone else, not even Butch. She told him how her father and her mother had gotten into an argument after her father had come home from the war. She had been three years old, and now, almost twenty-five years later, she still remembered that argument as clearly as though she was see-ing it on a movie screen. Her father had hit her mother, over and over and over, awful, sickening thuds of fist against flesh. Her mother screamed until she had no scream left in her. Melissa could still remember, as clearly as when it hap-pened, how her mother's screams turned into whimpers and then silence. She remembered the sound of her father's boots in the downstairs hall, how the door slammed. She still could see the upstairs hall mirror bounce on the wall over her head when he slammed the door. She remembered his footsteps on the porch, the squeak of the loose step, the crunch of his boots on the concrete sidewalk, his steps fading away. Her father had walked out of their lives. She had never seen him again.

Melissa was crying now, feeling sorrier for herself than she had for some time. Mr. Mausz listened attentively three thou-sand miles away. Melissa tugged a tissue out of a box on the windowsill and blotted her nose, careful not to snag the tis-sue on the two gold studs on the left side of her nostril.

What about her mother, Attorney Mausz had asked.

The neighbors had come to the house when they heard the screams, she told him. They took her mother to the hospital and found Melissa, huddled in the upstairs closet under coats that smelled like stale cigarette smoke. Whenever she smelled stale smoke or worn shoes she remembered that closet and that day.

She stood, now that the toenail polish had set, and moved the curtain aside so she could look down onto the street, still holding the phone against her shoulder. She and Butch lived on the second floor of a Spanish-style house where they had one big room, a kitchenette, and a bath.

Melissa told Mr. Mausz about Butch, and how she made jewelry to sell at the Saturday street fair under the tall palm trees. She told him her dreams about returning to Martha's Vineyard where she used to go summers. Her mother had never divorced her father, Melissa said. She told Mr. Mausz she was the only one in the family who knew that her mother was still in Santa Barbara, living with an abalone fisherman on a boat in the city harbor marina.

Mr. Mausz mentioned something she'd often thought about, and that was tracing her father. Her mother didn't want to. Vietnam had done a number on a lot of the guys who'd fought in it, Mr. Mausz said. But Melissa didn't have the kind of money a search like that would cost. Besides, she wasn't sure she wanted to find the bastard who'd beaten up her mother and then walked away from them like that. Yet she wondered sometimes what had happened to him. Did he ever think of his wife and daughter? Did he ever feel sorry he'd walked out on them years ago? Mostly, though, when it came to her father, she didn't give a shit.

She didn't realize until after she'd hung up that Mr. Mausz had said nothing about the possible sale of the family land and what she could do about it, the reason she had called him.

She re-read the item in the *Island Enquirer* and got still more concerned. She would have to see for herself what her grandmother was up to. This didn't seem to be something she could discuss with the old lady over the phone, since they usually argued within the first minute. She hadn't seen her grandmother for a couple of years. Even though this was February, perhaps it was a good time to visit, to talk to her in person. Melissa decided to wait until she got to Martha's Vineyard before she called, so her grandmother couldn't talk her out of the trip.

Melissa threw stuff into her backpack—her ski parka, underclothes, and a couple of sweaters—and caught the shuttle to Los Angeles, the red-eye to Boston, took the bus to Woods Hole, the ferry to Vineyard Haven. It was a lot colder in New England than she had remembered. The wind coming off the water brought tears to her eyes. She was wearing the gray sweatshirt with UCSB in large block letters across the front that had been plenty warm for California. Once she was on the ferry she went up the metal stairs into the snack bar, bought a cup of herbal tea, sat at one of the tables, took her down jacket out of her backpack, shook it out, and snuggled into it.

When they docked, she called her grandmother. There was no answer. Melissa hadn't eaten since yesterday noon, so she walked the short distance to the ArtCliff Diner to get some breakfast or lunch, she wasn't sure which. Time was all screwed up. Once she'd had something to eat she would hitchhike to her grandmother's.

When she entered the ArtCliff, Dottie, who'd been the waitress ever since Melissa could remember, greeted her, and Melissa sat at one of the small tables against the wall.

"How you doing, honey? Haven't seen you for some time." Dottie dropped a plastic-covered menu in front of her.

"I just got in from California," Melissa said. "I guess I want some lunch. I'm still on Pacific Time."

"The quahog chowder's fresh today. Pork chops, meatloaf, chicken-fried steak. You need something solid, cold day like today. They're calling for snow later."

"A salad," Melissa said. "No meat."

"I forgot you're one of those California gals now, alfalfa sprouts and tofu. Hope you brought warm clothes." Dottie scooped up the menu. "Visiting your grandma up-Island? I hear she's thinking of selling that property of hers."

"That's why I'm here. I was talking to Mr. Mausz about it just yesterday," Melissa said.

"Him!" Dottie practically spat out the word. "Why were you talking to him, for crying out loud? He represents the real estate guy who's been hounding your grandma."

Melissa felt blood drain out of her face. "He does? Harry Ness? Mr. Mausz represents Harry Ness?"

"That's what I hear," Dottie said. "Are you okay, honey? I didn't mean to give you a shock."

"He never told me he was representing that sleaze." Melissa looked up at Dottie, who was tucking a pencil behind her ear. "I told him all this stuff I shouldn't have."

Melissa was dimly aware of several men sitting at a round table in the corner, the same men who always gathered there. She heard the bray-like laugh of one of them. Heard male banter.

Dottie shook her head. "Mausz is a full-blooded sleaze himself, honey," she said. "Want Roquefort, Ranch, French, Italian, or Lemon Dill dressing on your salad?"

"I can't believe I told him all the stuff I did. And he listened! And he didn't say a thing."

"You could report him to the Board of Bar Overseers," Dottie said. "Only trouble is, they're all part of the same good-ole-boy network." She wrote something on her pad. "The Lemon Dill is nice. I'll give you that. And a couple of poppy-seed rolls."

While Melissa was eating, halfway listening to the kidding at the corner table, she noticed the sky had clouded over. A few flakes of snow drifted in front of the window.

Dottie came by with the check. "They say it's going down to the twenties for the next couple of days," she said. "Dress warm! Tell your grandma I was asking for her."

Melissa hadn't thought to pack gloves. When she stepped outside, her breath steamed around her face. A cold wind blew off the harbor. Back home, people who'd bought stuff from the nursery a couple of blocks from her place were probably planting their six-packs of flowers. She shivered, pushed her free hand deep into her pocket, and thrust her thumb out. Almost immediately, a red Volvo station wagon driven by an elderly woman stopped.

"Awfully cold to be standing out here," the woman said. "We can take you as far as North Road."

"Thanks," Melissa said. "That'll be great." Melissa climbed into the back seat. By now the snow was falling thickly.

"Where are you heading?" the man in the front seat asked.

"I'm going to my grandmother's," Melissa answered. "She lives off Tea Lane. Sachem's Rock."

"You must be Phoebe Eldredge's granddaughter," the man said. "Don't you live in California?"

"Santa Barbara." Melissa set her backpack on the seat.

"Bet you don't see weather like this often," the man said.

The woman turned on the windshield wipers, and hunched tensely over the wheel. Melissa found herself just as tense, waiting for a skid on the now slick pavement. No one spoke. The five-mile drive seemed interminable.

When they got to the big oak tree where North Road branched off, the woman slowed cautiously.

"Be careful now," the woman said. "It's awfully slippery."

Melissa lifted her backpack off the seat. "Bye. And thanks."

After the car had gone, Melissa got a ride in a pickup truck driven by a guy about her own age. She climbed in and blew on her chilled hands to warm them.

"How far you going?" he asked as he started up again.

"Tea Lane?" Melissa made it a question. "Mrs. Eldredge's?"

"I know the place," he said. "Nice property." He pronounced it *propahty*. "Be glad to take you right there."

"That's okay. I need the walk."

"You sure? It's a long hike."

He let her off where Tea Lane joined the main road. She thanked him and set off down the lane.

Tea Lane looked the same as it always had. Except for the trees that now overhung it, the lane had probably not changed much since before the Revolutionary War, when the tea smuggler lived along here somewhere. It was a sandy cart track with high banks lined with tufts of brown poverty grass. Sheep had once grazed on either side of the lane. Melissa still remembered hidden stone walls that once had fenced open pastures. When she was little she used to explore old cellar holes that were remnants of a small settlement. Her grandmother's was the only house still standing.

She turned left onto a narrow road that led up the hill toward the house. Melissa's were the first tracks in the snow. She had called her grandmother before she left the diner, but again there had been no answer. Her grandmother might be digging up parsnips this time of year, or who knows what.

At one point Melissa thought she heard voices, but decided it was the wind. No one would be around here this time of year, especially not on a day like this. She could remember wind-voices from her childhood that sounded exactly like people at a cocktail party. She had heard laughter and even distinct words. Now the wind-voices sounded like people arguing. She shivered and tucked her hands deeper into the pockets of her parka.

She came out of the oak woods into a clearing and there was the house, a curl of smoke coming out of the chimney. It was a typical old Vineyard farmhouse, gray-shingled, with a roof that sloped down to the first-floor windows, and a second-floor window at each end. She took a deep breath, not sure how her grandmother would receive her, and tried to walk confidently the hundred yards or so to the front door. She stepped up on the snow-covered granite stone and knocked.

Her grandmother came to the door, frail-looking in a large brown cardigan with sagging pockets and a soiled apron. One hand held a checked dishtowel, the other hand was braced against the doorframe as if to keep intruders out. She looked down at Melissa from where she stood in the doorway.

"Hi, Grandma, it's me, Melissa. From California." Steam puffed out of her nose and mouth. She smiled brightly.

"So I see." Her grandmother moved aside for Melissa to step up from the granite stone, and closed the door behind her.

"May I ask what brings you here? I suppose you just happened to be passing through?"

"I thought it was time I came to visit you," Melissa said. The two faced each other just inside the front door.

"In February?" Her grandmother's expression was pure disapproval.

"Well, it seemed like a good time, you know."

"No, I don't know," her grandmother said. "It wouldn't have anything to do with that item in last week's *Enquirer*, would it?"

"What do you mean?" Melissa avoided her grandmother's eyes.

"Never mind. Are you planning to stay here in this house? And for how long, if I may be so bold as to ask?"

"Well, I had thought so, you know, if it's okay with you."

"It's not convenient, if that's what you're asking, but I don't see that I have much choice, do I? And for how long?"

Melissa said nothing, simply stood there in the parlor with her backpack in her hand, her down jacket partly unzipped. The parlor looked the same, with its horsehair sofa, worn carpet, and mahogany table. Her grandmother moved into the parlor and flicked the surface of the table with her dishtowel.

"I don't suppose you've had anything to eat, have you?" Her grandmother clasped her hands together under her apron.

"I ate something at the ArtCliff. Dottie asked for you."

"That place. Well, put your things upstairs in your old room. It's not made up. I wasn't expecting company."

Once Melissa had swept away the cobwebs that hung from the bedposts, from the curtains, across the mirror, and from the sloping ceiling in the chilly room; once she had changed her clothes, put her things away, and made up her bed, she decided she should confront her grandmother directly.

"Are you really thinking of selling the land to that conservation group?" she asked when she found her grandmother in the kitchen scraping carrots.

"I don't see that's any concern of yours." Her grandmother continued to scrape.

"It's part of my heritage too." Melissa leaned against the kitchen doorframe.

"Oh? What makes you think that?"

"My father was the fourteenth generation on this land. I'm the fifteenth."

"Your father? Hah! Don't mention his name in this house."

"But I'm your granddaughter, you know. Your *only* grandkid."

"You are, eh? Fifteenth generation on this land? I don't think so. Look at you. Nose rings and tattoos like some Fiji Islander. Hair colored like a parrot. That may be the way they do things in California, but not in my house. You think I'd claim you as granddaughter? A greedy tart who comes to see me when she thinks she'll get something out of me, hey? You and your father."

"My father," Melissa said softly. "Have you seen my father?"

Her grandmother ignored her. "Don't think I don't know all about your mother living on some derelict boat with a fisherman. Whore! And still married to that man she calls your father."

"Where did you get that from?" Melissa asked, but she knew.

"I have my sources." Her grandmother brushed her wispy hair out of her eyes with the back of her wrist, the knotted veins of her hand standing out like cords. "I suppose you

13

want this land so you can start an artists' colony with that so-called tattoo artist you live with."

Melissa had a sick feeling in her stomach. What else had she told Montgomery Mausz? What had he told her grandmother? What could she do to stop him? Or was it too late?

Chapter 2

When Victoria Trumbull heard the crows, it was almost a month after Melissa's visit to her grandmother, Phoebe Eldredge. Victoria was hiking along the trail to Sachem's Rock, carrying in her gnarled hand an oak branch that she'd picked up to use as a walking stick. In her other hand she held a cloth bag with an orange, a notebook, and her navy blue baseball cap. Spring was in the air and she wanted to be out in it, writing poetry by the big rock. Victoria shifted the stick into her left hand and brushed her white hair off her forehead.

It was odd to hear crows so far from the hayfields where they usually gathered.

Tree roots stretched across the steep path where it wound among oaks and beech trees. Victoria put her feet down carefully, watching the ground beneath her, sandy soil with a covering of pine needles, acorns, and twisted rope-like roots. The beech trees still wore the bright gold leaves they'd kept all winter. Spring growth would push them off in a few weeks.

Sunlight filtered through the oaks and touched a bed of brilliant green moss, almost fluorescent in the drab brown and gray woods, a contrast to the tree trunks and rocks splotched with gray lichen. Victoria stopped to catch her breath and leaned on her stick.

The crows continued to squabble over something.

Above her, bare branches formed a lacework against the bright sky. Somewhere below her she heard a redwing blackbird carol in the wetlands. Another called in response.

Victoria had started up the path again, walking slowly, flicking acorns with her stick, when she saw the crows, a flock of them on the ground ahead of her and up to her right. They were worrying over something, carrion, she supposed, a dead skunk, or, when she got closer and the crows flew up in a raucous flurry, something much bigger. A deer, perhaps.

She moved slowly. At ninety-two Victoria was not as agile as she had been a few years earlier. She did not intend to fall and break something and have her granddaughter fuss about her walking in the woods by herself. As it was, Elizabeth was going to be upset because she had hitchhiked to the place where the overgrown path to the rock began.

More people should hitchhike on the Island, Victoria mused as she approached whatever it was the crows had found. All she had to do was stand by the side of the road, smile, and point her thumb in the direction she wanted to go. It was usually Islanders who picked her up, often someone she knew. This morning it had been a pickup truck, and the driver had gone out of his way to drop her off on North Road.

Perhaps she'd find a pair of antlers on the deer, if that's what it was. She would take them home in the cloth bag.

Victoria had to climb to reach the spot. She slid the bag up her arm to free her left hand, pushed aside the huckleberry bushes with her stick, and grabbed hold of a sassafras sapling to hoist herself up the bank. Thank goodness for her sturdy hiking shoes. Elizabeth had cut a hole in the top for her arched-up toe.

She noticed mayflower leaves underfoot, and thought how nonsensical it was to call them an endangered species. If you knew where to look, they were all over the place. She and Elizabeth would have to come back in another month when the sweet-scented delicate pink flowers would be in bloom.

Before she could identify what it was the crows had found, she smelled it, a putrid stench that drove the remembered sweet scent of mayflowers out of her mind and made her gag. Victoria reached into the pocket of her gray corduroy trousers and brought out a flowered napkin from Thursday's senior center luncheon. She held it over her nose. She hadn't realized dead game smelled quite so horrid. She wasn't so sure, after all, that she wanted to detach the antlers, even if they were perfect ones. But she would investigate what it was before she returned to the path.

When she reached the spot, a clearing floored with reindeer moss and wild cranberry, she didn't immediately absorb what she was seeing. What had appeared to be gray lichen, green moss, and brown twigs, turned out to have unnaturally straight lines. As she focused on it she realized it was a plaid wool shirt. What had at first glance seemed to be moss-covered rock, became tweed trousers. And at the bottom of the trousers were hiking boots with new-looking lugged soles. Only after she'd finished examining the shirt and what was below it, did she dare look at what must have been the face, the part on which the crows had been feeding.

Victoria hustled back to the road, her oak stick thrust in front of her, her feet stumbling over pine needles and acorns and roots. She flagged down the first car that came along.

The girl in the passenger seat looked at her uncertainly.

"I need a ride into West Tisbury." Victoria was out of breath. She didn't know either the girl or the boy who was driving, but they seemed nice enough.

"Are you okay?" The girl opened the passenger door and moved over to let her slide in.

"I found something up in the woods," Victoria said. "I need to get to the police station, quickly. Can you take me there?"

"Yes, ma'am." The boy reached across the girl to fasten Victoria's seat belt, and reached out still farther to slam the car door shut.

The girl looked at Victoria with concern. "What did you find?" she asked.

"I'm not sure," said Victoria. "It's something I need to tell the police chief about, though."

The boy pulled away from the side of the road with a squeal of tires on sand. The green cardboard pine tree hanging from the rearview mirror swung back and forth. Victoria held onto the window crank.

"Is there anything we can do?" the girl asked.

"No, thank you. I think it's a police matter."

The car's wide front seat was covered with furry material, patterned in black and white like a Holstein cow. Victoria took a deep breath. She would put out of her mind what she'd seen up at the rock until she talked to the police chief.

They flew down North Road toward town until they were slowed by a tractor inching along in front of them. The boy honked his horn, and the tractor driver, without looking around, held up his left hand in a gesture that clearly said, "What's your hurry?"

At a wide place in the road, the tractor pulled off to the side and the boy swerved around it. Victoria waved at the driver, Asa Bodman's oldest son, Ira. He returned her wave before they rounded the curve by the old ice pond and were out of sight of him.

On the left the hayfield at Seven Gates Farm was showing spring green through winter stubble, and the trees beyond were touched with a haze of pink. The hayfield was dotted with black crows. One flew up in a flurry of wings and settled back on the field again as they passed. Victoria wondered if the crows were the same ones she'd disturbed up on the hill.

She didn't feel like talking and the boy and girl were silent too. The car sped around the road's tight curves and plunged into the dappled lattice-like shade of overhanging bare trees. The girl sat with one hand on the boy's thigh, looking straight ahead except for an occasional worried glance at Victoria. Victoria shifted slightly in her seat.

"Do you have enough room?" the girl asked. She brushed her mop of curly hair away from her face and moved closer to the boy. Victoria nodded.

They crossed the narrow bridge over Mill Brook. Victoria could see the early hooded shoots of skunk cabbage, bright green fingers poking up along the marshy edges of the brook. She did not want to think about what she'd found near the big rock.

The boy slowed for the curve around the cemetery and sped up again on the straight stretch where the road tunneled under arching maples.

At Brandy Brow he turned left, passed between the mill pond and the old mill, and pulled into the oyster-shell parking area in front of the police station.

"Want us to wait?" The boy held the car door for Victoria, and helped her out.

"No, thank you," she said. "The police chief will give me a ride home."

Two Muscovy ducks nipped at her feet as Victoria hustled past, their mottled red and black heads outstretched. At the station house steps she turned and waved to the boy and girl.

The police station was a small shingled building that, years ago, had served as a one-room school. The front door faced the old mill across the road, the west windows overlooked the mill pond. Swans were feeding on something under the surface, their tails up in the air like white elfin caps.

Victoria opened the door. "Anybody home?" she called in. When she didn't see the chief, she went outside again. Chief Mary Kathleen O'Neill was behind the station house, scooping cracked corn out of a plastic trash barrel. She hurled a scoop full of corn toward the flock of ducks and geese that had gathered around her. Victoria watched the creatures flut-

19

ter around the chief's stocky figure, honking, quacking, and hissing.

The chief, who was called "Casey," dusted off her hands, wiped her boots on the back of her uniform trousers, and looked up with a pleased smile.

"Hey, there, Victoria. What's up?"

Victoria knew the chief well enough to come right to the point. "I think we have a problem at Sachem's Rock, Casey." Her voice was solemn.

Casey's smile faded. "Serious?"

Victoria nodded.

"Come inside." Casey climbed the wooden steps, two at a time, opened the door for Victoria, and followed her into the small office. Victoria sat primly in the wooden chair in front of the chief's desk, hung her cloth bag from the arm of the chair, and unbuttoned her blue quilted coat.

She told Casey what she'd found, the crows, the smell, and the plaid shirt. Casey listened, both elbows on her desk, hands clasped in front of her.

"We'll go there right away," Casey said when Victoria finished. "First I need to call the medical examiner." She ran her finger down a list thumbtacked to the wall under the calendar. "Doc Jeffers is on duty at the hospital this week." She picked up the phone. "Once I see what's up there, I'll radio him from the Bronco. If it's human remains, he needs to see them in place."

Victoria stood and buttoned her coat again. She fished her blue baseball cap out of her cloth bag and walked over to the small mirror on the closet door. She settled the cap on her hair and tilted her head until she was satisfied with the way it looked. Gold stitched lettering across the front read, "West Tisbury Police, Deputy."

"Looking good." The chief smiled at her ancient deputy and hung up the phone. She lifted her red-gold hair out from the neck of the Navy sweater she'd pulled on, and fastened her heavy equipment belt around her waist. She wrote a note for her sergeant, Junior Norton, and left it under a rounded beach stone on the tidy desk he shared with the two patrolmen. She followed Victoria out of the door, pulled it shut behind them, and pushed it to make sure it was latched.

"The selectmen still haven't decided to install locks," Casey said. "Anybody can walk in."

At Victoria's puzzled expression Casey added, "You've got to remember I come from the city where cops lock stuff up. I'm not used to people walking in any old time."

Once Victoria had settled herself into the passenger seat of the Bronco, Casey took off. Past the mill pond, past the cemetery, past Whiting's fields, onto North Road. Asa's son was turning the tractor in at the entrance to Seven Gates.

Casey parked the Bronco on the left side of the road near the path. She locked both doors, and Victoria laughed.

"I intend to lock up stuff, Victoria, whether you do or not," Casey said defensively.

They retraced Victoria's route next to the brook, past the overgrown field, and up the hill. The crows were still feeding. The stench was still awful.

Victoria waited beside the path. She sat on a fallen tree while Casey climbed to where the crows were assembled. When she approached they flew up in an angry black cloud, cawing curses at the chief.

Casey was gone what seemed to Victoria a long time. When she finally climbed back down the slope to the path, her boots slipping on the wet leaves under the huckleberry, her face was pale. She and Victoria walked back to the Bronco without speaking. Victoria lifted herself up into the passenger seat, and Casey called the hospital's emergency room on the radio.

"I need to talk with Doc Jeffers." She turned to Victoria. "I have to watch what I say. Half the people on the Island have scanners."

When Doc Jeffers responded, Casey said into the mike, "I'm where I told you I'd be. You better have a look."

"I'll be there, twenty minutes, a half hour."

While they waited, Victoria stared out of the passenger side window at the stone wall on the other side of the road and the grapevines that formed a twisted network behind it. She didn't want to think about why they were here. She thought instead about wild grapes. There would be a good crop this fall. She would come back in October and pick some for jelly.

Finally Casey broke the silence. "There's not much left of his face. A lot of fuzzy gray hair, beard, sideburns. His hair and beard must have stuck out five or six inches from his face and head. He's dressed in expensive clothes, Pendleton wool shirt, Irish tweed trousers, handmade leather boots."

Victoria thought for a while. "You know who fits that description, fuzzy hair and beard? Montgomery Mausz, the attorney for the real estate developer, Harry Ness."

" 'Loch' Ness?"

Victoria nodded. "Mr. Mausz lived on North Water Street in Edgartown up until a month or so ago. His wife tossed him out because of another woman."

"Yeah?" Casey looked at Victoria with interest.

"Someone said he's in Aruba with the other woman."

"Maybe not," said Casey.

There was a roar on the road behind them. Victoria looked in the rearview mirror and saw a huge motorcycle, its metallic blue finish glittering in the sun. The biker himself was encased in black leather and wore a helmet that matched the bike. Tiny blue lights across the top of the helmet blinked like Christmas tree ornaments. Two small white wings stuck out on either side. The biker pulled over, cut his engine, lifted his right leg over the seat of the bike, kicked down the stand with his booted foot, and pulled off his helmet to expose a thatch of white hair, rimless glasses, and a jutting jaw.

"Where's the corpse, Chief?" He detached a black leather medical bag from the carrier on the back of the bike and unzipped his jacket. Beneath it he wore a light green hospital scrub shirt with curls of white hair in the V of its neck.

Casey stepped out of the Bronco and strode over to Doc Jeffers, who was much taller than the chief. Victoria looked at his feet. His boots were festooned with steel chains.

Victoria led the way at first, then let Casey and Doc Jeffers go on ahead of her. She sat on a fallen log and waited until they returned.

"It looks like Mickey Mausz, all right," Doc Jeffers announced. "Whacked on the side of the head. Been dead awhile. Several weeks, I'd guess. Maybe a month." He sighed. "Would be the week I'm on duty."

"Not natural causes, I gather?" Victoria said.

Doc Jeffers shook his head. "Not unless he happened to hit the side of his head hard on something like a rock. I didn't see any rocks up there."

"I need to take some papers to Junior," Casey told Victoria, as she held the Bronco door for the older woman. Junior Norton lived down one of the unmarked roads that branched off the sandy Quansoo road.

"I must say, I'm glad to have you along to help me find places, Victoria. Without you it would take me months—years—to learn who lives where."

Victoria settled herself in the passenger seat and adjusted her cap with a faint smile. "What do you suppose Montgomery Mausz was doing at Sachem's Rock? He wasn't even near the path."

Doc Jeffers had examined the corpse. Casey called in the state police who brought in the state forensics people, and they, in turn, had gone over the scene. After that, Toby, the undertaker, drove the remains off-Island for an autopsy.

Casey lifted her shoulders in a shrug. Victoria continued.

23

"A month ago it was cold and snowy. It went down to the twenties. He wasn't wearing a jacket, was he? Only a wool shirt. Did he have a hat on? Or gloves?"

"Good question." Casey pulled off the road into the huckleberry brush to let a Jeep pass them. The driver waved. Casey waved back.

"Who was that?" she asked Victoria.

Victoria turned to look at the Jeep that was disappearing in a swirl of dust. "One of the women from the garden club."

Casey eased back onto the road. It had not rained for more than a week. Dust kicked up in the one-lane road settled on the Bronco and drifted in through the half-open windows. Victoria sneezed and blew her nose on the napkin from her pocket, then looked out at the undergrowth along the sides of the road.

"Stop!" she suddenly cried out.

Casey jammed on the brakes with a squeal. The Bronco bucked and stalled. She looked at Victoria, alarmed. "What's up?"

"Boxberries grow here. We should be able to find berries this time of year, if the pheasants haven't eaten them all."

Casey put her head down on the steering wheel in dismay, and her hair fell over her face. "Don't do this to me, Victoria," she muttered. "You're going to give me a heart attack."

Victoria opened the passenger door and slid out. "One doesn't usually get heart attacks at your age."

Dark red-green boxberry leaves carpeted the ground under the oak trees. Victoria brushed aside the leathery leaves and picked a handful of the red berries that dangled like miniature Japanese lanterns underneath.

"Better get back in, someone's behind us." Casey started the engine. Victoria turned and waved at the car behind.

She offered the berries to Casey, who looked away from the road briefly, took one and nibbled it. "Wintergreen. Nice." She looked in the rearview mirror. "Who's *that*?"

24

Victoria turned to look. "Zack West. He lives on this road not far from Junior. He's a biologist with the Conservation Trust." Victoria eyed Casey. "He's single. About your age."

"I'm not interested, Victoria. Once was enough."

Victoria settled her blue quilted coat underneath her. "I'll have you and Zack over for baked beans some Saturday night."

"No, no, no, Victoria. You tried that before, and the guy was gay."

Victoria changed the subject. "I haven't been down this road all winter." She cranked down her window.

"Junior probably isn't home, Victoria. It's his day off."

"I'm sure he doesn't lock his door." Victoria looked sideways at the chief, who smiled.

When Junior's father, Ben Norton, had retired as police chief, the selectmen, instead of promoting Junior, advertised off-Island and hired Casey O'Neill. After a few tense weeks things settled down and Junior had adjusted to working as Casey's sergeant.

Casey slowed and turned onto a rutted road with a grassy hump in the middle. Ahead of them the Great Pond spread out like a sheet of blue-gray glass.

"He told me he'd be fishing at the opening when the tide changes," Casey said. "Can you tell what it's doing now?"

Victoria sat up straight in the passenger seat so she could see across the Pond to the opposite shore. "It looks as though the tide has started to turn. It's beginning to run out."

"I'll leave the papers on his kitchen table, then."

Junior's camp was a one-story shack cobbled together with driftwood and scrounged lumber from construction jobs around the Island. It was on a low bluff overlooking the Great Pond. From the bluff Victoria could see Junior's father's place on the opposite shore. On clear days, Ben's gray shingled house stood out distinctly against the trees. Victoria could even make out Ben Norton's figure walking from house to barn. By boat, she thought, his house was about three-quarters of a mile from Junior's. By road it must be about seven miles.

Casey slammed the vehicle door and swished through the long brown grass to Junior's side door and knocked.

Victoria walked to the edge of the bluff. She could see, out of Ben's sight around the point and close to the opposite shore, someone working in a dory. She couldn't quite make out what the person was doing. She couldn't even tell whether it was a man or a woman from this distance. The figure was bundled up in a navy blue coverall and was wearing a brown knit cap. As Victoria watched, the dory moved from the cove into the main body of the Pond, and she saw the person drop something overboard. She couldn't tell what it was, nets or pots, something bulky. Shellfishing hours were over for the day, so he—or she—wasn't shellfishing. Not legally, anyway.

While Victoria was thinking about the figure in the boat, she turned to watch Casey, who knocked on Junior's door a second time, then, when there was no answer, opened it and went inside with the papers.

To her right, Victoria could see the grand sweep of the Atlantic. Over the narrow barrier bar that separated ocean from pond, breakers tossed foaming crests into the air before they curled and crashed onto the beach. She could smell the clam-flats exposed by the outgoing tide, a sulphurous smell that reminded her of greasy mud squishing up between her toes. She could feel the rumble of pounding surf, could hear, above the roar, gulls quarreling near the opening, a cut in the barrier bar that let tidal waters flow in and out to nourish the Great Pond's oyster beds.

She sat on an overturned rowboat at the edge of the bluff and watched the dory, which had moved almost as far as the opening. While she watched, it turned and headed back toward the cove, rounded the point, and disappeared from sight. She heard the putt-putt of its motor echoing against the shore.

The sun was warm on her back. She could work the subtle late-winter colors into a poem, a sonnet, perhaps. Contrast the brown and beige of grasses, dark green of cedars, black of wild rose and bayberry with the changing blue of sky and sea and pond. Maybe use the image of sleep. Winter was certainly not death, the way so many poets saw it. Dig into the ground a bit and you would see life burgeoning. For the final couplet, she might put in something about the person in the boat, the ambiguity of gender and purpose. She found an envelope and pen in her pocket.

She heard a sound from the house, a squeal, and looked up expecting to see Casey. It was the open door, swinging on its hinges.

When she was a child, Victoria had hunted arrowheads along the edges of the Great Pond. Junior's camp, or at least part of it, was here even then. His great-grandfather had built it as a duck hunting blind before Victoria was born.

She was pondering on the figure in the dory when Junior's door shut with a wooden thump and Casey strode through the grass.

"Sorry I took so long. I left Junior a note to explain what he was supposed to do."

"I don't mind the wait." Victoria lifted her wrinkled face to the sun.

Casey stood next to her at the bluff's edge. "It's clearer than I've ever seen it."

"This is the kind of day old-timers called 'a weather breeder,' " Victoria said. "We'll have a storm in a day or so. The surf sounds as if there's heavy weather offshore."

"I can feel it through my boots."

"I saw Ben heading to the barn, and I saw someone out in a dory." Victoria pointed to the cove. "The boat went around the point a few minutes ago."

"A fisherman?"

"I couldn't tell. The person was dropping something overboard, maybe bags of oyster cultch." Victoria got stiffly to her feet, holding a bayberry bush for support. "It could be the right time of year, I guess."

Casey stared at her. "Victoria, I have no idea what you're talking about. I'm a city girl. Remember?"

"Cultch is what oysters attach themselves to." Victoria picked up a driftwood stick near the rowboat to use for support. "Newly hatched oysters drift around in the water. After a bit they attach themselves onto something hard, like rocks or shells. That's 'cultch.' "

"Why *bags* of shells?"

"The bottom is muddy here. If you drop loose shells into the water, they'll sink into the mud. So they put scallop shells in bags of wide netting. The bags stay on top of the mud. The shells increase the surface for the oyster spawn to attach themselves."

Casey shook her head. "I have a lot to learn."

As they walked to the Bronco, Victoria poked at dried grass and leaves with her stick. "Signs of spring everywhere." She pointed to a small cluster of green leaves she'd uncovered. "Birdfoot violet. It won't bloom for another couple of months, but you can see it's getting ready." She covered the plant with leaves again.

As they headed home, thick clouds were beginning to move in. The few cars coming toward them had turned on headlights. Casey slowed going down Brandy Brow, passed the police station, and continued to Victoria's house, a quarter-mile beyond.

Victoria got down from the Bronco and glanced up. "I thought the weather would hold off a day or two, but it's likely to storm tonight." She slammed the car's door shut with a heavy thunk. "From the looks of it, a bad storm. Well, goodnight, Chief."

"Goodnight, Deputy."

As she went up the stone steps to the entry, Victoria held the railing tightly. Elizabeth had turned on the kitchen lights, and was waiting in the doorway, tall and wiry in worn jeans and gray sweater.

She's so much like her grandfather, Victoria thought. Jonathan would have been standing here, just like this, worried about me, but not wanting it to show.

"You had a phone call, Gram," Elizabeth said when Victoria had taken off her coat. "Zack from the Conservation Trust. Said it involved Mr. Mausz. He wants you to call back."

McCavity, the ginger cat, stalked in from the living room, where, Victoria assumed, he had been napping all day on the couch. He rubbed up against her corduroy legs and stretched, opening his mouth in a wide yawn to show his splendid teeth.

Elizabeth filled the teakettle and put it on the stove. "That cat brought you a present today. I have no idea what it was, something disgusting."

"Nice Cavvy," Victoria crooned. The yellow cat closed his eyes and purred.

CHAPTER 3

When the phone rang later that evening, Victoria and Elizabeth were eating supper. "Zack will be right over," Victoria said after she hung up. "Casey and I passed him on the Quansoo road this afternoon."

"What's he coming for, Gram?"

"Phoebe's sold her land. To developers."

"Oh no! What a shame. I thought the Conservation Trust was hoping to buy it."

"Apparently the developer got to her first."

"What does Zack expect you to do about it, Gram?"

Victoria dabbed at her mouth with her napkin before she replied. "I'm sure he thinks I can be of some help."

Rain was starting to ping against the windows of the cookroom, the room that had been the summer kitchen in Victoria's childhood. The small room, filled with hanging green plants and baskets, was where Victoria wrote her poetry and her weekly column for the *Island Enquirer*.

Elizabeth cut into her chicken then put her fork down. "Phoebe's family has had that land for ages. How could she ever think of selling out?"

"They offered her a million dollars, according to Zack."

"For two hundred acres of prime land on Martha's Vineyard? That's not much."

"It seems like a lot of money to me." Victoria helped herself to more salad.

The wind wailed through the loose window frame in the kitchen and rain began to slash against the glass.

"Someone should put tape over that crack." Victoria

looked meaningfully at Elizabeth, who grinned and left the table. Victoria heard a kitchen drawer opening.

"A hundred dollars seems like a lot of money." Victoria spoke up so Elizabeth could hear. "What is property in West Tisbury selling for these days?"

"Would you believe a hundred-thousand dollars or more an acre? Someone bought a house on a three-acre lot in Edgartown last week for eleven million dollars."

Victoria heard Elizabeth rip off a piece of duct tape and putter at the window. The wailing stopped. She did some quick calculating on an envelope she had retrieved from the wastepaper basket. "Two hundred acres would come to closer to ten million dollars than one million."

"Twenty million, Gram." Elizabeth returned to the table and sat again. "They took advantage of her. Developers are tearing this Island to pieces. It's just raw real estate to them, a way to make a buck."

Victoria nodded. "Apparently the deciding factor was when her granddaughter came to visit last month. Phoebe wanted to make sure neither her son nor her daughter—nor her granddaughter—would ever get the land."

"Nice family," Elizabeth murmured.

When Zack West came to the kitchen door a few minutes later Elizabeth was clearing the table. His yellow slicker glistened with raindrops. He hung it on a nail in the entry, where it dripped water onto the brick floor.

Outside, water poured off the roof and out of the overflowing gutters and hit the stone steps in a steady cascade. Lightning flashed occasionally, distant thunder grumbled.

Zack swiped his wet hair from his forehead, kicked off his boots, and padded into the kitchen, toes and heels showing through holes in his socks.

The warm kitchen air made his glasses steam. He removed them and wiped the lenses with a red bandana he'd taken out of his pocket. Zack was about the same age as Chief

O'Neill, and much too thin, in Victoria's opinion.

He blinked and put his glasses back on. "Filthy night."

"The fire's all set." Victoria handed him a box of matches. "Go ahead into the parlor and light it while I make tea."

Elizabeth loaded the dishwasher and turned it on. She yawned. "If you don't need me for anything, I'm going upstairs to read, Gram. Goodnight, both of you. Don't stay up too late."

By the time Victoria carried the tea tray into the parlor, the fire was blazing and Zack, who'd been squatting next to it, stood up and headed toward the ornately carved horsehair sofa.

"What on earth was Phoebe thinking of?" Victoria seated herself in the mouse gray wing chair and poured mugs of tea.

Zack watched the rain stream down the windows. "She was in a hurry to lock up a deal. The real estate people were nice, she told me. They were concerned about conservation."

"Hah!" said Victoria.

"She fell for it hook, line, and sinker. They sent her plants for her garden. This nice man, according to her, Roger Nordstrom, started dropping by. He was so attentive, more like a son to her than her own son." Zack paused. The wind shook the shutters and slammed against the house. "He even brought in a truckload of manure and spread it over her garden. When he gave her papers to sign, she signed them. She hasn't seen him since."

"She's along in years." Victoria smoothed her hair with her knobby hand. "Some elderly people can be quite gullible."

Zack's crooked smile showed large white teeth. "They not only offered the million dollars, but offered to pay all the taxes on the transfer." He leaned forward on the sofa. His knees, showing through torn jeans, were almost chest high.

"And they agreed to let her live there?"

"They told her the property would not be altered or touched or built on until after her death," Zack said. "Seemed like a good deal to her."

"Did she hire an attorney to go over the agreement?"

"Roger Nordstrom recommended an attorney." Zack paused and looked at Victoria.

"Surely not Montgomery Mausz?" She set her mug with a clink on the glass-topped coffee table.

McCavity came purposefully into the parlor and leapt into Victoria's lap. Victoria squinted as he kneaded his front paws on her thigh. "Ouch!"

"You okay, Victoria?"

"Yes, yes." She unhooked McCavity's claws. "You were saying Mr. Mausz represented Phoebe in the real estate transaction?"

"He was killed before the final closing, but he'd already done all the necessary paperwork. Did you know that Harry Ness was the principal owner of CARP, the real estate company? The developer? Phoebe didn't realize Ness was involved."

Victoria absently stroked McCavity, who purred.

"Don't tell me Mr. Mausz represented Harry Ness as well as Phoebe?"

"Yes." Zack stirred a spoonful of sugar into his tea.

Victoria shook her head. "It sounds as though Mausz had a serious conflict of interest."

Zack nodded.

"The deal went through?"

"The deed is signed and registered at the Court House."

"Weren't you and what's-his-name negotiating with Phoebe to purchase her land for the Conservation Trust?"

"Josiah Coffin. Yes. Loch Ness slipped in before we could get the money together. As I said, Phoebe was in a hurry. Ness's real estate agents sweet-talked her into believing they were working in the best interests of both her and the Island.

The Conservation Trust wasn't able to act fast enough."

"What happens now?" Victoria shifted McCavity slightly in her lap.

"He's filed a development plan with the Planning Board."

"Oh?"

"Ness intends to build sixty houses on the property."

"Sixty!"

The cat, startled, bounded off Victoria's lap, sat in front of the fire, and began to clean himself. He licked a front paw and scrubbed behind an ear.

"Sixty trophy houses, monuments to money, each on a three-acre lot. Each is to sell for three million dollars."

"Each house will bring in more than he paid for the entire property. Let's see." She scribbled on the clean side of an envelope. "Sixty houses times three million dollars comes to eighteen million dollars, am I right?"

"More like one hundred eighty million. Minus costs, of course."

Victoria was silent for long seconds.

"Are you still with us?" Zack said.

"I'm re-calculating." Victoria scratched with her pen. "One hundred and eighty million dollars. Eighteen million dollars. It doesn't matter, does it? It's all the same, too much money."

"The entire development—called Ocean Zephyr Estates, by the way . . ."

"Ooze." Victoria worked it out on her envelope. "Oz. N for Ness would make it Noze."

". . . will be surrounded by a chain-link fence with barbed wire on top, and will have a gate with a security guard."

"I thought you said they agreed to wait until after Phoebe dies before they did anything with her land."

"Buddie Keene on the zoning board called Phoebe to tell her Loch Ness had filed the plan. That's how she found out. They didn't honor what she thought was their agreement. She called me. Upset, of course."

"Can she do anything?"

"I'm not sure. The contract didn't state what Nordstrom had told Phoebe it did. She didn't read it, you know. All that fine print. Nordstrom said he had asked Mausz to read it and she trusted both of them. If we can prove somehow that she was deliberately misled, we might be able to delay things."

"But that's hard to prove, I suppose. You'd have to have documentation, and she's not likely to have any."

A fork of lightning lit up the room. Thunder rattled the windows. Victoria's mind flashed back to finding the lawyer's body. She remembered the awful stench, and shuddered.

"Storm's practically on top of us now," Zack said.

Victoria stared into the fire. "Was Mr. Mausz involved in anything else?"

"Who knows. Mausz had his fingers in so many pies, he'd made enemies in every one of the six towns. I can name a half-dozen people who are glad to see him out of the way."

"Me too," said Victoria. "I mean, I can name a half-dozen people, too."

"The fact that you found his body near Sachem's Rock seems to point to a connection. There's enough money and power at stake over the property to make people do crazy things."

Victoria gazed at Zack for several moments before she said finally, "Why are you coming to me?"

Zack shifted on the hard sofa. "I have a couple of ideas."

"Oh?" Victoria sat forward.

"You know Island plants better than anyone." He pushed his glasses back on his nose. His thick eyebrows almost met over the tops of the frame. He looked, Victoria thought, like a red-tailed hawk, with his large curved beak, his magnified eyes glittering fiercely, and his shoulders hunched as if he were about to pounce on prey.

"I suspect I know what you're about to suggest," Victoria said. "What do you want me to find?"

Zack focused his eyes on her and grinned. "That property must have at least a couple of endangered species on it."

McCavity finished cleaning himself and stretched out on the hearth rug so his soft belly fur faced the warmth of the fire. With each gust of wind, the curtains billowed, the fire blazed.

"I shouldn't be surprised to find a half-dozen rare plants," Victoria said. "They're putting everything on the endangered species list these days. Dandelions will be next."

"If we could only find one endangered plant or animal on the property . . ." Zack sat forward. He pushed his hair off his forehead with a quick gesture.

"We could stop them," Victoria finished. "They can't bulldoze rare plant habitats." She turned to Zack. "Well, I could take a look, if that's what you're about to ask me to do."

Zack settled back on the sofa and nodded.

"Will you come with me?" Victoria asked.

He shook his head. "I can't be seen on the property. The caretakers know me."

"Give me a checklist, then." Victoria's hooded eyes were bright. "A list that tells me what leaves of endangered species show this time of year. That sort of thing."

"We have a volunteer at the Trust, Robin White, an eleven-year-old, who can go with you weekends or afternoons when he's not in school."

Victoria heard a noise in the kitchen and got stiffly out of her wing chair to investigate. Zack unfolded like a carpenter's rule and followed. Water was dripping off the beam in the kitchen ceiling. Victoria put a saucepan underneath. "I asked Warren to fix that leak two months ago." She laid dishtowels in the rivulet that ran along the floor.

When they returned to the living room Victoria said, "Several ancient ways cross the property. Those are public rights-of-way. By law anyone can use them."

"You're right. Of course."

"Old cart roads and stage roads and sheep paths. I know most of them. Loch Ness can't stop me from walking on them."

Blinding lightning hit close by, with a simultaneous crash of thunder. The lights flickered. Victoria heard a long drawn-out cracking sound and a dull thud.

She and Zack looked at each other blankly, and both rose. Victoria grabbed the flashlight she kept next to the black bowl where Elizabeth put the bills, and they went to the kitchen door. Zack swung his yellow slicker over his shoulders and slipped his own flashlight, a long four-cell one, out of the pocket.

"Wait in the entry where it's dry, Victoria."

He flipped the hood of his jacket over his head and stepped out into the pouring rain. Lightning strobed. Thunder growled. In the brief flashes, Victoria could see a vague massive object on the ground.

Zack had gone only as far as the bottom stone step, moving his light around, when Victoria saw that the large silver poplar in the turnaround had toppled, completely blocking the drive.

Zack returned to the entry and took off his wet slicker. The storm had already moved farther away. The pause between lightning and thunder had lengthened.

"Looks as if you'd better spend the night," Victoria said. "There's no way you can get your truck out tonight."

"Thanks. I will. In the morning I'll cut the tree, if you have a chain saw. Clear your drive."

They returned to the living room, where the fire was dying. Zack added a log, and then folded himself onto the sofa again.

Victoria listened to the storm as it faded into the distance. "Sometimes the wind sounds almost human the way it moans around the windows."

"It's not surprising. These old houses are supposed to be haunted. A night like tonight I can imagine ghosts in your attic."

"A lot of nonsense." Victoria changed the subject. "Did you have supper?"

"I forgot."

"Put the screen over the fire and come into the kitchen. We have some leftover chicken."

After Victoria had made up the bed in the East Chamber for Zack and had gone to bed herself, she had trouble falling asleep. The storm had moved far off to the west, but she continued to hear a low moaning. At one point she started to get up to check around the house, then scolded herself for letting Zack's talk of ghosts bother her. It was the wind, she was sure.

The next morning Zack and Victoria were up before dawn. He set three places—one for Elizabeth, who had not come downstairs yet. Victoria cooked bacon and eggs, pancakes and toast.

"Wonderful!" Zack said, his plate clean, his mouth full.

Victoria passed the platter of pancakes and eggs. He helped himself to thirds, poured more orange juice. When Victoria saw the way the food was disappearing, she brought out a large box of Shredded Wheat and Zack ate two helpings and a fourth piece of toast with beach plum jam spread thickly on it.

"Don't you eat at home?" Victoria couldn't help asking.

"Not like this." Zack shoveled cereal into his mouth. "You said you have a chain saw?" Strands of Shredded Wheat stuck out like hay from a horse's mouth.

"It's in the cellar," Victoria said. "Open the bulkhead doors next to the fuel oil tank. There's gasoline in the shed."

The eastern sky still had the ragged dark remains of last night's storm clouds. The sun rose over the maple trees, late winter skeletons silhouetted against the sky. The gray scud lighted up with dawn colors—pink, lavender, red, and gold.

Zack filled the old chain saw with gasoline and started it up. It coughed a couple of times, spit out gray smoke, and whined into a ragged rhythm that gradually steadied. Victoria followed him out to the fallen tree.

She stooped down and picked something up. "Are these your spectacles, Zack?"

He shook his head and pointed to his own glasses. "I can't see two feet without them."

"Gold frames," Victoria said. "Bifocals. Someone's going to miss them. I wonder whose they are?" She wiped them off carefully with a napkin and put them in her pocket.

"I hardly know where to begin," Zack shouted above the noise of the saw. "That was one huge tree." He examined the top branches that filled the angle between the main house and the kitchen wing. "Ten feet in either direction, and you'd have had some major house repairs."

Victoria was behind him when he suddenly stopped the saw.

"Holy mackerel!"

Victoria hurried toward him.

"Call 911. Someone's pinned underneath the tree. Alive, I think."

"Good Lord," Victoria gasped. "That moaning I heard last night . . ." She hustled into the house and dialed. Zack started up the chain saw again.

By the time Casey and Junior arrived and the EMTs came with the ambulance, Zack had cut most of the smaller branches that pinned the unconscious man—nobody Victoria had ever seen before.

Zack carved away the thick tree trunk, careful not to shift more weight onto the man underneath, while Casey, Junior, and the EMTs held as much of the weight of the trunk off the man as they could. It looked to Victoria as if the tree had knocked him sideways. He was lying on his back with the heavy trunk across his chest. When they lifted it, he looked caved-in. Victoria put her hand on her own chest and took a deep breath. *I heard him,* she thought. *And I did nothing.*

Neither Victoria nor Zack could answer any of Casey's questions about the man, who he was or what he was doing there. They knew only that the tree had come down during the storm around nine-thirty the previous night.

"He lay there all night in the rain," Victoria whispered, her hand still on her chest.

"Don't think like that, Victoria," Zack said sharply. "What do you suppose he was doing there, anyway?" He set the saw down on the stone step.

Nobody answered.

The EMTs eased the stretcher under the man and gently moved him into the ambulance. Casey radioed the emergency room. This time Doc Erickson answered the call. "Lucky it was mild last night. Bring him in. I'll be ready when you get here."

The ambulance backed out of the drive, siren wailing, lights flashing, and sped toward the hospital along the Edgartown Road.

By the time Elizabeth appeared, rubbing sleep out of her eyes, the ambulance had gone. "What was all the commotion, Gram?"

Victoria told her what she knew. "He was standing under the tree in that thunderstorm for some reason. I wonder why? Who can he be? These must be his spectacles I found." She took the glasses out of her pocket and examined them.

Victoria, Zack, and Elizabeth stood around uncertainly. Normal activities somehow seemed inappropriate.

"I guess we have to take care of the tree," Victoria said finally.

Zack returned to work with the chain saw. Victoria pulled on her leather gloves and wheeled the garden cart next to him. The saw buzzed like a swarm of bees, too loud for conversation. Zack stopped occasionally to chuck fireplace lengths into Victoria's cart. Then he'd pull the cord to start the saw up again, and it roared and bit and chewed and whined. Chips flew.

The early clouds had cleared and the sky was a bright washed blue. Redwing blackbirds called from the wooded area behind the compost heap. On the south side of the house, green snouts of snowdrops poked up through the ground underneath the fuel oil tank. Perhaps this year her snowdrops would be the first in town to bloom, Victoria thought, then felt bad because she wasn't thinking about the man crushed under her tree.

Who was he and what was he doing there? She could think of no explanation. He had been dressed in new-looking foul weather gear, so he didn't seem to be a homeless man needing a place to stay out of the storm. He appeared to be in his early fifties, not a young person playing some game. He wasn't a suitor of Elizabeth's, as far as she knew.

She trundled the cart of green logs to the woodpile where Elizabeth unloaded them and piled them where they would season. Elizabeth was wearing an old plaid flannel shirt of her grandfather's. It still had the angular tear she had never mended. Jonathan wouldn't let her put his shirt in the rag-bag. She could see him now in his granddaughter, tall and slender, independent, stubborn, and decent.

The sound of surf on the south shore was gentler than it had been yesterday before the storm. She could still feel its vibration under her feet and in her chest, the ever-present surf, cresting and combing and tumbling onto the shore as it had for centuries. She wondered if that man would be able to feel anything in his chest ever again. He had looked so crushed.

CHAPTER 4

Josiah Coffin stood at the window of the small Conservation Trust office and looked down at the old cranberry bog at the foot of the hill, half-hidden in a rising ground mist. He thrust his hands into the pockets of his jeans. Zack leaned back in Josiah's swivel chair. The chair squealed. A lock of hair had fallen over Zack's forehead, and he peered out from under it through thick glasses and saw discouragement in his boss's slanted shoulders.

"We have so little to fight with." Josiah turned from the window. His large nose cast a shadow on the side of his pale face. His auburn hair needed trimming. He was about the same age as Zack, mid-thirties. "Loch Ness can buy off anyone who gets in his way. Damn Phoebe Eldredge. We were so close to getting that conservation restriction."

"It was her granddaughter's visit that triggered it," Zack said. "The granddaughter apparently swooped in like a vulture scenting a kill. Phoebe hadn't heard from her for at least two years. The granddaughter showed up with rainbow-colored hair, nose studs, and tattoos."

"So she was afraid the kid—how old is she, anyway?"

"Late twenties. She's not a kid."

"Afraid the granddaughter would end up with the property before we could get the conservation restriction on it."

Zack flicked his hair out of his eyes, pushed his glasses back onto his nose, and peered at Josiah. There was nothing he could think to say.

Josiah broke the silence. "Everybody was after Phoebe's land. For a golf course. For a millionaires' enclave. For a campground. The Wampanoags want it for a casino. Tom More still hopes to get it for a utopian housing complex. Ness got to Phoebe first. Damnation." Josiah stared out of the window again. "If she could only have waited another three weeks." He shoved his hands deeper into his pockets. "You wonder if it's worth it. Are we the only people on the Island willing to fight to preserve some small part of it? Does it even matter?"

Zack leaned back and the chair squealed.

"Well, hell." Josiah turned again and straightened his shoulders. "Let's look at the map and talk."

Zack unwound his legs from the base of the chair and stood up. He was a full head taller than Josiah.

The Island map Josiah referred to covered an entire wall of his office, twelve feet long and seven feet high. Parts of it were shaded in different colors, and it was stuck all over with colored pins.

Zack was responsible for about half the pins, which marked the locations of plants on the state's endangered species list. For ten years he had scoured the hills and moors and marshes and woodlands and grasslands and shores of the Island making an inventory of plants and animals and birds.

Josiah pointed to the area of Sachem's Rock. "The endangered species act is our only weapon. It would be a loss to the Island to have the two hundred acres around the rock developed. Sixty trophy houses."

"What do they say up at the tribal office?" Zack asked.

"I haven't spoken to Chief Hawkbill. I don't know how they can help. A casino would be worse than sixty homes."

Sachem's Rock was a house-size boulder that overlooked the two-hundred-acre property below it. It was a glacial erratic, dropped on top of a morainal hill by glaciers twenty thousand years before. It had been called Sachem's Rock long before white settlers came to the Island. The rock jutted out of the ground like a sperm whale broaching, split at the bottom to form what looked like a jaw. For generations, the Island's Wampanoags had come to the rock for ceremonial occasions, had revered it as a whale, and had named it "Sachem," the title of a tribal chieftain.

Zack leaned down to peer at the part of the map that showed the property, a large chunk almost in the center of the Island.

"Not many pins there," Josiah went on.

"I never had a chance to survey it," Zack said defensively.

"I didn't mean to fault you." Josiah turned from the map and gripped Zack's arm with a calloused hand. "It's so frustrating. No one expected Phoebe to sell out." He dropped his hand and turned back to the window. Swirls and tendrils of mist rose over the bog outside. "Ness has posted the land. He's hardly likely to give us permission to make a survey of rare species now. He knows that if we find anything on the land, it will, at a minimum, delay him."

Zack sat in the swivel chair again and rocked back and forth. He laced his hands behind his head. "You knew I was at Victoria Trumbull's the other day?"

"During the storm. The tree came down on that guy. How is he, by the way?" Josiah continued to stare out the window.

"Still alive, but still in a coma. The doctors think he'll recover okay."

Josiah shook his head. "What were you about to say?"

"I mentioned the subject of finding rare plants on the property to Victoria. She picked right up on it. She volunteered to help."

"She's ninety, for God's sake. I know she's tough, but still, we can hardly ask a ninety-year-old lady to tramp around the way we do."

"She's ninety-two, not ninety," Zack said. He thought of Victoria's bright hooded eyes and her pleased smile, the multitude of creases in her face that, strangely, made her look like a young girl. "She's related to you, isn't she?"

"Everyone on the Island is related to Victoria."

Zack waited.

Josiah stared out of the window. He jingled change in his pocket. At last he said, "I see what you mean. I guess. It's in the blood. Should we go to her place to talk to her, or bring her here?"

"I imagine she'd like to come here. We can show her maps and pictures, make copies of stuff she needs," Zack said.

"We've got nothing to lose." Josiah turned to Zack. "Who knows."

"I told her Robin White would go with her."

"A ninety-two-year-old and an eleven-year-old." Josiah laughed for the first time that morning. "I guess that averages out to fifty-one or so. Fifty-one isn't exactly combat age." He was quiet for several minutes.

Zack waited.

"What about transportation?" Josiah said finally.

"She hitchhikes." Zack pushed his hair off his forehead and linked hands behind his head again.

Josiah laughed again. For the first time in several days, Zack saw his boss's mood lift.

Zack went on, "When she's not hitching, she rides with Chief O'Neill in the police Bronco. The chief appointed her a deputy police officer, you know. After Victoria fingered that serial killer."

Josiah shook his head. "They don't make 'em like that anymore." He paced from the window to the wall map, glanced at it, and paced back to the window again. "She can ride with one of us. We have to be careful, though, not to let Ness's people associate her with the Trust."

"Harmless old lady strolling on the ancient ways with a little boy." Zack grinned and leaned forward.

"I must say, I'm concerned about her safety." Josiah became serious again. "We don't know why Montgomery

45

Mausz was killed, and not far from the rock. Was it something personal against him? His wife or mistress? Why there? Was he mixed up in some way with Ness? Double-crossing him, maybe? Does one of the Wampanoags feel their sacred rock has been violated? I don't know how Mausz's killer is going to feel about Victoria Trumbull innocently hiking the old trails."

Zack shook his head. "It didn't look like an accident, that's for sure."

"Did a stranger kill him, a tramp, maybe? A psycho? In which case, it's irresponsible of us to let an old woman walk around there on her own. She can hardly protect herself." Josiah's hands were in his jean pockets again, jingling coins.

"She can take care of herself," Zack said. "Maybe the killer is one of the doctors who hopes to build a golf course." Zack bared his teeth in a grin. "Half the members of the Park and Rec committee are crazy enough to murder someone over swings and slides and monkey bars. Tom More is a religious fanatic about his commune. Maybe one of the Indians— Native Americans—brained him. Maybe Mausz's mistress killed him. His wife."

"His wife had probable cause, I guess," Josiah said. "He wasn't exactly discreet about his fooling around. What was he doing on the property, anyway?"

"He was the attorney for the land transaction."

"I know. But that was no reason for his being there. Unless he was with Ness or one of his agents."

"You knew he was also the attorney for Phoebe?"

"No. I didn't know that. That's wildly unethical."

Zack shrugged. "That's our boy, Mausz. Maybe he liked to walk by himself and ran into a low branch."

Josiah went back to the window. "The medics in Falmouth say he was killed around the time of that hard freeze last month. Around the first week of February. They couldn't be definite about the time of death because of the cold." Josiah stared out the window. "If you recall, it got down into the twenties."

"Could they tell what killed him?"

"They couldn't be definite about that, either. Or at least, they wouldn't tell me. They said it looked like he'd been hit with something heavy and hard, like a stone or a chunk of metal. A tire iron, maybe."

"I don't see that Victoria's in any danger," Zack said. "Tramping around up there is nothing new for her." He got up from the chair and started toward the office door. "She certainly isn't afraid of a mere murderer. She was the one who found the body, after all."

"Well, we're desperate." Josiah left the window. "We've got to do all we can to prevent Ness from going ahead with that development. If Victoria can help, we'll put her to work."

"I'll give her a copy of the state's endangered species list." Zack ducked his head to go through the low door.

"She actually might find mountain cranberry on the property, it's the right habitat. Or goldenseal. If she could find a cranefly orchid, that would really stop Ness dead." Josiah reached up and brought down a thick book from the shelf in the hall outside his office. "I'm sure she knows the cranberry and goldenseal, but cranefly orchid is so rare, she's probably never seen it. It may not even be on the property." He put the book on a small table and thumbed through it until he came to a picture and a brief description of the rare orchid. "She should be able to recognize the plants this time of year. The leaves will be green now. The Vineyard is the only place in New England where they've been found. There are a few specimens on Seven Gates, one near the Great Pond, but nowhere else in the eastern U.S. until you get to North Carolina. The Great Smokey Mountains. If we could find one plant on that property, just one, it would be enough to trigger a cease and desist order."

Zack grinned. "And one hell of a lot of trouble."

Victoria unzipped her yellow slicker, unbuttoned her heavy sweater, peeled both of them off, and sat down with a plop in the chair next to Casey's desk.

"Whew!" Her white hair sparkled with droplets of condensed fog. She had walked the quarter mile from her house to the police station.

"Yesterday was quite a day!" She laid her coat and sweater over the back of the wooden chair. Her face was rosy from yesterday's sun and wind, and from this morning's hike.

From the station house window she could see the swans sail in and out of the eddying mist that rose over the millpond.

"You should have called me, Victoria. I'd have given you a lift." Casey stood up and went to the window. "The fog seems to be getting thicker. What's the weather going to do?"

"It'll burn off by afternoon," Victoria said with assurance. "Have you heard any more about the man under my tree, Spencer Kirschmeyer?"

Casey shook her head. "He's still in intensive care. Hasn't regained consciousness yet. The new surgeon repaired everything she could. It's out of her hands now, she said."

"Do they know anything about him besides his name?"

"He's a licensed private investigator from Bridgeport, Connecticut." Casey leaned down and brushed a speck of dust off her sharply creased uniform trousers.

"Investigating my house? How strange."

"He had a rental Jeep he'd parked on New Lane. He picked it up at the airport three days ago, rented it for a week. He'd put a hundred twenty-seven miles on it."

"Did he leave anything in the car?"

"Receipts. He was staying at the Harbor View in Edgartown. A briefcase with some electronic gear in it, a tape re-corder, ear phones. A couple of lined legal pads. Chewing gum wrappers. An empty Diet Pepsi can. Nothing else."

"Electronics," Victoria mused. "I don't know anything about electronics. Could he have been bugging my house?"

"Surely not you," Casey said with a smile.

"It's conceivable that someone might want to listen to my conversations." Victoria's mouth turned down.

"Yes, yes, of course. I meant . . . I don't know what I meant." Casey went to the small closet and took her jacket off a hook. "Let's go. I need to make my rounds. We can check your house for bugs at the same time."

She shut the station house door, gave it a small push to make sure it had latched, and shook her head at it.

"I'm tempted to invest my own money in a lock."

"The police station doesn't need a lock. It's a public build-ing," Victoria said.

Casey glared at her.

Victoria waited while the chief unlocked the Bronco's doors.

Casey backed out of the small parking lot and turned to-ward Victoria's house. On the way they passed the rock on the corner of Old County Road in front of Mabel Johnson's house. Mabel Johnson had been dead for at least fifty years, but no one called the house by the new owner's name, even though the new owner's children had grown children now.

The vehicle's tires swished on the wet road. The fog drifted in long ribbons with clear patches in between. As they passed New Lane, they saw a Jeep parked by the side of the road.

"Island Auto Rental was supposed to pick it up. I'll give them another call." Casey turned into Victoria's drive. "It looks bare without your tree."

"I remember when my grandfather planted it. Uncle Dan was cutting the horse and wagon too close to my grandmother's flowerbed. The tree would stop him, Grandpa said."

"So the tree was eighty-five, eighty-six years old?"

"About that."

"It was huge." Casey parked under the Norway maple. "I can't imagine what Mr. Kirschmeyer was doing here. Electronic bugging is about the only thing that makes sense. But I can't imagine why."

"Zack was working all around the tree. If there was a bugging instrument, you'd think he would have seen it."

"Maybe not. He didn't expect to find electronic devices. If he saw something like that, he probably would have thought it was some electronic game of your great-grandkids'. GameBoy or Pokémon."

The tree's roots had come out of the ground in a ball the size of a small car, leaving a gaping hole. Where Zack had cut up the fallen tree, there were heaps of fresh sawdust. The driveway was littered with leaves and small branches.

"There could be something underneath all this." Casey scuffed her boot in the litter covering the ground.

"I'll get the rake," Victoria said.

"Let me check the house first. Where were you the night the tree came down?"

"In the parlor."

From the main road Victoria's two-hundred-and-fifty-year-old house seemed neatly symmetrical. But from the back, it rambled off in a jumble of additions, ells, and crazy roof angles.

Victoria led Casey to the side of the main house. They started with the stone foundation, examining it carefully. Then the brick foundation on top of the stones, then up the weathered gray shingles toward the window.

"Who was here the night before last, you and Zack?" Casey asked.

Victoria nodded. "Elizabeth had gone to bed."

"Were you in the living room—parlor—most of the time?"

"Yes. That's the window right above you."

Casey searched along the bottom edge of the window frame with her hand. The window itself was above her head, just within her reach.

"Aha! Look at this, Victoria." She pointed to a small black box the size of a cigarette pack attached to the lowest pane of glass by a suction cup. She stood on tiptoe, pried the suction cup loose with her fingernail, and turned the box over. "It's a transmitter." She stepped out of the garden and away from the house. "Get the rake. We'll see if we can find the receiver under the debris. It wasn't in the rental car."

Victoria returned from the shed with two rakes and they cleared the ground around the stump.

"Here we are!" Casey held up what looked like a small tape recorder. "Let's take it back to the station house and see what we have."

"What was he listening for?" Victoria stared at the small black box. "Why? I certainly don't have any secrets."

CHAPTER 5

That afternoon Victoria met Robin White, her eleven-year-old assistant, for the first time. Zack and she picked him up after school. He seemed small, frail, and surly.

"Are you going to be warm enough?" she asked him.

The boy nodded without speaking.

Zack had let them off at the Sachem's Rock trailhead with a promise to pick them up in two hours. It was now about three o'clock. Days were noticeably longer, but the air was chilly and getting chillier as the sun dropped lower on the other side of the high ground.

Robin was wearing a brown baseball cap turned backwards so the band was across his forehead, almost touching his glasses. Above the band, a tuft of sandy-red hair stuck out in several directions. The front of the cap read "UPS" in yellow stitching. He was wearing jeans with the knees worn through to horizontal threads, and a dirty gray sweatshirt printed with a dog's skeleton and bold black lettering that read, "Dead Dog."

"Where on earth did you get that shirt?" Victoria asked, hoping to find some common ground so she could talk to this boy.

He shrugged and pushed his hands deeper into his pockets.

"It must be a collector's item," she said.

He shrugged again, shoulders lifting up and down.

"You don't have to go with me, if you don't want."

He looked at her through his glasses and grinned, showing big new teeth. "They're paying me."

"Who's paying you?" Victoria asked indignantly.

He shrugged again and looked down at his feet.

"Look at me, Robin White," Victoria ordered. "I don't want you to go with me any more than you do. You can sit there," she pointed to a rock beside the path, "and wait until I come back."

He shook his head. "I told them I'd go with you."

"For pay." Victoria frowned. "Who's paying you, Zack?"

He shook his head. "Mr. Coffin."

"How much is he paying you?" Victoria stood, feet apart, and leaned on her walking stick.

The boy hung his head. He thrust his hands still deeper into his pockets, shoulders up like the wings of a half-grown chicken. He looked down at his running shoes.

"Tie your shoelaces," Victoria ordered. "How much is Mr. Coffin paying you?"

He brought one hand out of his pocket. In it he held a deck of cards.

"Well?" Victoria demanded.

"Pokémon." He handed the cards to her, and she took them. He bent down and tied his shoelaces.

"You sold out for Pokémon cards?" she asked him.

He stood up again and nodded.

"If you're getting paid to guard me, I should think it would be worth more."

The boy glanced up with a worried look.

"Well, come on, then. We've got work to do." She handed the cards back to him.

They started up the path that led to the wooded area and high ground. Victoria walked carefully, making sure her footing was firm. Robin bounded ahead of her, then circled back. At one point Victoria stopped and opened out the folded topographic map. Robin loped back and looked over her arm.

"We're here." Victoria pointed with the hand that held her

stick. "One of the ancient ways branches off and follows the low land, you see here?"

Robin nodded, wrinkling his nose to lift his glasses into place.

A redwing blackbird caroled from the nearby marsh. Another answered.

"We're looking for any of five different rare plants," Victoria said. "Pay attention, Robin. Stop that." Robin had scooped up a handful of acorns and was flinging them at the trees next to the path. The acorns hit the trunks with a thunk.

"I'm listening."

"Mountain cranberry likes high ground. It's an alpine plant that's been here on the Vineyard since the Ice Age."

"Yeah?" Robin flung another acorn. Thunk! "Woolly mammoths lived here then."

"I suppose," said Victoria.

"Maybe they ate mountain cranberries. That's why they're rare." Thunk!

"We'll start with this path." She indicated it on the map. "You mark off the places we've been." Victoria handed him the map and a pencil.

He jabbed the pencil at the spot on the map she indicated, and the pencil point broke.

Victoria set her cloth bag on the ground with exasperation. "This partnership is not going to work. I can do this survey better without your assistance. I can't imagine what Josiah is thinking." She reached into the bag and handed Robin a small pencil sharpener shaped like a mouse.

"Wow!" Robin took the mouse sharpener, gazed at it in awe, and grinned. "Pikachu! Where'd you get it?"

"I have my sources," Victoria said tartly. "I suppose we're stuck with each other for the next two hours."

Robin was grinding the pencil round and round in the mouth of the plastic mouse. Pencil shavings curled off and dropped onto the ground.

"Isn't that sharp enough?"

"It works good," Robin answered.

" 'Well,' " Victoria corrected. "You may keep it. Come along, now. This path goes past a vernal pool, a damp place that's a pond in spring. In another month we should be able to find a lot of different plants there." For a brief stretch she led the way along the narrow path, then Robin ran ahead again.

Victoria stopped frequently and gently poked at the earth with her stick. She saw the bright green hoods of skunk cabbage at the edge of the marsh, and tight fiddlehead curls of ferns. Unkempt cattail heads showed white fluff beneath their brown velvet coatings. A breeze riffled the tall dry grasses on the other side of the wetland.

"What are we looking for, anyway?" Robin called out.

"The best discovery of all would be a cranefly orchid," Victoria told him. "If there are any here—and this is the kind of place they like—we should be able to find green leaves lying flat on the ground. They might have purple dots on top. The undersides of the leaves are purple." She stopped as Robin leaped up to catch an overhanging branch. "Pay attention."

"I am. Purple dots. What's the big deal?"

"They're endangered. The Vineyard is only place they've been found in all of New England."

"Yeah?" He leaped into the air and slapped at a branch. A shower of dry red berries dropped around their feet.

"There used to be cranefly orchids on Cape Cod, but when developers built houses there, they destroyed the orchid's habitat. That was only about twenty years ago."

"That was in the olden days. Before I was born."

Victoria glanced at him. "That was only yesterday. Not even a hairline in geologic time."

Robin shrugged. He picked up a small rounded stone and

flung it into the marsh, where it landed with a plop. "How do they know they're here, in this spot?"

"They don't. That's why we're looking. But they've found a few plants in other places on the Island, so it's possible there may be some, or at least one, here."

"Mr. Coffin wants us to find them so nobody can build houses here?"

"I suppose so."

They continued along the old trail. In places it was marshy, and Victoria stepped carefully from one tuft of dry grass to another. A stand of beetlebung trees arched over the path.

"What kind of plants are these, Mrs. Trumbull?" Robin pointed to a clump of bushes with dry seeds in clusters like miniature upright bunches of grapes.

Victoria glanced over. She had been watching the ground to make sure of her footing. "Clethra," she said. "Sweet pepperbush. When it blooms in the summer, it's one of the most wonderful scents on earth, spicy and clean."

"Oh," Robin said.

They passed swamp maples and oak trees, sassafras and viburnum. Victoria recognized their winter skeletons.

"Look!" Robin shouted. "Holly! I know holly."

Victoria nodded. "Look under it for green leaves."

"With purple spots," said the boy.

They stopped under a beech tree, the gold-brown leaves of last autumn still clinging to the branches, and they searched the ground carefully, pushing through catbrier, bright green with wickedly sharp thorns, to get a better look.

"I don't see anything," Victoria said finally. "But this is the sort of place they like."

Robin looked up suddenly. "What's that noise?"

Victoria stood still and listened. She had heard a rustling that only nudged at her mind, a chewink scratching in the dry leaves, perhaps, a noise that didn't really register. When she stood still, the sound she wasn't sure she'd heard stopped. They waited, both of them holding their breath.

"Perhaps it was a deer," Victoria whispered.

"Maybe it was a person. That's why Mr. Coffin said I should guard you. Some person might try to attack you, he said."

"He said that? That someone might attack me?"

"Not exactly, but that's what he meant, I know."

Victoria looked at her watch. "We have only a half hour left before we need to turn back."

"I bet it was a person we heard. Sneaking up on us." Robin ran on ahead, Victoria followed slowly.

The ancient way skirted the hill of the great rock, wound slowly up between beech trees and oaks, rising gently, an old cart path, away from the wetlands where the beetlebungs and catbrier kept their feet wet. Bright green moss contrasted with the golden beech leaves and the austere browns and grays of early March.

"I heard it again," Robin said. "I think he's following us."

Victoria listened and heard nothing, not even the remembrance of hearing something. The sun was settling behind the hill, and the path was in deep shadow. She shivered.

"You cold, Mrs. Trumbull?" Robin sounded anxious.

"Not really, but we should be getting back. Mark the map. Carefully, now. No more pencil holes."

"I can't help it."

"Here, lean on my notebook." Victoria stopped walking and brought her notebook out of her cloth bag. As she did, she heard the sound, a stealthy rustling of dry leaves that stopped an instant after she did. It wasn't the leaping sound of a deer. Nor the scratching, rustling of a chewink, hunting for something in the fallen leaves. Nor did it sound like a dog or a skunk following along with them. It was the sound a person might make if he wanted to see without being seen.

"Let's go back," Victoria said abruptly. "Right now. It's getting dark and cold. Come on, now."

"You think he's going to attack us, Mrs. Trumbull?"

"Don't be silly." Victoria stepped along as fast as she could, holding her stick in front of her like a blind person to feel the roots and stones that were hidden now in shadow.

"I've got a weapon." Robin held up a large oak branch that he'd picked up.

"That won't do. It's rotten. You'll simply enrage him if you hit him with it and it smashes. Come along." She had heard the sound again, and it did sound like footsteps. An occasional snap of a dead stick. A rustle of leaves. She looked up quickly in the direction the sound came from, thought she saw a flick of movement in the dusky woods. They came out of the shadow to the marshy place where they'd searched for the orchid. Victoria was slowed by having to step carefully from one grass tuft to another. She heard the rustling now, almost steadily. It was as if the stalker no longer needed to be stealthy. Would he come out into the open, she wondered? There wasn't much she could do to defend herself if he did. Perhaps Robin could run for help; she certainly couldn't. She moved faster, tripped over a grass tuft. Robin reached his scrawny arm out as if it were spring-loaded, and she fell against it. His arm gave like a sapling, and he helped her to stand upright again.

"Well." Victoria caught her breath. "Well. Maybe you *are* earning your pay. Thank you."

He looked around behind them. "We better keep moving. Want to hold my arm?"

Victoria heard the rustling, closer now. "Yes. I'd better."

While Victoria and Robin were scouting for an orchid that might not exist, the gang on Alley's porch was basking in the warm spring sunshine.

Joe unzipped his windbreaker and shoved his grimy hands into his pants pockets. "Where's Donald at?" He was standing at the edge of the porch, pelvis thrust out, rocking back and forth. He shifted a wad of something from one side of his mouth to the other.

"Down at the boatyard," said Lincoln, bending and straightening his long legs to scratch his back on the door-frame.

Sarah had unbuttoned her coat, exposing a black T-shirt printed with a slogan for the Two Braves Trucking Company in Day-Glo pink and orange. She was sitting on the bench, drinking a Diet Coke. She wore her hair in an inch-high crew cut.

Joe jerked his head toward the T-shirt. His hair curled in dark ringlets that Sarah envied. "How come you're always wearing that Indian shit? You ain't no Indian."

" 'Native American,' " Sarah said primly. "I work for the Tribe, in case you forgot."

Joe shook his head.

"Anybody heard any more about the Mausz murder?" Lincoln stopped scratching his back and straightened up. He had a long, horsy face topped by blond hair that was beginning to gray. "It's been mighty quiet."

A black pickup truck pulled up in front of the store and a short bearded man in jeans and a jean jacket got out. He nodded at the three on the porch and went into the store. The door banged shut.

"Who's the short guy in the high-heeled cowboy boots?" Lincoln indicated the door with his thumb.

"Tom More," said Sarah. "The one who wants to build that commune at Sachem's Rock."

"I thought Ness had that locked up."

Sarah shrugged. "You never know."

"You was saying about Mickey Mausz," Joe turned back to Sarah.

"Toby took his body off-Island in the hearse and they did an autopsy in Falmouth." Sarah took a sip of her Diet Coke. "All they found out was what everybody already knows. He was hit on the head with something, and he'd been dead about three, four weeks. A month maybe."

A red Volvo went past headed toward Chilmark. The driver waved. Lincoln nodded.

"How's his wife taking it?" Lincoln said. "They weren't getting along too good, last I heard."

"That's putting it mildly." Sarah finished the last of her soda and set the empty can on the bench beside her. "She was suing him for divorce."

"Yeah?" Joe looked at Sarah with interest. "Because of his girlfriend?"

" 'Woman friend,' " Sarah corrected.

"Who's the woman friend, anybody we know?" Lincoln started rubbing his back against the doorframe again.

"Get a splinter, doing that," Joe said.

Lincoln ignored him. "I heard she was someone from the Island. A mystery lady."

"He must be about the first person on this Island who kept his girlfriend's name a secret," said Joe.

Sarah brushed a speck off her black trousers. "If you've got money, you can always fly to the Caribbean. That's where his wife thought they'd gone. At least that's what she's saying."

"Did his wife know who the other woman was?" Lincoln asked.

"Who knows what she knew." Joe wriggled his hips. "Minerva Peabody is Edgartown Yacht Club, dahling. Tennis. Sailing. Pink shirts and flowered drawers. Mausz married her for her money."

"Yeah?" Lincoln leaned forward. " 'Peabody?' "

"She kept her maiden name," Sarah explained.

Joe guffawed. "Wouldn't you if you was her? Minerva Mausz?"

Lincoln shrugged. "Where's her money come from?"

"Old money," said Sarah. "Railroads or oil or mergers or something."

Joe spit off to one side again and wiped his mouth with the back of his hand.

"That's disgusting, Joe." Sarah shifted on the bench as if to distance herself from him.

"Want me to swallow it instead?"

Sarah shuddered. "Animal."

Joe guffawed. "You got that right, lady."

"Any more news about the guy Miz Trumbull's tree fell on?" Lincoln asked.

"They say he's still in a coma," Sarah replied.

"What's her and that nerdy kid doing?" Joe took his penknife out of his pocket and began to clean his fingernails. "They been walking up to Sachem's Rock."

Sarah set the soda can down again. "She's always walking places. That's why she's in such good shape."

"Probably scouting for something." Joe rocked, heel to toe.

"Everybody wants that land," Lincoln said. "The golfing docs. The tribe."

"Well, it's Ness's land. He bought it," Sarah said.

"Don't mean he's going to keep it." Joe finished cleaning the nails on one hand and started on the other. "Park and Rec wants the town to buy it for a kiddy park and campground."

"How'd you hear that?" Lincoln asked.

"My wife's cousin is on Park and Rec. And then there's that religious freak in there." Joe jerked his head toward the interior of the store, where Tom More had gone. "Alfalfa sprouts cooked by solar energy in a community kitchen. Red plot."

"It's not communist, it's communal," Sarah said.

"Same thing."

"Don't forget the Conservation Trust. That quiet guy has something up his sleeve, too," Lincoln added.

"Josiah Coffin?" Sarah raised her eyebrows. "What about him?"

"Mark my words. Coffin is going to tangle with Loch Ness." Lincoln said.

"Coffin don't have two cents to rub together." Joe started down the steps. "I gotta get back to work."

"Want to take bets on what happens next?" Sarah asked.

"Only thing I'm betting on is Old Lady Trumbull," Joe said over his shoulder. "She's some smart, for an old bird."

CHAPTER 6

When they got back to the Conservation Trust office, Victoria sat heavily in the armchair at the head of the conference room table. "Someone was following us," she said to Josiah. "At least it sounded that way."

Josiah turned to Zack who was standing behind Victoria. "This is foolish. We have no idea who's out there. Maybe it's Ness's caretaker or maybe not. Until they determine who killed Mausz we shouldn't send anyone out there. I'm calling this off. We'll have to find another way."

Robin, who was circling the table, stopped. "You mean you won't let us go back there?"

Josiah shook his head. "I don't think it's wise."

Victoria drummed her fingers on the table. "If Robin and I stay together, there's no danger to either of us. The person who was following us this afternoon could easily have attacked one of us today and didn't."

Zack turned to Josiah. "Suppose I go along with them?"

"We've got to come up with some other plan," Josiah said, still shaking his head. "You'd be a dead giveaway, Zack. Everyone on the Island knows you're with the Trust. It won't work for you to go along."

Robin had stopped by the bookcase and was running his fingers along the backs of the books. He turned around. "That's not fair," he said to Josiah. "You promised . . ."

Josiah glowered at him and Robin didn't finish.

"It seems to me," Victoria said, "since I'm the one involved, since it's my safety you're worried about, that it's my decision whether to continue or not. You've told me your concerns, and I thank you. But I intend to continue my survey of the property. I have no right to speak for Robin, of course."

"Me too," Robin said quickly.

"That's not up to me," Victoria said.

Josiah stared down at the map in front of him. Zack looked out at the cranberry bog. From the window the bog was a dark red blanket below them. Victoria continued to drum on the table. Robin's glasses had slipped down to the end of his nose.

"It's not your decision," Victoria repeated. "It's mine. If you won't take me, I'll get Elizabeth to take me. Or Casey."

"Me too," said Robin.

Victoria turned her head. "That's up to your mother."

Josiah stood. "All right, Victoria. We need your help, that's for sure. And you're the only person I can think of who can get away with the search. You and Robin, that is."

Zack leaned against the bookcase. "What about letting her take a hand-held radio, Josiah?"

"I've never worked one of those," Victoria said.

Zack grinned. "You can learn."

"I don't need a radio," Victoria insisted.

"Can we take a radio, Mrs. Trumbull? Can we? I can work it for you."

" 'May' we," Victoria said. "Not 'can.' "

And so it was decided. Josiah showed Victoria and Robin, both of them, how to work the radio, and from then on, Victoria carried it with her in her cloth bag.

On their second day out, Victoria and Robin went beyond the marsh, followed the gentle slope of the old cart path, and came out of the woods into a clearing. Boulders the size of automobiles dotted the overgrown field, left there by the glacier. The grass moved in the breeze like russet and tan ocean waves. A song sparrow sang a snatch of an almost recognizable aria. Victoria unbuttoned her heavy sweater, the one

Fiona's parents had given her. She was still too warm.

"Hey," Robin shouted. "Here comes a dog." He held out his hand. "Here, dog!"

A large black and white dog trotted toward them, tongue hanging out. It stopped a few yards from them and growled.

"What's the matter, dog?" Robin kept his hand out.

The dog growled.

"Here's a piece of bread." Victoria gave Robin a crust from their sandwiches, and he held it out to the dog.

The dog growled.

"He doesn't seem very friendly," Victoria said.

Suddenly, the dog started to move, and moved swiftly toward Victoria. Taken by surprise, she stepped back, and the dog leaped at her, grabbed her open sweater in his teeth and snarled. Robin snatched up a fallen branch from the ground and clobbered the dog on the head. The dog, still growling and snarling, let go of Victoria's sweater, and turned on Robin, who swung the stick at him again and again until the dog backed away, teeth and gums showing. It finally turned and slunk away, looking over its shoulders at Victoria and the boy.

"Are you okay, Mrs. Trumbull?"

"Yes. Thanks to you. And you?"

"He didn't scare me."

"Was he wearing a collar?" Victoria asked. "It happened so quickly, I didn't see."

"A red collar," the boy said, "With metal tags."

"It wasn't a feral dog then. It must be somebody's pet. It must think we're trespassing on its territory."

"Do you think his owners are around here someplace?"

"Perhaps they're hiking," Victoria said.

"Maybe they're camping out. Maybe they built a cabin and live here and nobody knows about them. Maybe that's who we heard the other day. Maybe it's like that man who lived in an underground house, and nobody knew about him until one day somebody tripped over his stove pipe."

"Hmmm," Victoria said.

Robin paused. "I didn't hurt him, I don't think."

"I'm sure you didn't."

Later that afternoon, when they sat around the table in the Trust office with the map spread out in front of them, Victoria told Josiah how the dog with the red collar had attacked her.

"That's strange." Josiah leaned his elbows on the table. "The caretaker has a dog, but it's a black lab. Doesn't sound like his."

Robin said, "I bet somebody's camping out. That's what I think." He ran his hand along the polished surface of the table.

"Sit down," Victoria said. "We can't think with you doing that."

Robin sat in a chair in front of the window that looked out over the cranberry bog. He immediately jumped up again. "Look, Mrs. Trumbull. Cedar waxwings. That's what you told me they were. There's a million of them in that tree!" He pointed.

Both Victoria and Josiah got to their feet and looked at the birds in a red cedar to one side of the bog.

Josiah patted the top of the boy's baseball cap. "You're absolutely right. That's what they are."

Robin knelt in the chair and stared out the window. Victoria and Josiah returned to the table and the open map.

"There are only a few more places I can think to search," Victoria said. "Here," she pointed with her gnarled finger, "and here. And over here."

"That's precisely where Ness wants to put several of the houses." Josiah circled the area lightly with his pencil. "It would be great if you found something there."

"When we got this far today," Victoria pointed, "the way was blocked by a fence."

"A fence?" Josiah sounded puzzled. "Those ancient ways are public rights-of-way. They're not supposed to be blocked."

"It's a new board fence, about six feet tall. We turned back when we came to it."

"Try to get around it if you can," Josiah said. "That area should be good orchid habitat. If it's anywhere on the property, that seems like a probable place."

The next day was rainy.

"Are you sure you want to go walking today, Victoria?" Zack took off his glasses and wiped them with his bandana. "It's nasty out."

"It's not going to rain hard." Victoria walked outside to Zack's truck and looked up at the sky. In the driveway a robin hopped three or four times, stopped and cocked his head, hopped again, cocked his head. Victoria watched. The robin darted at something, leaned back on his tail, the end of an earthworm in his bill, and tugged. The worm was anchored in the ground.

"March showers," Victoria said. "They don't amount to anything." The worm was stretching, longer and longer. Suddenly, it let go, and the robin flopped back onto its tail, shook itself, and flew off with the worm.

"That slicker looks as if it will keep you dry unless it's pouring, Victoria. If it starts to rain hard, I'll come back early for you."

They drove to the school. Robin was waiting for them where the yellow school buses lined up. A sea of kids in yellow and blue and red slickers were milling around the school entrance, throwing punches at each other, shouting, running, pushing.

" 'Bye, Robin," said a girl Robin's size in a shiny powder blue slicker. "Call me this afternoon!"

"Maybe." Robin said.

Zack looked over at the boy. He had climbed into the passenger side next to Victoria, who slid to the middle. "Girl friend?" said Zack.

"She's a dork. A retard. A nerd. She's ugly and she's a psycho."

"Sounds as if you like her," Victoria said.

Robin made a gurgling noise.

"How was school?" Zack asked, and Robin chattered on about Magic cards and GameBoy and Pokémon. Victoria felt as if she were in a time warp.

Robin pulled something out of his book bag and turned to Zack. "See what Mrs. Trumbull gave me?" He held out the mouse-shaped pencil sharpener.

Zack, who was just turning onto State Road from Old County Road, took a quick look and grunted. "A mouse."

"Not a mouse," Robin said. "Pikachu. Jeez, even Mrs. Trumbull knows who Pikachu is."

Victoria smiled faintly.

The sky was blotchy gray and overcast. It had sprinkled off and on during the morning, and looked now as though it might rain again. The air smelled fresh, of wet earth and germinating seeds and plants ready to emerge.

After they turned onto State Road it started to sprinkle again. Zack turned on the windshield wipers and looked questioningly at Victoria.

"This won't last long."

The rain let up and Zack turned off the wipers.

He dropped them off at the usual place and agreed to meet in two hours. Victoria checked her watch before she moved across the passenger seat behind Robin, and, holding the sides of the door, slid off the seat until her feet touched the ground.

Robin and she had gone along the trail several times now and were familiar with its branches. Only once had they seen anyone—the caretaker, with his black Lab. He'd greeted them pleasantly. Victoria had asked how his new grandbaby was doing, said she was showing her young friend, Robin, Audrey White's grandson, some of the places she'd known as a child, hoped it was all right if they walked the ancient ways. She promised to be careful. He'd tipped his cap, lifted the visor slightly, and said sure, any time she wanted to walk the place, it was okay with him. Robin had patted the black Lab, whose name was Pepper, and they went on their way.

They walked past the marsh, where the tiny tree frogs Vineyarders called "pinkletinks" had started shrilling in the past day or two. The tufts of dry grass where Victoria stepped to keep her feet dry showed green shoots close to the ground. She hated the thought of crushing the fragile new growth. The trail wound around the base of the hill, then branched off onto the path that was blocked farther along by the new fence.

Rain had softened the crisp fallen leaves and turned the pale new wood of the fence a reddish gold. Victoria sniffed the vanilla scent of the new lumber and the rich smell of wet leaves and earth.

She suddenly sensed that someone was watching them. She stopped and listened. She could hear Robin walking carelessly through the undergrowth, the squish of damp leaves and the slap of branches. She heard the sound of water dripping from wet limbs, the distant rumble of surf on the south shore. Far away and below them she heard a car go by on North Road. A crow called. She heard the sleighbell sound of pinkletinks in the marsh. Was she simply imagining a sound that did not belong?

They stopped at the fence and Victoria said to Robin, "I'll wait here while you see how far it goes." She looked around for something she could sit on and found a lichen-covered rock. "See if there's a way around it."

Robin darted off through the huckleberry and catbrier that grew next to the fence. The briers snatched at his jeans with a sound like fabric ripping.

While she waited, Victoria took out her notebook and pen, alert for sounds and smells. The gray sky and gray trees, the gray of the rocks around her and the gray lichen formed a silvery grayness that was broken by patches of green moss and golden beech leaves. She heard only the sounds of the woods and the sea. Within a few minutes Robin returned along the fence, running a stick along the new boards with a clacking sound.

"It stops at the brook, Mrs. Trumbull. You can get around okay. I'll help. There are big stepping stones."

He held the briers aside so they wouldn't slap across her corduroy-clad legs and they walked beside the new fence.

Before she saw the brook she heard it burble over its rough bed. The brook was narrow, only five or six feet across. Four large stones led from the end of the fence to the other side of the brook. On the upstream side was a thick growth of bright green watercress.

"On the way back, we'll pick some for your mother and Elizabeth." Victoria pinched off the tip of one of the plants and nibbled it.

"You can eat those leaves?" Robin turned up his nose.

"Ladies serve watercress sandwiches at tea parties."

On the downstream side of the rocks, long streamers of green grass-like weeds trailed and waved in the current.

"Hey, an eel!" Robin said, leaning out over the rock he was standing on.

Victoria bent over to look. "It's a lamprey," she said. "I think that's supposed to be rare. Be sure to tell Zack."

"It looks like an eel."

"It's not. Its mouth is a sucker. Some kinds of lampreys

latch onto other fish and drink their blood, but I don't think this kind does."

"Vampires!" Robin hopped across the stepping stones to the other side and back. "Sweet!"

Victoria held one hand on the post that supported the fence, set her stick in the brook, and stepped cautiously onto the closest rock. Robin was beside her instantly, and held his arm out to her in case she wanted to take it. Victoria set her feet firmly on the mossy bank, took a few steps, and sat on a fallen log to catch her breath.

"Do you really think those vampire fish are rare?" Robin asked. "Will you tell them I was the one that found it?"

"Yes, yes," Victoria said in between breaths. She stood up again. "Let's go."

They heard the soft patter of rain on the beech leaves off to one side, and felt a sprinkling. Before they reached the path where it continued on the other side of the fence the rain had stopped again.

As they walked, Victoria kept listening for the sound she thought she had heard, but there was only rainwater dripping from trees, the frog chorus, the sea. She concentrated on searching for the elusive leaves with purple spots.

Then, as if it were quite ordinary, just another green leaf on the ground, she saw it. The leaf was under an old oak tree that spread long low branches far out from its trunk, and next to a large beech tree. A single dark green leaf lying flat on top of last autumn's fallen oak leaves. The leaf, which was only an inch or so long, was spotted with dark purple blotches. Its edges were slightly ruffled. "Look. Robin. We've found it!"

Robin dashed over to her, and when he saw it he jumped up and down.

"Careful!" Victoria cautioned. "Don't trample it." She got down onto her knees carefully, holding her stick for support, and gently turned one of the leaves over. "Look at this."

"It's purple. Just like Mr. Coffin said. Just like you said. Cool!"

"We need to mark this exactly." She handed a pencil and the folded map to Robin with her notebook for backing.

A few feet farther on near a cluster of clethra she found three more leaves. And a quarter mile farther up the path she found another single leaf. Then it was time to turn back.

They hurried down the trail, skirted the fence, carefully went around it at the brook. The lamprey still clung to a rock on the bottom of the brook, looking much like the green weeds that pointed downstream. Its eely tail waved in the current.

They followed the fence back to the path.

Then Victoria heard something again. Her neck hairs lifted. She looked over at Robin, and held a finger to her lips. His eyes opened wide.

She whispered, without making a sound, "Do you hear anything?" and raised her eyebrows in question.

He shook his head.

They moved steadily along the path. At one point Robin veered off to the right to follow a deer trail, and came bouncing back holding a box turtle about eight inches long with a high domed shell. The turtle had drawn in its head and feet and closed its hinged lower shell.

"Hey, Mrs. Trumbull! Look what I found on the path!"

He put the turtle down on the ground, and they watched it while it gradually stuck its head out. Its eyes were a fierce red, its beak turned down in a sort of sneer. It ventured its feet out, one after another, four toes on each. Its dark brown shell was boldly patterned with yellow and orange streaks and splotches that matched streaks on its legs.

"Pretty," Victoria said with admiration. "I shouldn't be surprised if you hadn't found another special creature. They're calling everything rare these days."

"Can I take him home?" Robin asked, picking the turtle

up again. The turtle immediately withdrew its head and feet and snapped its lower shell shut.

"Leave him here. He probably has a family somewhere."

"Turtles? Families? They lay eggs and bury them. That's not a family."

"Leave him alone," Victoria said more sharply than she intended. She had heard a distinct sound on the other side of the path. "Come along." She reached into her cloth bag to make sure the hand-held radio was where she could get it easily, and moved as rapidly as she could.

"Hey," Robin said. "Wait for me!"

They rushed along the path, Victoria watching where she put her feet, Robin matching her speed silently. Down the gentle hill, where she felt, rather than heard, the presence of someone. Over the grass tuft steps next to the pinkletink marsh. Across the open meadow, over the stone wall, to the road, where Zack waited for them.

Victoria was out of breath and leaned against the truck for several minutes while Robin chatted excitedly.

"I found a vampire fish that Mrs. Trumbull said is rare."

Zack looked out from under the fall of straight hair, through his thick glasses. "Vampire fish?"

"An eel in the brook. It was holding onto a rock or something with a suction cup. Mrs. Trumbull said they drink blood."

"A lamprey?" Zack asked.

"Yeah! That was it!" Robin jumped up and down and then stopped. "And I found a turtle, but Mrs. Trumbull said I had to leave it there."

"How big was it? Did it have a high shell?"

"That big." Robin held out his hands. "And this high."

"Orange and yellow and red splotches?"

Robin nodded.

"Think you can remember where you saw him?"

Robin nodded.

"If you've found a brook lamprey and an eastern box turtle, that was great work for today."

Victoria was leaning against the fender of the truck, listening. She breathed deeply. "Tell Zack what else we found."

"Oh yeah. Mrs. Trumbull found a whole bunch of cranefly orchids."

CHAPTER 7

In the senior center later that afternoon, the heavyset woman in the flowing black-and-brown caftan was knitting, making a clicking sound that was irritating to Tom More. "Is there any chance of buying the Sachem's Rock property from Harry Ness?" she asked without looking up from her work. Tom studied her before he answered. Her white hair, worn long and loose, floated partway down her back. Her gold-rimmed granny glasses rested on her nose. When she finished speaking she finally looked up and her knitting needles paused. She was knitting the bulky sweater of speckled brown wool she had been working on as long as Tom More had known her, a year now.

Tom More had called this meeting of investors in Cranberry Fields, his cooperative housing project. Twenty of his investors were seated on folding chairs arranged around him in a semicircle in the senior center's basement.

Tom More himself was sitting in an armchair under a large watercolor of geese standing by the millpond. Members of his group were talking to each other and the noise level had grown to a low roar with an occasional tinkle of laughter.

"I'm hopeful, Marguerite." Tom More's eyes fixed on her intently before he looked from one to another member of the group. He stood up, a short stocky man in blue jeans, a jean jacket, and cowboy boots that gave him an additional two inches in height, and held up his hands for silence. On one wrist he wore a heavy Rolex watch, on the other a thin copper bracelet. The flock stilled.

"I have an announcement to make." He waited until all

eyes were on him, then waited a few moments more, gazing from one face to another with hypnotic eyes. "An anonymous donor has offered to put up a considerable sum of money if we can get Mr. Ness to sell Sachem's Rock to us." There was a soft murmur from the group. Individuals looked at each other, then back at Tom More.

"What's Ness's price?" a young man with untidy dark hair and farm-grimy hands asked.

The knitting needles clicked.

"As you know, Sanders, Mr. Ness bought the property for one million dollars." Tom More sat down again. He leaned forward, elbows on the arms of the chair, hands clasped in front of him. His hair waved thickly around his face and hung down to his shoulders. His beard covered the lower half of his face. His glasses magnified his intense eyes. "We had offered Phoebe Eldredge one-point-five million."

"How come she turned it down, sir?" asked a blond young man in white painters' overalls standing by the far wall.

Before Tom More could answer, a balding middle-aged man sitting on the far side said, "She told me she thought Cranberry Fields was a hippie commune."

"How ridiculous." Marguerite twitched a length of speckled yarn out of a tapestry bag on the floor beside her chair.

"How much would we need to offer Ness to get the property, do you think?" Sanders asked again.

Tom More unclasped his hands and held them out, palms up. "It's anyone's guess. I'm prepared to offer him two-and-a-half million."

"That's a sizeable profit for Ness," the balding man said.

Marguerite's knitting needles clicked. Tom More considered asking her to stop, and decided not to.

"How much will each of us have to ante up?" Sanders asked.

"Our donor has offered to contribute one million dollars

to the Cranberry Fields project." Tom More looked over the group until his eyes met those of a lean tan woman wearing a cashmere blazer that matched the sun-streaked blond of her hair. She smiled at him. He leaned back in his chair and waited.

The group was silent. Then there were murmurs. A young woman in the back row of chairs raised her hand.

"Deborah," Tom More acknowledged her. A small girl, probably two years old, clung to Deborah's jeans-clad legs.

"One of us? Offered a million dollars?"

Tom More nodded.

"Thank you, somebody," Deborah said.

"Yes! Yes!"

The tan blond in cashmere folded her hands in her lap.

"Are there any conditions on the grant?" Sanders shuffled his boots, and a chunk of dried mud fell onto the floor.

"Only that we acquire the land and build our community." Tom More looked around the group, which had started murmuring again. "This individual believes in Cranberry Fields." He stood again and raised his hands. The group quieted. "This person believes in a simple life, as do we." His deep voice was growing louder. "Believes in a community of brothers and sisters. Believes in family. Believes we have the only lifestyle that can survive on this frail planet in this new millennium."

"Yes! Yes!" said several voices.

"We will live in harmony with the earth, as Native Americans did before white settlers came. We will not waste the earth's precious resources. Cranberry Fields will be a life of harmony."

"Yes! Yes!"

Tom More's voice dropped down from its preaching level. "Does anyone want to ask any further questions before we get down to business?"

"Will this discovery of the endangered orchid affect Cranberry Fields?" a thin, almost scrawny, forty-ish woman asked.

"You mean the layout of our houses, Evie, community center, and carpentry shop?"

Evie nodded.

"Good question," Tom More said. "It should help us, actually. We believe in maintaining the existing ecosystems. We intend to keep human intrusion to a minimum. Cranberry Fields concentrates our houses in one small area, and leaves the rest of the property untouched. Ness's plan subdivides the property into three-acre lots with a large house on each lot. You can imagine how that would disturb the ecosystem. A septic system for each house. Swimming pools. Lawns. Gardens. Garages. Our community will not be built on the sacrificed corpses of other species."

"Suppose they find another orchid, or some other rare plant, on our site?" Evie asked.

"That's not likely," Tom More said shortly. "Any other questions?"

There was a general head-shaking.

"We're going ahead with our plans for Cranberry Fields as if Sachem's Rock is ours. Positive thinking, guys and gals?" He raised both hands in a sort of benediction.

"Yes! Yes!" the group responded.

"To business, then." Tom More reached behind his armchair and brought out rolls of maps and charts and blueprints. Sanders got to his feet and clumped to Tom More's side, leaving a trail of dirt. Together, they unrolled charts and taped them over the paintings on the wall.

That done, Tom More turned back to the group. "Harmony. We could almost call our new community 'Harmony,' rather than Cranberry Fields."

"Someone already did that," the balding man said, and laughed. "That one didn't work."

Tom More ignored him. "Here's the overall plan." He turned back to the charts and blueprints taped to the wall. "Here's the carpentry shop, off to one side where no one will be disturbed by the sound of saws and hammers. About half of the people who have signed up for Cranberry Fields already work in the old carpentry shop. They'll be able to walk to work, walk home to the community center for lunch, take a quick nap or whatever, and go back to work."

There were titters and smiles.

"Here's the community center." He placed his hand flat on the schematic. "This is where we'll want to spend most of our free time. On this side is a community kitchen with a commercial-size stove and refrigerator. We'll take turns preparing food. Here's the dining room. We'll eat family style. And over here," he pointed, "is the community recreation room. We'll have a fireplace with couches arranged around it, and over on this side a place to set up tables for writing letters or playing bridge or board games. And over here," he moved to the other side of the chart on the wall, "we'll have a teen center, where the kids can do their homework or do their thing without bothering the rest of us."

"Is there a place where I can keep my sewing machine?" one of the women asked.

"Over here," Tom More pointed, "we'll have a hobby area for sewing or working on stamp collections or making models or whatever. Big work surfaces, unlike what most of you have at home now, right?" He turned to the group.

"Right! Yes!"

"Any questions about this so far? I know we're going over some of this for the third or fourth time for some of you, but for others, this is new."

"Have you assigned any of our homes yet?" the bald man asked.

"I'm getting to that." Tom More turned to a second drawing taped to the wall. "Our homes are simplicity itself. A comfortable bedroom or, in the case of those of you with children," he nodded to Deborah and her child, "more than one bedroom. A place to sleep. A lavatory with composting toilet. Showers and baths will be in the community center. A small kitchenette for preparing breakfast or snacks. Simplify, simplify." He slapped his hand against the sketch taped to the wall.

"Laundry?" someone asked.

"Washing machines will be here, in the community center. No dryers. We'll have a drying yard over here, where our clothes and bed linens will get plenty of sun and the good west wind." He turned back to the group. "I'm sure you want to know where you'll be living."

"Yes! Yes!" said the group.

"The houses are arranged in a square around the community center, so no one has too far to walk for dinner. Or a shower."

General smiles.

"Jeff, you and your wife and kids have a three bedroom. Here, on the northwest corner of the square. And Marguerite, yours is a single bedroom next to Jeff."

"Tom, is it all right to be totally frank and open?" Marguerite stopped knitting.

"Of course. Now's the time."

"This is a bit uncomfortable to say," said Marguerite, "and I realize it's my problem, not anyone else's. But I don't like being around small children."

Jeff's wife made a choking sound. "Then why did you sign up for Cranberry Fields? We're supposed to be a family, and families have small children. Even if you don't remember, that's how you started."

"I know, I know," Marguerite looked down at the pile of knitting in her lap. "I realize this is my problem. I don't mind being three or four houses away, or on the other side of the community center, but I really don't want to be right next door to children. That's one reason I signed up. The brochures said this would be a wonderful place for older single people."

"We'll see what we can do," Tom More said soothingly. "Perhaps you'll feel differently once we're all settled. Older members of our community have so much richness to bring to our younger members. We envision surrogate grandmothers reading to and playing with the little ones. And baby sitting. Older people are a truly wasted resource."

"That's not my vision of my life. I'm a painter. I don't want somebody else's grandchildren. I don't have any of my own and don't want them. With all those houses," she pointed with a loose knitting needle, "I should think I would have a choice whether or not to live right next door to squalling brats with sticky fingers and dirty faces."

Jeff's wife stood up abruptly and started to say something. Before she could, Tom More said, "We can work this out. Don't worry about it. Naturally we all feel a bit of pressure, especially since we don't even have a piece of land yet. Let me go on. I'll work on your location, Marguerite."

Marguerite took up her knitting again, her face a bright pink. Jeff's wife sat down again, her eyes glittering, her mouth a tight line. Jeff patted her knee.

"Chris, you'll have the third house—we'll decide later who'll be in Marguerite's."

"It's okay to fence my backyard, isn't it?" Chris said. "I got two German shepherds."

"Do they hate kids, too?" Jeff's wife called out.

Chris turned to her. "They're real good with kids, as long as the kids don't tease them. They may bark a little, but they're real good dogs, Fluffy and Muffin."

"Moving on," Tom More said. "Sanders, you'll be next door to Chris."

"Are your dogs going to bother my chickens?" Sanders said.

"I don't think so. You'll have them fenced in, won't you?"

"No," said Sanders. "They're free-range chickens."

"Wait one damn minute," the balding man said. "This is turning into some damn barnyard. Are we going to wake up before the sun when his damn chickens start crowing?"

"You advertised this as an environmentally aware community," Sanders said. "Birds sing. Roosters crow. If people don't want to hear country sounds, move to South Boston or Braintree. All you have to listen to there is traffic and horns blaring and rock music out of boom boxes, for crying out loud."

Marguerite's knitting needles clicked.

"We can settle all of this later," Tom More said. "This is a first cut."

That same afternoon the gray weather had lifted slightly as the sun burned through thinning clouds over Edgartown. The road in front of the Harbor View Hotel was striped with wet and dry pavement from passing cars. Three men and a woman were seated at one of the tables in The Coach House, the hotel's pub, where they could look past the wide porch with its empty rocking chairs and see the lighthouse and Chappaquiddick on the other side of the harbor.

"Will Dr. Jeffers be joining us this afternoon, Dr. Erickson?" asked the elegantly slim woman. "I'm in a bit of a time crunch."

Doc Erickson stroked his sand-colored mustache. "He should be here any minute." He adjusted the collar of the rumpled linen sports coat he wore over a pink and blue madras shirt. "What's the outlook for your crushed-chest patient?"

"Kirschmeyer. That's my chief reason for being on-Island today, to check on him. He's coming along slowly."

"Curious case," Doc Erickson said. "I can't imagine why he was standing under Mrs. Trumbull's tree in that storm."

"It's not my job to worry about motives." Dr. Gibbs placed her hand on the table and flexed her long fingers.

"Why don't we go ahead and order drinks." Doc Erickson beckoned to a bartender who came over to the table promptly. "I'll order for Jeffers. He takes ginger ale with a twist."

From where they sat they could see the Chappaquiddick ferry shuttling back and forth on its two-minute run across the narrow part of the harbor. A large sailboat came in while they waited, motored around the bend and out of sight into the inner harbor. The Edgartown light flashed its beam, watery-looking in the late afternoon light.

"It's good to be back on the Island," said the youngest of the group, a pudgy man with a shiny bald head. "Especially out of season like this."

"You ought to come over more often, John. We could use an orthopedist at the hospital," Doc Erickson said. "More moped accidents every year. Enough broken bones to keep you happy."

"Got plenty of those on the Cape now." John turned to the woman, who was sitting on his right. "It's nice to see you again, Kate. You're looking good—as always. Last time was at the Boston AMA meeting, wasn't it?"

"On the golf course after the meeting, actually." Dr. Gibbs smiled. A sudden ray of sunlight picked out highlights in her glossy black hair. Two streaks of white fanned out from her temples, giving her a distinguished look.

"Well," said Doc Erickson, "that's why we're here, after all." He turned at a clanking sound. "Here's Jeffers now."

Dr. Gibbs's eyes opened wide.

Doc Jeffers, who was well over six feet tall, was wearing his leather motorcycle jacket and trousers. He had taken off his metallic blue helmet and was holding it under his arm. As the others stared, he reached into an inside pocket and the small blue lights that blinked across the front of his helmet went out. He unzipped his jacket, exposing a bunch of curly white hair in the V-neck of his hospital scrub shirt.

Dr. Sawicki and the fourth person at the table, an elderly man wearing a Harris Tweed jacket over a starched white shirt and regimental tie stood as the biker came to the table.

The biker stuck out a great paw to the white-haired man in tweed. "Jeffers," he said.

"Russ Billings," the man said.

"Kate Gibbs," the woman said, keeping her hands in her lap.

"Dr. Gibbs the surgeon. Delighted to meet you," Doc Jeffers said. "Lucky you were on-Island that day. No one else could have saved him. Nice piece of work." He grinned, showing great strong teeth.

"Thanks. He's coming along nicely."

Doc Jeffers turned to the plump young doctor. "You must be John Sawicki. Orthopedics. I suppose Erickson has already tried to enlist you?"

Dr. Sawicki smiled, his small mouth like a dimple in bread dough.

Doc Jeffers pulled out a fifth chair and sat, with a final clank. He stowed his helmet under his chair and settled his booted feet firmly on the floor.

Dr. Gibbs looked at her watch again. "I'm afraid I have to catch the six-thirty boat. If you don't mind, perhaps we can get right down to business."

Doc Jeffers leered at her.

Doc Erickson reached down for a folder that was leaning against his chair and opened it on the table. "This is a map of the Sachem's Rock property. Ideal for an up-scale golf course. Put the clubhouse here, right behind the big rock. Nice landscaping around the rock, Island plants, that sort of thing, make it the theme for the golf course. Parking here in a circle around the rock. There's a house here presently," he pointed, and Dr. Gibbs and Dr. Sawicki leaned forward for a better look. "It belonged to the former owner, a Mrs. Eldredge. We'll raze that and on the site, which has a great view, construct a small country inn, eighteenth-century flavor, twenty-first–century conveniences. Big fireplaces at either end, a common room, a dining room, no more than ten to twelve guest rooms, each with its own bath."

"What about acquiring the property from Ness?" Dr. Billings smoothed his hair and straightened his tie with a gnarled hand.

"I don't think that will be much of a problem," Doc Erickson said, shuffling the top papers onto the bottom of the stack. "He paid one million for it. We're prepared to offer him two-point-five for it, maybe go as high as three million. It's probably worth ten."

"From what I hear of Ness, he's not likely to sell out at bargain rates." Dr. Sawicki pursed his lips.

"We'll turn up the heat," Doc Jeffers said. "Nothing like social pressure. We know how to apply it." He winked at Dr. Gibbs, who looked back at him stonily through almond-shaped dark eyes. "We've got, how many investors, Erickson?"

Doc Erickson peered over his half-frame glasses. "Fifty investors have already pledged two-hundred-thousand each for membership. We're limiting membership to five hundred, so that gives us room to grow."

"All physicians?" Dr. Sawicki placed his elbows on the table and laced his plump hands beneath his chin.

"Physicians or health care professionals," Doc Erickson looked up from the papers. "Ah, here comes the bartender."

Dr. Gibbs was making notes with a slim gold pen in a slim leather-bound notebook with gold edges. "Ten million. Those are firm pledges?"

The bartender set down coasters and drinks. Doc Erickson signed the tab with his illegible signature and the bartender left.

"Firm pledges," Doc Erickson said. "Acquire the land for two-point-five, maybe three. That leaves seven million to develop the golf course, put up the buildings. Memberships and fees, the restaurant and the inn will sustain it."

"It looks pretty good to me," Dr. Sawicki said. "Good investment, a healthy choice, not like putting up a gambling casino, which is what I understand the tribe wants to do."

"An opportunity for the physician investors to get a much-needed vacation in an unspoiled spot," Dr. Billings said. "You've done a good job, Erickson. I commend you."

"Thanks. I've been working with DufferPro," Doc Erickson said. "They get the credit. They have a track record of developing golf courses for professionals who have the money but not the time or know-how."

Blue-black highlights glinted in Dr. Gibbs's hair as she turned to Doc Erickson. The white strands were brushed carefully away from her temples. "What do you need from us? A check?"

"Not yet," Doc Erickson said. "Let me show you what else we have here."

Dr. Sawicki moved drink glasses to one side so Doc Erickson could spread out the papers, and they leaned over to see better.

"Looking good!" Doc Jeffers lifted up his glass in a toast and took a swig of his ginger ale. "The greatest selling point, that I can see, is that the course will be open to Islanders, at cut rates."

Doc Erickson nodded. "I agree. For years, I've been urging my patients to get out there on the links and swat at a few balls. With this," he slapped the papers in front of him, "they won't be able to say they can't afford it."

"A grand scheme," Doc Jeffers agreed.

Doc Erickson ran his pen lightly around the map. "One of our greatest selling points will be this system of public paths that wind around the golf course."

"Somebody's going to get hit in the eye with a golf ball." Dr. Sawinski's bald head reflected the overhead light as he bent over the drawings. "Trying to get us more business, are you?"

"No, the paths were designed by the DufferPro people to be well away from the line of fire. No, we see this as a way to stem public criticism of an elitist golf club." Doc Erickson peered over the top of his glasses at Dr. Sawicki.

"It certainly isn't elitist if we allow the public at large to play." A frown creased Dr. Gibbs's smooth forehead. "Did I hear you say it will be open to Islanders at cut rates? I should remind you that one of the reasons I agreed to invest was to get away from the great unwashed public. I see enough of them every day at the hospital."

"I agree." Dr. Billings stretched his turkey neck out of the constrictions of white collar and tie. "This was intended, if I understood correctly, to be a retreat for overworked physicians. We all know what will happen if the general public is encouraged to join. Every hypochondriac on the Island will be asking for a free consultation. Every visiting tourist. We'll have no peace at all."

Doc Erickson put the papers back into the folder. "The only way we're going to be able to build the golf course is by getting public support. There's already a public backlash over the No Trespassing signs that are going up all over the Island. That plus fences and lack of access. We need public support."

"Well, go ahead and get your public support, then. Sounds as if you don't need mine." Dr. Gibbs rose to her feet. "I've got to go."

Doc Jeffers rose also.

"Don't be so hasty." Doc Erickson looked up at Dr. Gibbs. "We're still in the initial planning stages. Lots of room for negotiations and adjustments. Don't harden your position, Doctor."

"She has a point, though," Dr. Billings said. "If we're talking about a public golf course, I'm not interested, either. I can invest in a public golf course closer to home and a hell of a lot cheaper. Two-hundred-thousand bucks will buy me and my wife quite a few nice vacations away from it all."

"Why don't we sit on this for a week or so," Doc Erickson said. "Before we can take any further steps we have to be sure we can buy the land. I'll have the DufferPro people see what they can negotiate with Ness and then I'll get back to you."

Dr. Gibbs was still standing. She pulled on thin black leather gloves, slid her fingers together smoothing the soft leather in a way that Doc Jeffers watched with bright moist eyes.

"How are you getting to the ferry?" he asked her.

"I'll ask the concierge to call a cab."

"I've got an extra helmet," Doc Jeffers said. "Be glad to give you a thrill ride on my Harley."

Dr. Gibbs stared at him in horror. "No thank you. I've stitched up too many hotshot bikers. I have no intention of ruining my assets." She held up her black-gloved hands and wiggled her fingers. "Good day, gentlemen."

While the golfing doctors were meeting in Edgartown and Tom More was meeting with his community housing people downstairs in the West Tisbury senior center, the Park and Rec committee was having a heated discussion on the senior center's sun porch.

"Forget the Sachem's Rock property, kiddo. Find another site for a campground." The speaker, Julius Diamond, a recently retired gasoline dealer from New Jersey, was involving himself in the politics of his newly adopted Island town, starting with Park and Rec. "The town doesn't need two hundred acres of swings and slides and tent sites. Let Ness build his houses. It's his land. He can do what he wants with it."

Julius smoothed his new L. L. Bean checked shirt over his slight paunch.

Page Bachwald, chair of the committee, was standing beside the round glass-topped table. "I can't believe you said that, Julius!" She thrust both small fists straight down by her sides and stamped a foot. "West Tisbury has a greater percentage of young children than any other Island town."

"I think Mr. Diamond is right, honey," a sharp-nosed older woman wearing a broad-brimmed purple felt hat said. "We should put up swings and slides next to the library and encourage our wonderful young people to read books."

Page turned to the fourth person at the table, a vague-looking woman with frizzy hair and round glasses. "You agree with me, don't you Fanny, that we should get the town to purchase Sachem's Rock from that developer? I mean, we don't want another suburban development, do we?"

"Well," Fanny looked down at the yellow-lined pad in front of her on which she was drawing a row of stars, "On the one hand Sachem's Rock would make a nice campground, since we lost one of our two campgrounds to that golf course down-Island, so now families don't have any place to stay if they want to spend their vacation in a tent, which I don't, but many people do, and it would give families a Vineyard experience that would be unlike any other Vineyard experience, since we don't really have any low-cost places for families to stay." She stopped and took a breath. "On the other hand, we'd probably have to ask the town for more than a million dollars, since that's what Mr. Ness paid for it, and I'm not sure the taxpayers would want their taxes to go up that much, although if we divide a million dollars up among all the people over several years it won't be so bad, but I don't think they'll like it."

"Oh for God's sake." Julius, who had been sitting next to Fanny, wrinkled his nose and shifted away from her in his seat.

"It's a matter of saving open space," Page insisted.

"A family campground isn't open space," Julius said. "Trailers, RVs, kids, boom boxes. Look at what happened to Yosemite. Ruined it. Sheets hanging on lines between campsites. People arguing about the neighbor's TV. Smoke from hamburgers grilling over those damned briquettes. You're talking about a ghetto. Muggings. Robberies, rapes. Believe me, I know."

"This isn't Yosemite with waterfalls and Half Domes and a highway that goes right to it," Fanny said. "We don't need to squash people right next to each other, Julius. We can plan nice sites that will give everybody privacy and have public trails and Page can have her swings and slides and even a jungle gym. My only problem with it is who's going to take care of it? I mean, do we have outhouses and garbage pails?"

"For God's sake," Julius said again. "That's exactly it. People urinating in the bushes. Polluted wells. Trash everywhere. Candy wrappers and used condoms."

"Please," Lucy, the older woman, shook her head. "We're getting off the subject, and Julius, I don't think what you just said was nice at all." She fixed him with a severe look.

"Nice!" Julius sputtered. "What do we need a campground for? That's ridiculous. It's not for the people in town. Except for some people's junkie kids, a place to shoot up." He looked meaningfully at Fanny, who was drawing her stars and didn't notice.

"We'll charge them twenty-five dollars a night for a tent site," Page, still standing, said. "That way we can make money for the town."

"Are you out of your mind?" Julius leaned forward in his chair. "How many tent sites are you planning on? Fifty?"

"That sounds about right," Page said. "That's a good number. Somebody multiply that out."

Fanny had her calculator out. "That comes to twelve-hundred and fifty dollars a night."

Page counted something on her fingers. "So over the season, Fanny, from May through October, let's say it's a hundred and eighty days, what does that come to?"

"Two hundred twenty-five thousand." Fanny looked up from her calculator.

"How wonderful!" Lucy reached up to straighten her hat, which was slightly askew.

"See?" Page said. "We'd be putting all that money into the town's economy."

"Listen, sweetheart, you don't know beans about business." Julius shifted his chair back and crossed an ankle over his leg. "Take it from me, you'd be lucky to realize one quarter of that amount from a campground. It's not going to be occupied one hundred percent every night from May through October. You'd be lucky to have a twenty-percent occupancy. On top of that, don't forget you have to pay trash pickup and maintenance, someone to man the entrance booth . . ."

"We don't say 'man something' these days, Julius," Lucy said. "We need to be sensitive to the feelings of people." She tucked her white bangs under the brim of her hat.

"To continue," Julius said. " 'Person' the entrance booth. Security. You'll be paying more in salaries than you take in. And for what? Not a benefit for the town, that's for sure."

"It *would* be a benefit for the town," Page said, thrusting her fists down. "We'd have a picnic area. . . ."

"Yeah, and swings and slides. You going to drive your kids all the way up there after school to play on the swings and slides? I don't think so." He uncrossed his leg and set both feet flat on the floor.

"He's right about that, honey," Lucy said. "It would be so much nicer to have the swings and slides right next to the library. You could walk there with your little ones after school, and when they get all rosy-cheeked and tired from swinging and playing on the jungle gym, they'll be so happy to have you take them into the library where you can read to them. Parents are not reading to their children today the way I did to my children."

"Fanny, you understand what I'm trying to do, don't you?" Page was close to tears.

"Well yes," Fanny said. "I don't think any of us want to see that awful man Ness build all those disgusting trophy houses on one of the most beautiful pieces of land on Martha's Vineyard—with a gate and a guard—and it will be like every other expensive suburb on earth and we'll have lost what we're all about."

"Exactly." Page wiped her nose on a tissue she'd taken out of the sleeve of her pink sweater. "I want your support in asking the selectmen to put a request on the town meeting warrant to buy the Sachem's Rock property from Mr. Ness. For the benefit of future generations." She blew her nose and put the tissue in her pocket. "I need you to be on my side, Julius."

"I'll vote with you," Fanny said. "Basically it's a good idea, only I think the voters may have a problem with it, but it's up to them to decide after all, and, I mean, who are we to tell them how to vote?"

"I will too, honey, but I believe we ought to spend a little more time thinking it over." Lucy tugged on the brim of her hat. "We care so much about our town's children, and, well, I just don't know, but I'll vote with you."

"Oh hell," Julius said. "The town will never go for it. I might as well vote with you to make it unanimous. But you're making a mistake you'll live to regret."

CHAPTER 8

Josiah opened the folded map that Victoria had been carrying in her cloth bag the day before and flattened it on the conference room table. He and Zack studied the marks she and Robin had made on it.

"Hand me the aerial photo, will you Zack?" The overhead light picked out the auburn highlights in Josiah's thick hair. He had recently shaved off his beard, and Victoria was surprised to see how strong his chin was, definitely a Coffin feature.

Zack slid the aerial photo across the table, a square of heavy paper that curled stiffly at the edges. Josiah pointed to a distinctive line on the map that marked a turn in the trail and then to the same distinctive turn, half-hidden by trees, on the same path Victoria could see on the photo.

"From your marks on the map, it looks as if the orchids are in this area." He pointed to the photo with a grease pencil.

Victoria had seated herself in front of the spread-out map. She looked carefully from map to photo, and nodded. "Yes. That looks about right."

"Victoria, can you pinpoint the place you found the plants?" Josiah leaned over, both hands flat on the table, and looked from the map to her.

"You see that large tree here on the photo," she pointed with her pencil, "and this one. It looks like the beech that was right next to the first orchid. The second orchid was over here on the other side."

Josiah circled both spots with his grease pencil. "This is

great, Victoria, better than we could have wished for." He stood up straight and stroked his chin as if the beard were still there. "I want to take a look myself, confirm what you found, make some notes of my own." He flattened the folds in the map, set the photo next to it, and put a heavy book on top.

"I'm sure Robin would like to come." Victoria noticed for the first time that Josiah's eyes were hazel, almost green.

"When does he get out of school?" Josiah asked.

She looked at her watch. "School lets out at three. It's only ten o'clock now."

"I'd like to go there now," Josiah said. "I'm afraid we can't wait for him. The sooner we get this discovery on record the better. Everybody in town seems to know about it already."

"I'll stay here at the office," Zack said. "Call on the radio if you need anything."

Josiah and Victoria crossed the wooden bridge that led to the parking area that was hidden among trees. Josiah helped her into the pickup truck. She moved a pair of binoculars and a bird book onto the shelf behind her, where there was a collection of shells and seedpods, and an old oriole's nest, woven with shreds of blue plastic that might have come from a tarp at a construction site. She settled her quilted coat under her and smoothed her corduroy trousers over her knees.

They jounced down the rutted dirt road until they came to the paved main road where they turned left. They drove past the bog, overgrown now, where Victoria used to glean cranberries after the late October harvest. Grasses and shrubs had turned the once-wet bog into a meadow.

Josiah had apparently noticed her wistful look. "One of these days we'll restore it," he said. "There's so much to do and nowhere near enough people and money."

They passed the cemetery and the tiny Methodist Church, passed the path that led to the Lambert's Cove Beach, passed

Uncle Seth's Pond where parents brought their toddlers in summer to paddle in the shallow water.

They turned right onto State Road. A great spreading oak tree marked the beginning of North Road and Seven Gates Farm. A winter storm had split the tree almost in half, had ripped the ancient trunk, exposing raw heartwood. A host of volunteers had patched the wound, splinted the bleeding trunk, bandaged it, fed it tree delicacies, and watched it until it sent out leaf buds the following spring, more than anyone could remember.

"That tree has always been the same size, except for what the storm did to it," Victoria told Josiah. "It was a giant tree when I was a girl."

Josiah glanced over at her. "That tree is probably two hundred years old. You've known it through half its life."

"Not quite," Victoria's face creased in a smile.

They parked at the usual turnout by the trailhead.

"Aren't you worried that someone will see you with me?" Victoria said. "Zack was afraid he'd be associated with me."

"We didn't want to be seen time after time searching for plants. It won't be a problem now, one walk. You said the orchids were immediately off the ancient way?"

"Practically on it."

They retraced the route past the marsh and shrilling pinkletinks, over the tufts of grass, noticeably greener only one warm day later. Up the gentle slope. When they came to the new fence, they skirted along it to the brook.

"This is where Robin found the lamprey." Victoria pointed to one of the stepping stones. "It looked so much like one of the weeds it was difficult to see. It seemed to be hanging on to a rock with its tail pointing downstream."

Josiah leaned over one of the big stones, his hands on his knees. "There it is now," he said. "Just where you saw it. *Lampetra appendix*, American brook lamprey. It's a threatened species that needs clear, clean running water." He had taken his notebook out of his shirt pocket and started to write. "It's sensitive to very low levels of pollution. Quite a find." He was smiling broadly. Deep creases lined his cheeks. Victoria thought how attractive his and Casey's children would be if she could only get those two together. He continued to write. "Do you need help to get around the end of the fence, Victoria?"

Just as she started to say, "No thank you," she slipped on the slimy algae that coated the stepping stone. Josiah caught her as she started to fall.

"That was stupid of me, showing off. By the way, it was right around here that I thought I heard someone yesterday."

"I can't even guess who that might have been," Josiah said thoughtfully. "A hiker or one of Ness's caretakers or maybe someone who was simply curious. I suppose we'll never know."

They followed the fence to where the path continued on the other side.

"I'll have to talk to Ness. He can't block this path."

They retraced Victoria's and Robin's route up the path to the spot where Victoria had found the first orchid.

"It was right here," Victoria said, looking around in bewilderment. "I'm absolutely sure. I recall the clethra next to it and that distinctive beech."

"Perhaps it was farther on."

"There were other plants farther on, but this is where I found the first one, I know." She poked around the fallen leaves. "Right here. I even recall some of the individual leaves. It was here, Josiah, right here. I know it was."

Josiah brushed aside the leaves in the spot she had indicated. "Someone was digging here."

"You don't suppose they uprooted the orchid, do you? I am absolutely sure it was here."

"I believe you, Victoria." He bent down and examined the

ground. "This is the right habitat. The ground has been disturbed." He stood up straight. "Someone must have heard you and Robin. Perhaps that was who was following you."

"Why?" Victoria leaned on her walking stick. "Why?"

"A very good reason. If we were to make such an important find on this property, Ness's development would be held up for months, perhaps even halted permanently."

"So it must have been Ness or one of his people?"

"That's the only thing that makes sense." The creases that had made Josiah's face look so young and happy only a few minutes earlier now made him look grim and older.

"You knew, didn't you, that I'd found other plants?"

They walked solemnly up the trail to the second site, where the cluster of leaves had been. The same thing. The plants had been dug up, and last autumn's leaves smoothed over to conceal the disturbed ground.

"This represents a huge loss. The last recorded *Tipularia* population in Massachusetts other than here on the Vineyard was on Cape Cod, and that's gone now. They're nowhere else in New England."

"For petty gain," Victoria murmured.

"To Ness, it's millions of dollars, hardly petty gain." Josiah dropped his head so far his chin rested on his chest. "I wonder what they did with the plants they dug up? I hope to hell they didn't destroy them."

"Can they be transplanted?" Victoria asked.

"Yes. But they've got such specific habitat needs, someone would have to understand what they need in order to transplant them successfully."

"I'm afraid we made a fuss about finding them. If somebody was following us he must have heard. Robin was so excited he jumped up and down. I was afraid he might trample them."

Josiah shook his head and said nothing.

"I found two other plants farther on," Victoria said quietly.

He looked up bleakly. "We might as well look."

They walked along the path in silence.

"We'd better assume someone is watching," Josiah said. "If the plants are there still, we don't want those dug up too."

When they came to the places Victoria had found the orchids, they had to search before they saw the characteristic spotted leaves, lying flat on top of last fall's leaf litter.

"Keep walking, Victoria." Josiah scuffed dry leaves over the orchids, covering them. When they had moved up the path well away from the plants, he turned to her with a smile. "We may yet be okay," he said. "Let's keep going up the trail. . . ."

"In case anyone is watching."

"Yes. Then we can turn around and head for home."

The way back was a gentle downhill slope, much easier for Victoria. Josiah was in an exuberant mood.

"They're odd, Victoria, not like most other plants. This time of year when other plants have died back, the cranefly orchid leaves manufacture food for the corms, which are something like gladiolus bulbs. Then in spring, when other plants are putting out new green leaves, the cranefly orchid leaf dies back, and you won't see anything for a couple of months."

"Yes, I read that in the papers you gave me," Victoria said.

"In June the orchid sends up a stalk that flowers in mid-July," Josiah continued. "It has numerous small flowers along a slender stalk."

"I read that," Victoria said.

Josiah went on. "In the south, where it's common, it may have forty blossoms."

Victoria was walking slightly ahead, flicking leaves and acorns out of the path with her stick.

"Up north it will have fewer." He paused and Victoria looked around. He was smiling.

"I've read all that," Victoria said again. She leaned on her stick, more tired than usual.

"Sorry," Josiah said. "I'm getting carried away. I was thinking about the best way to protect the last two plants that are still there."

Victoria started down the path, then stopped again to catch her breath.

Josiah was right behind her. "If you'd like to sit, there's a log not too much farther on."

"I'm fine," she said.

"They do produce seeds," he said. "The seeds are like dust."

They continued to walk down the path again. "An interesting aspect of the cranefly orchid," Josiah went on as if he were lecturing to an undergraduate botany class, "is that it's pollinated by night-flying moths . . ."

"Yes, yes," said Victoria, slightly out of breath. "Noctuid moths. I read that, too."

". . . noctuid moths," Josiah went on as if he hadn't heard, "like the kind that fly into your porch light. Theoretically, the flowers could self-pollinate, but it's probably rare."

Victoria was becoming increasingly irritated. "I know all that, Josiah. About how the pollen sac the moth picks up has a thin cap over it that prevents it from adhering to the flower's stigma."

"Absolutely right, Victoria," Josiah said. "And then . . ."

"And," Victoria continued, somewhat louder, "a half-hour after the moth picks up the pollen, the protective cap falls off, and the pollen is able to stick. You see, I've done my homework."

"Yes, well," Josiah said, "Nature's way of preventing inbreeding."

"Astonishing, isn't it," Victoria said. "Our own reproductive method seems strange until you hear how other organisms reproduce themselves."

Josiah laughed.

Victoria said, "Can't you see a moth professing undying love to one orchid plant before it sweeps the pollen up on its tongue, or whatever it does, flies around for a half hour, and then transfers it to another plant? It's a wonder any survive."

While they were walking back to the truck, Victoria kept listening for the rustling she and Robin had heard before, but the woods were still except for an occasional chickadee calling its winter call, the sound of pines sighing in the light wind, the distant sound of the surf.

Apparently Josiah was too wound up to stop talking. "Actually, the orchids here on the Vineyard seem to reproduce by cloning, rather than by seed. A professor in North Carolina thinks our Vineyard cranefly orchid is related to the same species found near him, only one species spirals clockwise around the stem and the other spirals counterclockwise."

Victoria was beginning to feel ashamed of herself for trying to cut Josiah off when he was so obviously elated. "I suppose, then, you can tell by looking at the flower stalk whether they're Vineyard plants or not."

"Yes. They're common in the southeast," he said. "But the Vineyard is their northernmost range." He stopped. "Are you all right, Victoria?"

"I think I do need to sit for a minute or two." She stopped next to a fallen log, and eased herself onto it. "Whew!"

While she caught her breath she could hear the steady bell-like sound of pinkletinks. A car hummed far away on North Road. She heard crows arguing, and thought about Montgomery Mausz. She wondered if he had been aware of someone following him. She had heard nothing this afternoon. She was sure a person had been following her and Robin. Perhaps it was the same person who had followed Mausz and had killed him. Perhaps it was the killer with no motive other than madness. She shuddered.

"Are you all right, Victoria?" Josiah sounded worried. "I'm afraid we've overdone the walk today."

Victoria got up as quickly as she could. "I just needed a moment to catch my breath." She wanted to hear Josiah's voice talking about matter-of-fact things. She was sorry she'd tried to one-up him about how much she knew. "You were thinking how we can protect the plants we found," she said.

"The best protection is to publicize it," Josiah responded. "It's a balancing act between arousing curiosity and informing the public of the value of this discovery. We have to let people know they mustn't trample it or pull it up."

"Perhaps the *Island Enquirer* will do an article," Victoria said. "I can write it up in my West Tisbury column."

"Good. I'll contact the state endangered species people. They'll want to send a botanist here to confirm the find."

Spencer Kirschmeyer regained consciousness that same afternoon. When he opened his eyes and looked around, one of the orderlies was straightening his room, and immediately called for Doc Erickson, who was on duty.

The bandages on Kirschmeyer's head covered his hair and his cheeks and his chin like a football helmet. It was difficult to tell what he looked like normally, or even how old he was.

"Where am I?" He said when Doc Erickson came into his room.

"You're in the Martha's Vineyard hospital," the doctor answered.

"Martha's Vineyard? What the hell am I doing on Martha's Vineyard?"

Doc Erickson shrugged.

"I don't remember anything."

Doc Erickson wrapped a blood pressure sleeve around his

patient's upper arm, held a stethoscope in the crook of his arm, looked at his watch and listened. He nodded. He peered into Kirschmeyer's eyes and mouth. "It will come back to you. In the meantime, welcome back to the real world. You had us worried for a few days."

Kirschmeyer shook his head. "Ouch!" He put his hand up and felt the bandages. "Did a job on myself, didn't I."

"Yep. A tree fell on you."

"Where else did I get it?"

"You have a few stitches in your chest."

Kirschmeyer moved his hands from his neck down toward his stomach. "Holy shit. I'm in a cast."

"Yep." Doc Erickson wrote something on a clipboard.

"Funny. I don't recall a thing."

"Don't worry about it. It will come back in time. Are you hungry?"

"Starved."

"We'll start you out slowly on solid food. Mashed potatoes, applesauce, and Jell-O." He noted something on the clipboard.

"How about a steak? Rare."

Doc Erickson cracked a tight smile. "If the applesauce and potatoes stay down, I'll order you a steak in a couple of days."

"Days!"

"Something to look forward to."

"Is there a TV in this place?" Kirschmeyer asked.

"I'll see that you have one." Doc Erickson made a note on the clipboard. "This afternoon, if you feel up to it, we might get you out of bed. I want you to take it easy for now."

"Wish I knew how the hell I got here."

"So do a lot of other people," said Doc Erickson.

CHAPTER 9

Harry Ness had grown up in South Boston, the youngest of eleven children. When he turned sixteen he dropped out of school, got a job loading freight onto boxcars in the South Boston yards, and left home. He put every cent he could save into buying land. In ten years he had accumulated a fair amount of property.

When he made his first million, he married a long-legged Nevada showgirl, Crystal Payne, the daughter of a Mormon bigwig. She was taller than he and a lot smarter than she looked.

Harry Ness, not yet fifty years old, now saw his logo, a sea serpent twined around a world globe, in almost every city and town east of the Mississippi. He intended to make that *every* city and town, not *almost* every. He planned to spread out from there, truly circle the globe.

He built a large house on the Vineyard for his wife, its windows paned with lead crystal in honor of her name. He built a dock and parked his sixty-five-foot seagoing motor yacht alongside, where everyone could see it. At night the lights in his house turned on automatically, one at a time like theater lights, and stayed on until midnight when they went off, one at a time. The neighbors, the entire town, complained about light pollution. Let them. It was his house and he'd damn well turn on any lights he wanted.

He bought land on the Island, more land, and more land. For several years he had been aware of the Sachem's Rock property, one of the largest tracts of undeveloped land on the Island. He knew that Phoebe Eldredge was getting along in years, knew that she wasn't speaking to either of her kids. He knew about the conservation group negotiating with her about buying a conservation restriction. What a waste that would be. Why would the town go along with that, taking the land off the tax rolls completely? Build exclusive housing on it and the land would be as good as preserved, plus adding some heavy-duty taxpayers who would be here a month, two months, five months at most during the year. Their taxes would pay for educating the town's kids.

Whenever he thought about kids in school, he'd have a pang of regret that he and Crystal didn't have any. Crystal would have been a good mother, and, he thought, he'd have been a hell of a lot better father than his old man. He thought sometimes that they didn't have kids because Crystal didn't want any. Well, whatever. It hadn't worked out that way.

Before he bought Sachem's Rock from Phoebe Eldredge in February, he had considered joining forces with the physicians' golf club consortium that was also looking at the property. He got hold of their prospectus, and decided the doctors were naive, the managers incompetent.

He looked into the town's Park and Rec Committee, the group that wanted to build a campground. He had thought when he acquired Sachem's Rock he might carve off a few acres near the road and sell it to the town at a fair rate. Not only a tax write-off, but good public relations. But when he looked into the membership of the committee, he decided they were airy-fairies, well-meaning do-gooders who had no concept of politics, finances, or management. He crossed them off his list.

One of his people looked into Tom More's housing scheme. Several of the units would be set aside for affordable housing, something the Island needed. "More Homes," the company was called. The guy was a competent enough builder, had been putting up touchy-feely solar homes for ten years, long after the hippies of the sixties and seventies had become stockbrokers. Tom More wanted his commune, Cranberry Fields, to be an experiment in group living, as if that hadn't been tried before. And why, for God's sake, why pick the most expensive chunk of real estate on the East Coast for an experiment in group living? Why not Maine or Vermont? Or someplace out west like Idaho or Nevada?

In case there was something he had overlooked, Ness examined everything he could find out about Tom More and his plans, and found there was a gap in his background that no one was able to penetrate. Except for that, a period of five years, the guy seemed to be exactly what he said he was, a builder out to make a buck under a cloak of environmental blarney, only More had not put it that way. Ness decided he'd better not underestimate the guy. Tom More had an almost religious following, the kind of people who would probably leave their homes and families and go off with him in a space ship.

Ness also investigated the Conservation Trust's plan to put a conservation restriction on the entire property. Josiah Coffin was young, quiet, and idealistic. He had both a law degree and an environmental science degree. His followers were every bit as rabid as Tom More's, but they were lawyers, bankers, and investors, professors of economics and hydrogeology, practical people with brains, money, and power. After studying the reports that came back on Josiah Coffin, Ness marked him down as formidable.

After all his research, Ness felt, quite reasonably, that his plan was the wisest and best use of the Sachem's Rock property, and two months before he finally closed the deal, he had set about wooing and winning Phoebe Eldredge.

About that time his attorney, Montgomery Mausz, disappeared for what everybody thought was a Caribbean vacation.

The day after Victoria and Josiah had found the cranefly orchid missing, Elizabeth dropped her grandmother and Robin off at the trailhead.

"Have a good walk. I'd go with you, but I'm late for work. Can you get home okay?"

"Of course," Victoria said. "Josiah or Zack could pick us up. I still have the radio." She rummaged in her cloth bag and brought it out.

Victoria had not told her granddaughter that Josiah had expressly forbidden her to go to Sachem's Rock. She had done her part, Josiah had said. It was time for the state endangered species people to take over. He warned her to stay away from the property, especially since they didn't know who had been following them.

The Island spring, always so unpredictable, had finally settled in. The meadow grass was greening. A meadowlark sang.

Before she asked Elizabeth to take them to the trailhead, Victoria had told Robin about Josiah's warning. "He thinks it's not safe," she said.

"He's nothing but an old lady." Robin tugged his UPS cap off and tossed it into the air, caught it, and plopped it backwards onto his tousled hair.

"I think we need to check those plants," Victoria had said.

"I think so too."

So it was set, and Elizabeth, unsuspecting, had driven them to the trailhead.

Now, Victoria watched Robin dart across the familiar meadow, sweet-smelling in the warmth. He jumped from one green tuft of grass to another. She followed slowly, her own heart skipping and jumping with each step of Robin's. They moved up the gentle incline into the beech woods to the new fence, went around it where it ended at the brook. The lamprey seemed to have attached itself permanently to the rock, for it was still in the same spot, its tail waving in the brook's current. They edged along the other side of the fence and back onto the path.

A bird Victoria didn't recognize caroled a few notes, and Victoria, glad to be out on this glorious day, repeated the bird's notes, her mouth pursed in a whistle.

"Wow, that sounded exactly like him," Robin said with admiration, and leaped into the air, slapping a high branch.

A soft breeze shook pine needles onto them and onto the path. Above them the sky was clear spring blue.

They came to the patch where Victoria had found the first orchids, where only yesterday she and Josiah had found them missing, dug up, and the ground covered over with fallen leaves.

And there, almost exactly where she had found them the first time, were two cranefly orchid leaves. The dark green leaves, splotched with purple, lay flat on top of the leaf litter as if they had always grown there.

"What do you make of this?" she asked Robin.

He shrugged. "Maybe somebody was sorry they dug it up and planted it again."

"It's a different plant."

Victoria knelt next to it.

Robin bent over her, hands on his knees. "Yeah. It's got two leaves, not one."

Victoria took out her notebook and started to write.

"I'll see if the other plants are okay," Robin said.

Victoria nodded absently. What was going on? None of this made sense. In the back of her mind she heard Robin racing up the path, heard him jump, heard him slap a tree branch overhead, heard his light-hearted whistle at a squirrel or a bird fade away down the path. She heard a quail call, "bob white! bob bob white!" The call of the bobwhite always sounded like summer meadows and hayfields, a nostalgic sound that brought back the scent of new-mown hay. The first call of the quail came right around haying time and the fields would echo with their whistle, "bob white! bob white!" She heard it again, off to the left side of the path.

She returned to the new orchid plant, noted its exact position, sketched its leaves, then moved a few feet over to where she had originally found the second plant, where she and Josiah had found it missing, dug up. Sure enough, a new plant had been set in the old one's place.

Victoria tried to reason this out. Someone must have known the plants were there in the first place, must have been following her and Robin, and must have dug them up. But who set new plants in the same place? Were the woods full of people following other people, digging up and transplanting plants? And where were they getting the new plants? They were, after all, rare. At least here in New England.

With this, she thought about Robin. He should be back by now. She listened for his footsteps on dry leaves and heard nothing. There was no sound of underbrush slapping across small-boy jeans, nor his whistle. She got to her feet with difficulty, hoisting herself up with her stick, and listened again.

A beech leaf fell. A hawk cried high in the blue sky. Bees hummed. Blood pounded in her ears. But no boy noises.

"Robin?" she called.

No answer.

She started up the path again, stiffly at first from having knelt on the ground, then faster as her muscles limbered up.

"Robin?" She stopped and waited. She heard a faint echo from the woods and thought it might be Robin, but it was only her own voice coming back to her, bounced off tree trunks.

She hurried now. Where could he be? She thought of the footsteps they had heard before, Robin and she, the footsteps in the woods beside the path that had made them hurry back to where Zack had parked at the trailhead. She thought about the concern in Josiah's voice when he had warned her not to go back to Sachem's Rock.

Her breath was coming in short gasps. She stopped and rested on her stick and listened. She heard only the sounds of the woods and the call of birds and the far away whish of tires on North Road. She heard the sound of surf everywhere around her, in her ears and in her being, the beat of surf keeping time to the beat of blood pounding through her arteries. Where could Robin be? Had he jumped up for a branch and hit his head and knocked himself out? No, she would have found him in the path. Why had she let him go off by himself? They were strong together, but so vulnerable alone, he, a very small boy, and she, not as agile as she once had been. She continued up the path until she had passed the point where she and Josiah had turned back, where the gentle hill started to curve downward again. From the top of the hill, she could see over a wide area through the trees, as far as the pond and the ice house. But there was no sign of Robin.

"Robin? Robin!" she called.

She was tired. She knew she could go no farther. She rested both knobby hands on her stick and leaned on it until she caught her breath again and could think. Her knuckles showed white through the skin of her hands, dirt-stained from gardening, the winter cracks on her fingertips that hurt so much she no longer felt the pain, the brown age-blotches she didn't really mind, the prominent blue veins that coursed over the tops of the frail-looking bones.

She could not hope to find him by herself. She had to get help, and right away. She moved back down the trail until she came to the first site, where the newly transplanted orchid plants seemed as fresh as if they'd always grown there. She sat on a fallen tree on the other side of the path and scrabbled around in her bag until she found the hand-held radio. She examined it. Turn this button on the right, that should switch it on. Turn it farther to the right and that will increase the volume. Turn the button on the left until you hear static, then move it back just a bit. Josiah had said the radio was set to reach him or Zack, all she had to do was press a flat bar on the side and speak into the perforations of the leather case.

Josiah had told her what to say. Identify yourself. So she held the flat bar on the side and spoke clearly into the radio. "Victoria Trumbull to the Conservation Trust." She released the bar and waited. You were supposed to wait two minutes, Josiah had said, but that seemed much too long. The second hand on her watch had ticked off one minute. She spoke into the radio again, held the flat bar and released it. No answer. Were the batteries dead? Was she too far away? Did the hills between them block reception?

Victoria left the radio on in case someone had heard and might try to call her, and moved down the trail. She paused as she came to the end of the fence. Someone had always been with her before and she hadn't worried about falling. Now, she froze. The stepping stone looked slippery, and probably was. She had almost fallen there yesterday. But Josiah had been there to catch her. Should she take off her shoes and wade so she wouldn't have to trust the slippery rock? *No, I've got to take a chance*, she thought. *Time is critical.* She thrust her stick into the streambed and gingerly placed her foot on the rock, leaning on the stick. So far her footing was secure. *This should take two seconds*, she mumbled to herself, *and here I am, acting like an old lady, taking two entire minutes. And if I don't act boldly, it will be two hours and who knows what will happen to Robin?* She put her second foot on the rock and balanced there, holding her stick. She repositioned the stick on the other side of the rock, took a deep breath, and stretched her long leg over the space that separated the rock from the bank and the other side of the fence. She reached for the fence post, clutched it, and there she was, around the barrier, as easy as that. She was shaking. She was out of breath. She was annoyed with herself for being so tentative. She stood up straight and took a breath, tossed back her shoulders, and marched ahead through the briers and huckleberry back to the path, and down the path to the trailhead. It seemed an aeon ago that she had made almost this same journey, when she had heard the crows and found the body of Montgomery Mausz. But it was only a couple of weeks.

When she reached the trailhead she stopped where she could flag down a car, if she needed to, and tried the radio again.

This time the radio crackled with static and she turned the squelch down. It was Zack. "Victoria? Where are you?"

Victoria said cautiously, "In the usual place. Come as quickly as you can, and bring help."

"Roger," Zack said. "Ten minutes."

It was a long ten minutes. Victoria paced back and forth. She sat for a time on the stone wall, and picked with her ridged fingernail at the flat gray lichen that covered the surface of the rock on which she sat. A car approached, slowed, Victoria lifted her hand in a wave, and the car sped up again and went on. A bicyclist passed, leaning over his handlebars, his feet alternating like pistons. The sound was the swish of oiled machinery. The bicyclist didn't seem to see her. She watched him disappear bit by bit, first his tight black legs, then his tight blue jacket, then his white helmet, toward Seven Gates and the intersection where the great oak grew.

She stood again. She was stiff. She paced partway up the path toward the meadow, then back again, then up the path, then back. The day didn't seem as springlike and innocent as it had only an hour ago. The crows sounded sinister, not clownlike. The breeze seemed to have a bite. The sky had a milky tinge. She heard the mournful summer cry of a chickadee, "Pee-wee."

She looked at her watch. She took out the radio again. She had left it on in case she was called. She held down the flat bar and said, "Victoria Trumbull here."

Zack's voice came on immediately. "I'm rounding the bend now. Be only a second."

And within a second Victoria saw the familiar pickup truck, saw Zack's glasses reflecting the light, his beaklike nose, his black hair falling into his eyes, his nestlike beard. In the passenger seat next to Zack she saw Josiah, his bare chin and deep-set eyes, his thick auburn hair.

Zack pulled on the emergency brake with a squeal, turned off the ignition, opened the door, and leaped out as if he were on a spring, and Josiah followed him.

"Casey is on her way," Zack said. "I called her."

"What are you doing here, Victoria? Where's Robin?" Josiah's concern tumbled out with the questions.

"Robin's missing. He went on ahead of me. He's gone." Victoria looked up at Josiah with a pained expression.

The police Bronco pulled up behind the Conservation Trust truck, and Casey and Junior joined them.

Victoria sat on the stone wall again while Casey and the others questioned her. She fidgeted as she answered.

"We've got to know exactly what happened before we rush off in all directions, Victoria," Casey said.

Victoria picked at the skin around her nails while she answered Casey's questions. She looked at her watch. Time was going by too slowly and too fast. She would never forgive herself if Robin had gotten hurt. He was so small and so bright and such good company. His Pokémon cards. The half-dozen pencils he'd ground down with the Pikachu pencil sharpener she'd given him. She was scarcely listening.

"Let's go." Casey held out her hand to Victoria.

"Robin might be hurt or unconscious." Victoria took Casey's hand and got to her feet. "He may have fallen into an old cellar hole. He may have been attacked by that dog.

He may have fallen into the brook. That person who was following us may have kidnapped him."

"We'll find Robin." Casey put her arm around Victoria's shoulders. "Don't worry. There's probably some simple explanation."

For the first quarter mile Victoria led until she began to tire and flag behind. Casey walked with her.

Victoria told Casey about finding the orchids in the first place. About finding them dug up when she returned with Josiah. About finding new plants there now.

Josiah listened. He stroked his chin as they walked. "It doesn't make sense. None of it."

They got around the fence safely. They passed the first group of newly planted orchids and reached the place where Victoria had found the second group, the ones Josiah had protected with leaves. When she had passed by earlier, Victoria had been so intent on finding Robin she had not noticed that the ground had been disturbed. Nor had she seen that the two cranefly orchid plants she and Josiah had identified and carefully covered were now gone.

Josiah bent down and ran his fingers through the leaves, and shook his head. "What in hell is going on?"

"Victoria, stay here, and don't move," Casey pointed to a rock in the path. "The rest of you start searching uphill," Casey ordered. "Fan out through the woods. Keep in sight of each other."

Victoria could hear their voices fade away. At first she heard them talking to each other, could hear what they were saying. She heard them call Robin's name. Then, their voices died away and she heard only the mournful cry, "Robin! Robin!" and then that, too, died away and the noises of the woods returned, a thrush, a towhee, a chickadee. Then she heard the quiet woods noise, a rustle of a leaf dropping, the whisper of pine needles falling, the sound of growing things pushing aside the winter mold.

Victoria poked the ground with her stick. What could have happened to Robin? At the time he disappeared she had been concentrating so hard on the new orchid plants she had paid no attention to him. Was there anything she could recall? A sound that didn't belong? A noise that had meant nothing to her at the time? She thought back to the call of crows, the chickadees, the bobwhites. Bobwhites? Calling this early in the spring? She didn't remember ever hearing them much before June. And, now she thought of it, the bobwhite had called from the woods on the left side of the path, not from the open meadow. Had it been a signal from Robin? She got to her feet, holding her stick for support. She turned slightly to peer through the woods to the right of the path, the uphill area that Casey and Junior, Josiah and Zack were searching. They would return and search the other side of the path, she knew. But that might be too late.

Victoria studied the ground, the undergrowth, the branches to the left. She noticed a scuffed area just off the path, where soggy leaves had been flipped over, dark undersides showing. Why had she not thought of this before?

She called. "Casey! Josiah?" and waited. Nothing. Not the sound of voices or footsteps or branches snapping.

I've got to search for Robin myself, she thought. *Time is running out. I must find him.*

Victoria laid an arrow of small branches in the path to point in the direction she intended to go, then started through the undergrowth, watching for disturbed leaves in front of her. Robin might have made those marks, bouncing through the woods, leaving broken twigs, torn briers, turned-over stones. The trail was easy to follow. It moved downhill gradually, angling along the side of the gentle slope. Here, the trees were smaller than on the other side of the path, with an occasional clearing. Victoria had to stop often to rest and rather than take the effort to sit and get up again, she leaned on her stick, breathing heavily, annoyed with herself for having to rest so frequently. She broke branches to mark her route. The trail would be easy to follow. While she was resting this last time, she decided to take the trouble to sit. She examined the ground around her for a rock to sit on or a log, so she wouldn't have so far to get up.

Victoria was in a clearing where she could look through bare trees and see ahead and down the slope. The clearing was covered with reindeer moss, soft gray and plump from the recent rain. The only raised surface where she might be able to sit was a large clump of grass, a tuft that stuck up about two feet high, oddly solitary in this glen of reindeer moss, cranberry, low poverty grass, and bare blueberry plants.

She was starting toward the clump that looked almost like a seat, when something moved down the hill. She put her hand up to her forehead to shade her eyes. It was a person, limping up the slope toward her. As the figure came closer, she could see it was Robin, covered with mud as if he had been dipped in chocolate.

Victoria called to him. Robin looked up. His glasses had slipped down his nose and his eyes were white spots in an umber mask. He moved faster and Victoria could see his limp was more pronounced.

She waited for him in the clearing. When he reached her he stood with his head down, not saying a word, until Victoria bent down to him, dropped her stick, threw both arms around him, and hugged him tightly.

"Hey," he said, snuggling against her, "You'll get all dirty."

Victoria hugged him more tightly. "Where have you been?" she said into the top of his muddy head. "We've got people searching for you."

"You didn't need to do that. I was okay," he said gruffly, still clinging to her.

"You know you shouldn't . . ." Victoria stopped.

Robin nodded his head against her and she saw he was crying. Light brown streaks ran down the side of his nose through the darker coating of mud.

CHAPTER 10

"Tell me what happened," Victoria said gently. Robin handed the walking stick to her and they started back up the path, side by side.

Robin put his hand in hers. "You remember the dog? The black and white dog with the red collar?"

"The one that attacked me."

Robin nodded and wiped the back of his hand under his nose, leaving a broad light stripe. His glasses were blotched with mud. Victoria handed him a paper towel from her coat pocket. He took it from her and blew his nose.

"Let me have your glasses," she said. He tugged them off, and his eyes stared myopically out of the pale mask where they'd been.

"I'll clean some of that muck off you." Victoria took the paper towel from him, and rubbed it across his face. He shut his eyes and clamped his lips together. When she had finished he took the muddy paper towel from her and held it in his clenched fist. She breathed on his glasses to mist them, and lightly wiped them with a napkin from her pocket, careful not to scratch the soft glass. He put them back on.

"Now tell me what happened."

"Well, I was walking up the path to see if the second batch of orchids was okay, you know?"

Victoria nodded. "And then you saw the dog?"

"Yup. The dog came up to me, real friendly. He was wagging his tail and everything."

"Then what?"

He put his hand back in hers. "Somebody whistled to him, and he charged off into the woods."

"Was the whistle like this?" Victoria puckered her mouth and whistled, "Bob white! Bob bob white!"

"Exactly like that, only loud."

"And you followed the dog?"

"Well, yeah."

"Let's rest a bit." Victoria leaned on her stick.

"I'll get something for you to sit on." Robin bounded off through the woods.

"Don't go too far away!" Victoria called after him.

She heard him drag something through the underbrush, and when he appeared he was tugging a stump that he set upright for her. She sat, first spreading the bottom of her quilted coat over the rotted top of the stump.

"Whew! Thank you. How far did you follow the dog?"

"To right about where you were when you saw me," Robin said. "Only farther down the hill."

"Did the dog's owner appear?"

"Nope. The dog went racing down the slope and popped into a hole." Robin hunkered down next to Victoria.

"Really?" Victoria stared at the boy, who nodded his head up and down vigorously.

"He just popped into a hole in the side of the hill."

Victoria looked closely at Robin. His shirt was coated with drying mud. His jeans were slick with mud. Where the mud had dried, it had fallen off in chunks, leaving square patches of faded blue jeans.

"If I had been you," Victoria said thoughtfully, "I probably would have found that hole and tried to follow the dog."

Robin looked up at her with awe. "That's exactly it. That's what I did."

"How far did the hole go?"

"I couldn't tell. The dog just disappeared."

"You mean it didn't open into a cave or cellar hole? How big was it?"

Robin held his arms in front of him, touching his fingers

together to form a circle two feet in diameter.

"Did you get stuck?" Victoria asked.

"Yes."

"And you couldn't move forward and you couldn't move backward, and it must have been dark and scary."

He nodded and wiped his nose again. He stood again and shifted from one foot to the other in front of Victoria, who was holding her lilac-wood stick in front of her.

"Could you hear the dog ahead of you?"

"Not exactly. I thought I heard a voice, but . . ."

"I know," Victoria said. "It's an awful feeling to get stuck in a dark hole. You imagine things. How did you finally get out?"

"The hole kept getting smaller, so I couldn't go forward. I couldn't turn around." Robin was breathing heavily as if he was stuck in the hole again. "All I could do was push back with my hands and toes." He demonstrated, standing on the tips of his toes and waving his hands over his head.

"It must have been slippery," Victoria said.

"It was. I couldn't find anything to push against, just mud. Yuck!" Robin stopped and took a deep breath. "I dug my fingers in and tried to push back that way. It was really, really dark and slimy and my arms were out ahead of me. I couldn't move them back because there wasn't room for my elbows to bend."

He looked up, and Victoria realized his brown UPS cap was missing. "I kept imagining things. The earth closing down on me. Me being stuck there forever. I thought I heard the dog and I figured he might come back and chew on me and I couldn't do anything about it. I thought I heard some-body talking, like a radio or something, and I thought maybe somebody really, really small lives at the end of the tunnel in an underground house. And I thought maybe they would find me and kill me and nobody would ever know what happened to me."

Victoria reached her arm out and Robin stepped toward her and leaned against her. She tightened her arm around his narrow shoulders and he nestled against her.

"What time is it?" he asked, abruptly squirming away from her. "How long was I gone?"

Victoria looked at her watch. "I reported you missing around four and it's almost five-thirty now. We'd better get going again. They'll be worried about us."

But Victoria was thinking to herself. The dog had vanished down a narrow tunnel and had not come out again. Suppose somebody did have an underground house on the side of the hill. Maybe even used an old cellar hole and roofed it over and planted sod on top. No one would ever suspect. Perhaps the tunnel down which the dog had disappeared was for extra ventilation, or for the dog to come and go. Or for drainage. There must be another entrance, certainly. The more she thought about it, the more it made sense. But who would the dog's owner be? The person who had killed Attorney Mausz? Whoever lived like that, hidden away from the world in an underground house, would have to be a bit different from other people.

"You aren't listening to me," Robin said.

"I'm sorry, my mind was somewhere else. What did you say?"

"I said, we could come back tomorrow and I'll show you the tunnel." He stopped abruptly. "I can't do it tomorrow. I have a stupid music lesson."

"Let's make it the day after tomorrow," Victoria said, and her heart lifted.

"I should have known," Casey said, when the four searchers returned to the path and found Victoria missing. "She won't listen to anybody." Casey pointed to the arrow of sticks that Victoria had laid on the ground. "Look at that."

Junior looked down at the arrow, his thumbs in his trousers pockets. The gold stitching on his baseball cap picked up glints of the low-angled sunlight filtering through the trees. The usual crinkles of good humor around his eyes and mouth drooped with concern.

"Now we have to find two people." Casey paced.

Josiah stared at the stick arrow. Zack squatted down in the path and picked up a handful of sandy earth mixed with pine needles and shreds of dry leaves, and sifted it through his fingers.

"She thinks she's a Boy Scout or something," Casey went on. "She thinks she's a real cop." She shook her head. "Once we're done with all this she's going back to school to learn proper police procedures, and that's that."

Zack sifted the handful of dirt into his other hand. Josiah scuffed the toe of his boot into the ground. Junior tipped his cap onto the back of his head.

"Well, let's not just stand here," Casey ordered. "Let's find her."

Zack stood again and looked in the direction Victoria's arrow pointed. "She's marked her trail plainly enough."

"Zack, you come with me. Junior, you and Josiah follow to one side. Who knows what she's stumbled into."

They had gone only a few hundred feet through the tangled brush when Casey heard a faint "Hello!" coming from below her on the slope and saw two figures trudging through the undergrowth.

"Victoria!" Casey called out.

"He's safe." Victoria and the boy stopped and Casey saw her lean on her stick.

"Are you okay?" Casey tore down the slope. Huckleberry bushes slapped against her trousers and boots. Branches stung her face.

"We're fine. You don't need to come down here. We'll be up there in a minute or two."

"Robin?" Casey slowed and waited.

"Robin needs a cup of hot cocoa and a bath. That's all." Victoria and the boy were moving up the side of the hill again, hand in hand.

When all six had assembled back on the path, Robin told them how he'd followed the dog and had gotten stuck in the tunnel.

"Could it be an entrance to a cave?" Casey asked. "Like the caves in Kentucky?"

"Not likely," Josiah said. "The Island is glacial moraine, a rubble of rocks and sand. There's no limestone to form caves like the ones in Kentucky or Indiana."

Victoria sat with a sigh on the moss-covered stone beside the path. "Cellar hole," she said.

"You could be right," Josiah turned to the others. "There was a small settlement here at Sachem's Rock in the early 1700s. Six or seven houses."

"Do we know exactly where the settlement was?" Casey asked.

"Not precisely," Josiah continued. "Phoebe Eldredge's is the only house left."

"Did the rest burn down, or what?" Casey asked.

"They burned or they were abandoned," Josiah answered.

Victoria rose to her feet. "We'd better get this young man home to clean up and do his homework."

"Awww, man!" Robin groaned.

Between the time he walked out on his wife and baby daughter in California and the time he came back to life, the man who called himself Ulysses could remember nothing but fleeting images. He'd worked on a freighter, he recalled. But what freighter and what ports he'd visited were blanks. He'd worked as a roughneck in the offshore Louisiana oil patch, as a parking lot attendant somewhere, slept on top of a steam grate in front of an art gallery in D.C., stole a shopping cart from a store in Virginia to hold his bundle of clothes. He'd built himself a shack of cardboard and hammered-flat juice cans under a bridge. He had a vision of rain pouring off the roadway above him. He scavenged for food in restaurant trash barrels and grocery store dumpsters. He fought with wild cats and dogs for food, growling and clawing the same way they growled and clawed.

He moved, always moving, hitchhiking, riding the rails, walking, from one coast to the other, from north to south. He headed up the East Coast. Caught a ride on a freight train, sat in an aluminum lawn chair he'd scrounged from a dumpster and looked out at scenery flying past him through the big open door. That was an image he recalled. The car shook on the rails as the train picked up speed and he had felt a motion sickness the likes of which he had never felt before, an awful jarring, curdling feeling, so awful he wanted to hurl himself out of the big open door onto anything solid. But his body wouldn't let him. The car built up a sickening rhythm as it swung and shook, faster and faster, until the train was moving so fast the sympathetic vibrations stepped up a notch and it was as if he had broken through some barrier into calmness.

He got off the train in a freight yard and heated a can of tomato soup over a fire a hobo had left burning next to the track. Nothing was connected in his mind—not his body, certainly. His body was an organism that fought for life without help from his mind. His body fed itself. It eliminated what it couldn't use. It slept. And his mind raced off into images and impressions, shattered colored glass that formed itself into focus briefly, then whirled out of focus again. He saw a cave in Nam. The freighter. Saw pieces of his buddy flying through the moist air. Blood and body parts dropped onto him. The parking lot. Rice paddies. The steam grate. Green hills and denuded hills. Rain pouring off a bridge above him.

He awoke in Vermont. It had started to snow. He was

squatting on a street corner in his rags with a cup in his hand. Occasionally someone would drop coins into his cup, and he would shake the cup and mumble, "Thank you, miss" (or sir). At first the snow was only a few specks that he was not sure he saw or felt. The specks dotted the sidewalk and vanished, and the morning or afternoon, he wasn't sure which, was gray and raw and colorless and damp, and it was the first time he had felt anything for as long as he could remember, except for the sickening ride in the freight car. He looked up and snow hit his face and he blinked his eyes. He stuck out his tongue and the snow, now big fat flakes, dropped onto it with a hiss, and he heard it and felt it and tasted it. He got to his feet unsteadily and looked down at himself. Who was he? And where was he? He was disgustingly filthy. He had a long scraggly beard, his hair was a tangle almost down to his waist, his teeth felt like moss-covered stones and they hurt. His clothes were nothing he could remember acquiring, they were horrid-smelling rags that hung on his gaunt body in layers of plaids and stripes and checks and tweeds, all melded together into a uniform mud brown.

My God, how did this happen?

He stumbled along the sidewalk toward a church he saw midway down the block. The men and women he passed veered out of his path, and he suddenly felt ashamed of himself, of the way he looked and smelt. Smelt was a good term, he thought, rotten smelt is how he smelt, and he realized he was thinking and even making a small joke, and he held his face up to the snow that was now falling in great fat flakes, and rubbed the wetness around with his black, calloused hands. How had he got those callouses? The sidewalk had a thin white coat of snow. The street was black. A car swished past. Another car. A dozen cars. He was alive again and there was hope.

He found his way to the soup kitchen in the back of the church, to the homeless shelter. Someone gave him a small wrapped bar of soap and a toothbrush and led him to a shower. He dropped his clothes outside the stall and turned the handle all the way around, and stood under the blast of hot water, soaping himself and his hair, watching rivulets of gray water and soap bubbles pour off him. He stood there, his mouth open, swishing the water around in his mouth and spitting it out again and again. He used up the small soap bar on his hair, his beard, his crotch, under his arms. The longer he stood under the stream from the showerhead the more he felt life returning, felt his mind reconnecting to his body.

They had left a towel and a comb and a razor on the bench outside the shower for him. He scoured himself with the towel until his body was raw. He found another scrap of soap and a pair of scissors on the sink under a steamed-up mirror in which he could see himself only as a blur of dark hair and dark eyes, and he used the scissors to hack off his beard, almost pulling it out by its roots, then the scrap of soap to lather what was left of his beard and shaved it off. He chopped off his hair until it stuck up like a brush all over his head, an inch tall, no longer snarled and knotted. He wiped the fog from the mirror with the end of his towel and stared. My God! He would never have recognized himself.

Someone brought him clean (and new) underwear. How long had it been since he'd had clean clothing next to his body? He couldn't even guess how much time had gone by. They brought him new tan work pants. New! Why? And a T-shirt that smelled of newness. And a jacket, a worn jacket, but a clean one.

When he first saw the calendar on the wall of the soup kitchen, he was sure he had misread it. Then he thought the calendar must be wrong. He asked everyone he met what date it was. He finally came to terms with it. It had been seven years since he had left California and his wife and daughter. Seven years.

Slowly, slowly, he'd healed. And then he got a part-time job with the sanitation department collecting trash and lived in the shelter at night. He worked in the soup kitchen, cutting up carrots and onions and potatoes to pay for his food. He mixed cement for a bricklayer. He hauled shingles for a roofer. He tacked up insulation. He painted. He carried boards for a carpenter. And after he had carried boards and nailed up framing and taped sheetrock, he got a job with a construction company. The other workers left him alone. He was strange, odd. That was fine with him. He didn't need or want their company.

He got himself a cheap room and started to save his money, and began to think about getting home to his family's land on Martha's Vineyard. He needed to save enough to get back there and build himself a place on the family land, and enough money to hold him over a year or so, or until he got a job.

Sometimes, not often, he thought about his wife and daughter. By now they must have forgotten him. They were only an infinitesimal part of his life, a fleeting moment. He wondered how his mother would feel about his return, and did he really care? He and his mother had never seen eye to eye.

Eventually he bought a used pickup for cash. And eventually he headed home to the Vineyard.

The morning after Robin discovered the tunnel, Victoria was reading about cranefly orchids in the Conservation Trust library when the phone rang. Josiah, who was working at the other end of the table, answered. After he hung up he made a thumbs-up gesture. "That was the state botanist, Dr. Cornelius. He's in Woods Hole now, and is catching the ten-thirty ferry."

Victoria looked at her watch. "That's less than an hour from now. Is he bringing his car?"

"No. I'm to meet the boat. Want to come? I'll leave in about a half hour."

During that time, Victoria finished writing up notes and made sketches from a photograph in a journal article she'd found.

Josiah looked over her shoulder at the drawing. "Not bad. I'm writing an article for the newsletter. Your sketches would be good illustrations."

Victoria cocked her head to one side. "I suppose I could polish them a bit." She gathered up the notes and stowed them in her pocketbook.

"They're great just as they are." Josiah headed toward his office. "I'll get my camera equipment and then we can go."

Victoria started down the steep stairs that led to the back of the building where the pickup truck was parked, holding the railings on either side tightly. She didn't intend to keep Josiah waiting. When she reached the truck, she turned to see if he was behind her. The building was built against a hill, two stories high in back, one story in front. As she looked up she could see into Josiah's office windows on the second floor, and thought, at first, she saw him standing next to the window, staring down at her. She couldn't make out the figure clearly because it was in shadow, but she had the impression it was deliberately staying out of sight. She had convinced herself it was Josiah, and was wondering why he would conceal himself from her when she heard the heavy metal door at the foot of the stairs clang open and Josiah strode out with his camera case and tripod.

"Sorry to keep you waiting, Victoria. Another phone call. What time do you have?"

She lifted the cuff of her blue coat to look at her watch. "Ten-twenty."

"We'll make it in time."

Josiah helped her into the passenger seat and went around to the driver's side and slammed the door shut behind him. The truck jounced down the rutted track that skirted the old cranberry bog, and turned right onto the Lambert's Cove road. Victoria forgot to ask him about the figure at the window.

They reached the steamship terminal as the ferry was pulling into its slip. Dr. Cornelius, who had been standing on the upper deck, was one of the last passengers to disembark.

He greeted Victoria with a bear hug. "This is a significant find, Mrs. Trumbull." His enthusiasm seemed at odds with his white hair and gold-rimmed glasses.

"They're quite excited about it at the Endangered Species Office," Dr. Cornelius continued as Josiah led the way to the truck. "Martha's Vineyard is getting quite a name for itself."

"I'm afraid so," Victoria said.

"I'm referring to endangered species." Dr. Cornelius sounded amused. "This is great!"

Victoria glanced at him as he helped her up into the truck. He was probably in his mid-sixties, her daughter Amelia's age, lean and leathery and distinguished looking.

"We'll go right to the site, unless you want to stop at the office first." Josiah backed out of the parking space and merged into the line of cars coming off the ferry.

"The sooner the better," Dr. Cornelius said. "Haven't been on the Island for ages. Good to see it hasn't changed much."

"It's changed," Josiah said. He waited for the Five Corners traffic to clear. "It's a constant battle to keep it from changing too much, too fast, and in the wrong direction." Traffic moved and he turned right onto State Road. "And who are we to decide what's the right direction? Harry Ness, who bought the property, isn't a demon. He thinks he's doing the right thing by building a housing development." He passed a car that was turning onto Main Street and continued up the hill. "A millionaires' housing development, true."

"I'm sure you've seen a lot of change on the Island, Mrs. Trumbull," said Dr. Cornelius. "What are your thoughts about all this development?"

Victoria, who'd been thinking of something else, namely how to get back tomorrow with Robin to explore for the tunnel, looked over at Dr. Cornelius with a smile. "I don't mind change. I'd like to be around for a while to see what happens next."

Josiah followed State Road through the outskirts of Vineyard Haven and into the rural countryside. He passed the split oak on North Road and pulled over onto the wide place where the trail to Sachem's Rock began.

It was a bright warm day. The sun was high. Birds sang. Overnight, miniature leaves had burst out of fat pink buds on the wild rose canes. Spring perfumed the air.

When they came to the brook, the lamprey had moved over to another rock, but there it was, hanging in the current, its eely tail moving with the flow of the water.

Dr. Cornelius bent low to examine it. "My God, what a find this is. Brook lamprey. It would be criminal to build on this land."

He helped Victoria across the stream. "You talked to Ness about this?" he asked Josiah.

"I have an appointment with him tomorrow," Josiah said. "I wanted to get your confirmation of Victoria's discovery before I spoke with him."

When they reached the site where Victoria had found the first group of orchids, Dr. Cornelius knelt and brought out a small magnifying glass that was on a chain around his neck.

"These are not the same plants that were here originally," Victoria said. "When I brought Josiah here to see the ones I found, they were gone. Someone had dug them up."

"And later these were planted in their place?" Dr. Cornelius asked.

"Yes."

"Very strange," he said after he had examined the new plants minutely. "I can't be sure until the orchid blooms, but I could swear this is not the same variety of cranefly orchid that occurs on the Island."

"Are these similar to ones that grow in the south?" Victoria asked.

"It's possible," Dr. Cornelius said. "I'll photograph this one and document it, take a sample of the leaf to the lab for analysis."

"Here's another plant," Victoria said, standing over the second newly transplanted orchid.

"Same thing," Dr. Cornelius said, after he had examined it. "Curious. I can understand somebody digging it up if they thought the orchid would hold up construction. But why replace it? And with a different variety?"

When he had finished writing notes and making sketches and had photographed the plants, they moved up the path to where Victoria had found the second group, and where, just yesterday, they had found the second group dug up also. There were three new plants, looking as though they had been there always.

"I'll be damned!" Dr. Cornelius said. "What on earth is going on?"

CHAPTER 11

While Josiah and Dr. Cornelius set up the camera and adjusted lights, made notes and conferred over the newly dug-in plants, Victoria hiked up the gentle slope that led to the big rock, through the beech and oak wood that grew to the right of the path. She was still within sight of the two men when she noticed something bright orange on the trunk of a large beech tree in a clearing, a strip of fluorescent surveyors' tape. When she got closer, she saw that strips of tape fluttered from trees all around her forming a large square.

She walked back and forth across the clearing. In a grassy spot in the dead center she saw a flat green leaf with ruffled edges and purple spots. She bent down to examine it. It was the leaf of a cranefly orchid.

She called down to Josiah and Dr. Cornelius. "Come up here and see what I've found. The trees are marked with orange tape."

"Damn," she heard Josiah mutter. "Ness doesn't let any grass grow under his feet."

"Or cranefly orchids either, apparently," said Dr. Cornelius.

"You might want to see what else I've found."

"Be right there," Josiah called back.

She heard the scraping sound of the telescoping tripod being put away and the two men came toward her through the huckleberry brush, Josiah in his worn jeans and sweater, Dr. Cornelius in his pressed tan trousers and plaid wool shirt.

"Good heavens!" Dr. Cornelius looked around the clearing

at the tape-marked trees. "Does this mark the lot or is it one house?"

"One house," Josiah said after he'd looked around. "The tape is on the trees that are to be cut. The stakes for the house are over there." He pointed to orange plastic stakes ten feet beyond the largest beech tree.

"This beech is gigantic." Dr. Cornelius walked to the tree. "I hope they don't plan to cut this down. It must be two hundred years old."

"Afraid they intend to," said Josiah.

Victoria leaned on her stick while she waited for them.

"What else have you found, Mrs. Trumbull?" Dr. Cornelius strode through the grass toward her. She pointed to the leaf. He knelt down next to it. "I can hardly believe what I'm seeing. Come here, Josiah."

Josiah ambled over and stared. "Damn!"

"It's not the normal habitat, would you say?" Dr. Cornelius got to his feet and brushed off the knees of his trousers.

"It's been planted here," Josiah said. "Recently. What the hell is going on?"

Victoria pointed to the plant with her stick. "The first plant I found, the one that was dug up, had the same distinctive heart-shaped spot near the center leaf vein and the same ruffles on the leaf edges."

Dr. Cornelius tugged his magnifying glass out of his shirt pocket and examined the leaf. "If I'm not mistaken, this is the variety I would expect to find on the Island. But this is definitely not its normal habitat."

"It's right in the middle of the marked-off area," Victoria said.

"Dead center." Dr. Cornelius got to his feet again, dropped the magnifying glass into his pocket again. "I'd like to look around some more, Josiah. Can you show me other house sites?"

The day had grown warm and Victoria unzipped her

heavy sweater. She started to walk with the two men when she heard a rustling in the woods. She stopped.

"Are we going too fast for you, Mrs. Trumbull?"

"No," Victoria said. "You go on ahead. I'm going to rest for a minute or two."

"We'll wait with you," Josiah said. "We're in no hurry."

"No, go ahead. I'll catch up if I feel like it." She heard the faint rustling again.

"If you don't mind, I'll take Dr. Cornelius up to the rock, then, and we'll be back in a few minutes. Are you sure you don't want us to stay with you?"

"Go ahead, please." Victoria seated herself on a rock to one side of the cleared area and waited. She watched until the men were out of sight and listened to the sounds in the woods, twigs snapping and branches swishing. A song sparrow called. A beech leaf fluttered to the ground. Another twig snapped.

"I know you're there," Victoria called out softly. "They've gone up to the rock and won't be back for a while."

Something moved.

"I won't harm you. I'm going to sit here until they come back. I'd like to see you."

Quite suddenly, there he was in front of her, a tall, gaunt man with dark sunken eyes. His short hair was streaked brown and gray and white. Except for a large mustache, he was clean-shaven. He seemed to Victoria to have more lines in his face than she had in hers.

She held out her gnarled hand for him to shake. "I'm Victoria Trumbull."

"I know who you are." He kept his hands by his side.

Victoria put her hand back in her lap. "You're Phoebe's boy, James, aren't you?"

"I am called Ulysses." His hands were still by his side.

"The wanderer." Victoria put her hands on the top of the lilac stick. "Where's your dog? He attacked me, you know."

133

"I'm sorry. He's not a mean dog."

"Where is he?"

Ulysses put two fingers into his mouth and whistled, "Bob white! Bob bob white!" And within a few seconds the black-and-white dog came bounding through the undergrowth toward them, tail and rear end wagging, tongue hanging out. Victoria held out her hand to the dog, who sniffed it and nudged his head under it.

"It makes a difference, I guess, if the boss is here," she said.

"He's defending his territory." Ulysses shifted from one foot to another, as if he were about to take off.

"You've been tracking the boy and me, haven't you?"

"Yes, ma'am." Ulysses stared at her.

"You knew the boy followed your dog into the tunnel?"

"Yes, ma'am." His eyes were set so deep they were almost like holes in his face. "I have his cap."

"And you live in one of the old cellar holes."

He said nothing, but continued to stare at her.

"Does your mother know you live here?"

"I've seen her."

"But she doesn't know you're here?"

"I don't know what she knows." He shifted from one foot to another, still staring.

"How long have you been here?"

He shrugged. "Two years. More or less."

"Do you work?"

He shrugged again. "Carpentry. Odd jobs."

"And nobody recognizes you, not even your mother." Victoria looked into his eyes. "How sad. Don't you think she'd want to see you? To know you're near her?"

"I'm dead, as far as she's concerned."

"Children never are." Victoria looked down at the dry grass at her feet. "If I were to come back with the boy sometime, would you let us see your home?"

Ulysses was silent.

"If we promise not to tell anyone else?"

"Nobody's ever been to my place."

"The boy and I are coming back tomorrow afternoon by ourselves."

"I know. I heard." Ulysses glanced up and Victoria followed his gaze. She heard voices from the direction of Sachem's Rock. When she turned back to Ulysses, he had faded away like a figure cut out of her imagination. She heard the clump of boots and Dr. Cornelius and Josiah appeared.

"Sorry we took so long," Josiah said. "We checked out four of Ness's house sites."

"And you found cranefly orchids?" Victoria asked.

"On three of the four sites."

"Damndest thing I've ever seen," said Dr. Cornelius. "As if somebody else is trying to use the endangered species act without knowing what it involves. You can't simply plant a rare specimen and halt whatever it is you're trying to halt. Whoever is doing this is working against us, actually. We've got to find out who it is and stop him."

The next afternoon Josiah went alone to meet with Harry Ness in his house on Edgartown Harbor. An iron gate that hung from white-painted brick posts barred the entrance. To the left of the gate was a speaker set into the gatepost. Josiah announced himself and the gate slid open silently and closed silently behind him. He drove down a long approach paved with Belgian block that bisected a green meadow. Three chestnut horses grazed on the bright new grass. The road dipped slightly and then, ahead of him, filling his view from one side of the windshield to the other, was an Italian villa of white marble. A curving double stairway led up to a second floor. Josiah's impression was of overwhelming expense, of dozens of dazzling windows, of costly gold leaf, of a slate roof, of at least six tall chimneys.

He pulled up next to a Porsche with a yellow finish that seemed to consist of many coats of lacquer, and headed toward the grand stairway. Before he reached it, a wiry man in shorts and T-shirt jogged toward him from a side road. He was about the same height as Josiah. Sweat dripped from beneath a terry cloth headband.

He jogged in place. "You must be Coffin." He extended his hand, which Josiah shook, a hard, big, sweaty fist. "Ness," he said, still jogging in place. "Loch Ness. Doing my daily dozen," he explained, puffing slightly. "Want to see the place?"

"Yes, certainly. Of course."

Ness took the marble steps two at a time. Josiah trailed behind him, thinking that Ness, who was at least fifteen years older than he, was in better shape.

They went through a massive oak door that opened directly into what seemed to be a huge kitchen. Through an archway in the kitchen he could see a bank of windows at the distant front of the house that looked out over the harbor. Between him and the windows were several groupings of couches and easy chairs in pastel chintz, each grouping arranged on a large Oriental carpet that was placed with meticulous carelessness on the marble floor.

"I didn't mean to be so late," Ness apologized. "Have a seat at the kitchen table while I run upstairs and change. Can I get you a beer first? A diet soda?"

"A glass of water would be fine." Josiah looked around for the kitchen table and decided Ness meant the one beside him, a table three times the size of the conference room table in the Trust office, made of some exotic wood inlaid with arabesques of lighter and darker wood.

"A man after my own heart. Nothing beats good fresh H_2O."

Josiah turned so he could look behind him into the kitchen where he heard water splashing into a sink. Under the windows that faced onto the driveway was a twenty-foot-long counter topped with green marble. Stainless steel refrigerators, freezers, and cupboards lined the wall next to the counter, and in the center of the floor was an island with an eight-burner commercial stove. Pots and pans hung from a low beam above it.

"I'm the cook in the family," Ness explained. "The wife doesn't go in for kitchen duty, but I love it." The water continued to flow. "Have to let it run a few seconds. Well water, you know. A hundred feet deep. Good and cold. Takes a while to get up here." He went around the stove and reached into a cabinet opposite the sink, filled two glasses, and brought them to the table. Josiah noticed that the glasses, frosted by the cold water in them, were crystal.

"Practically everything in the place that can be crystal is crystal," Ness said almost apologetically. "The wife's name is Crystal. She likes it when I give her that sentimental stuff." He left the vast kitchen area and padded across the inlaid marble floor. "Slippery," he said over his shoulder. "Have to watch your step. I'll be back as soon as I change. Make yourself at home. Look around."

He walked lightly from the marble onto the Oriental carpet that muffled his footsteps and disappeared around a corner.

Josiah didn't move from his seat at the table. He could not imagine making himself at home in this palace. He sipped his water and gazed out the windows at the green lawn on one side, saw one of the horses lift its head high into the air and trot closer to the house. He could see the blue harbor through the front windows, saw a white sail pass below the house into the inner harbor. He was startled when, much sooner than he had expected, he heard Ness return.

"I suppose you want to get down to business." Ness had come around the corner, crossed the carpet, and his worn boating shoes slapped on the marble floor. He had changed into a yellow knit shirt and rumpled tan cotton trousers that looked as though they had been left too long in the dryer. "We can look around the place later, if you want."

After a few polite remarks, the house, the Trust, the horses, the car, the truck, Ness's background, Josiah's background, Ness sat back in the armchair at the head of the table, rested his elbows on the chair arms, and held his fingertips together in a sort of tent. "What did you want to see me about?"

Josiah, who usually had no trouble dealing with power, started to stutter.

"I suppose it's about the Sachem's Rock property?" Ness said, as though to put him at ease.

Josiah nodded. "It's one of the most beautiful unspoiled large tracts on the Vineyard."

Ness nodded. "Yes, it is."

"You probably know our position at the Trust." Josiah sat forward, hands in his lap. "We don't want to see that land developed."

"Your opinion is certainly valid, I'll give you that," Ness said. "I'm sure you recognize your opinion is only one of many." He tapped his tented fingertips together as he spoke. "Other people have ideas about the best use of that land. I happen to believe mine is the best and wisest use."

"Sixty houses is high density," Josiah said, moving his hands from his lap to the inlaid top of the table. "Sixty houses means roughly two-hundred-fifty people. It means, at two cars per household, a hundred-and-twenty cars. Probably twenty dogs the same number of cats. The impact of that intensity of development will destroy the habitat of a lot of plants and animals, both rare and not so rare."

"Each house will be surrounded by about three acres," Ness said, tapping his fingertips. "They'll scarcely be in sight of each other."

"Each homeowner will want to landscape his property,

plant specimen trees and exotic shrubs, put in a lawn, use fertilizers."

"Quite frankly, Coffin, I don't see anything wrong with that. Human beings are a species too, after all."

Josiah had avoided saying anything about the cranefly orchid. He was not sure how much Ness already knew, and he needed to learn more about who was moving the plants and why. "There may be rare species of plants on that land."

"Fine. I'll have a plant expert go over the property a couple of weeks from now with a fine-tooth comb. See what's growing. If it's rare, I'll build a shrine over it. No problem." Ness tapped his fingertips.

"If there are endangered species on property about to be developed," Josiah pushed a lock of hair off his forehead, "the state's endangered species act kicks in. The state people will need to make their own survey."

Ness's tanned face showed a faint flush. "This is a free country, Coffin. I bought that property. I own it, free and clear. I paid cash for it." He put his hands flat on the table with a decisive slap. "No one, not even the state, can tell me what to do with my property." He pushed his chair back, stood, and paced the length of the table and back again. "I like nature as well as the next guy. Look at my place." He swept his arm toward the manicured lawn. "I hunt. I fish. By the way, I'm going after oysters tomorrow afternoon on the Great Pond. Care to join me?"

Josiah shook his head.

"Almost the end of the season. Months with the letter R in them, you know."

"Yes, I know. But no thanks."

"By the way, I am fully aware that you've engaged Mrs. Trumbull and that kid to trespass on my property and I've said nothing. I respect the old-timers on the Island who think they have a right to walk anywhere they please. But I must tell you, she's trespassing. And sooner or later I'm asking her to keep off my property."

"Mrs. Trumbull has been walking only on the ancient ways," Josiah said. "Ancient ways are public rights-of-way."

"We'll see about that, won't we?" Ness stopped pacing and stared at Josiah. "I'm not sure you want to engage in battle with me, Coffin. Go along with me and I'll see that your Conservation Trust is rewarded. We'll carve off a nature sanctuary on the property, bring in rare plants, that kind of thing." He turned to the window that overlooked the driveway, then swung around again. "But if you fight me, I'll exercise my rights to do what I want with my own property. I have one hell of a lot larger budget for legal expenses than the Trust does, even though I realize you, its director, are an astute and competent attorney in your own right, and can probably hold your own with any two of my attorneys. But I've got six attorneys. Eight. Ten. Can you fight that?"

Josiah stood up. "The Trust would like to make you an offer, Ness. We're prepared to pay you what you paid for the land, one million dollars cash, plus another million in installments."

Ness laughed. "And what do you plan to do with the property?"

"We had been negotiating with Mrs. Eldredge to put a conservation restriction on it, keep it in an undeveloped state in perpetuity. She would have a right to live on it for the rest of her life. Her children too, if she wants."

Ness laughed again. "She doesn't want anything to do with that cuckoo son or that flaky daughter of hers. Or her tattooed granddaughter, for that matter."

Josiah went on. "She said you had agreed to let her live in her own home for the rest of her life, that you would not be building in her lifetime."

"She misunderstood." Ness put his hands in the pockets of his slacks.

"I don't think so." Josiah stood too, put his hands flat on the table, and leaned on them.

"Think whatever you want to think." Ness jingled change in his pocket. "I paid Mrs. Eldredge one million dollars, a fortune for her. I had my lawyers put the money into annuities and trusts to protect her—we didn't need to do that—we paid all the back taxes and all the fees, we had all the paperwork drawn up at our expense. She's got a fixed income of a hundred thousand dollars a year minimum, living on interest alone. She can travel, buy a place in Florida, keep an apartment here on the Island, if she wants. If she misunderstood us, I don't know what more we could have done. It was all in writing. All she had to do was read it."

"It was my understanding that Montgomery Mausz represented both you and Mrs. Eldredge." Josiah leaned forward over the table.

"That was between Mausz and Mrs. Eldredge," Ness said. "Mausz was on a retainer to me. Mrs. Eldredge had a right to pick any lawyer she wanted. I can't answer for Mausz's ethics, especially not now." He jingled the coins in his pocket. "Better leave that one alone, Coffin. If you want to save some plant or bird or fish or butterfly, I'll work with you. But I do it on my terms, you understand? You remember that so-called endangered fish that stopped that billion-dollar dam? As I recall, a couple years later the stream biologists found a whole colony of the damned things upstream and in other streams where they hadn't even looked before. So much for endangered species." He turned again to watch the horses. They had stopped grazing and were rollicking over the green lawn. Josiah could see the glint of steel horseshoes in the sunlight as they kicked up their feet.

"Pretty," Ness said, and turned back again. "As I was saying, I don't want some sophomore in biology at Boston University holding me up because she thinks she's found some species of rare ragweed or something. I'll work with you,

141

Coffin, but I'm not taking orders from you or any of your minions, you understand?" Ness jabbed his forefinger at Josiah for emphasis. "Understand?"

"I think you've made your point, Ness. I've got to go."

"I haven't shown you the rest of the place." Ness was the cordial host again.

"I'll take a rain check, thanks." Josiah headed through the kitchen to the big oak door.

"Let me get that door for you," Ness said. "It's alarmed."

While Josiah was engaged in the one-sided duel with Loch Ness, Page Bachwald of Park and Rec had stepped up onto the porch at Alley's with a pen and an official-looking document in her hand. She addressed Joe, the plumber. "You live in West Tisbury, don't you Joe?" she asked. Although the afternoon was warm and the four people on the porch were in shirtsleeves or sweaters, Page was wearing a pink parka with its fake rabbit-fur hood thrown back.

She held the document out to Joe, who was leaning against the post watching Taffy. The dog was in the pickup, snapping at flies. "Early for flies," he said to Lincoln, who was standing with his back to the sign lettered, "canned peas." Without looking at Page, he reached for the petition, which had about six signatures on it. "I'll sign. What's it for?"

"Don't make the X too big," Donald said.

Sarah flicked an Oreo crumb off her black sweater, embroidered with turquoise and red Navajo-inspired designs. "You're not a West Tisbury resident." She was sitting next to Donald.

"Who cares? It's all one Island."

"What's the petition for?" Donald asked.

"To ask the selectmen to place an article on the town warrant to buy Sachem's Rock for a park." Page reached a small hand behind her neck and lifted her hair away from the neck of her parka.

"It'll never fly." Joe held out his hand. "Lemme sign it."

"You can't, Joe," Sarah said. "They'll throw out her petition."

"Ness has that land already sewn up," Lincoln said. "He's even got the lots surveyed. He won't sell."

"If we get the whole town behind us, we have a chance. People *can* make a difference." Page emphasized the word *can* with a downward thrust of her fist.

"I'll sign," Sarah said. "Doesn't mean I'll vote for it. This town is spending money faster than we earn it."

"Thought those Indians paid you pretty well for that job up to Gay Head," Joe said.

" 'Native Americans,' not 'Indians.' 'Aquinnah,' not 'Gay Head.' And yes, they pay me just fine, thank you." Sarah turned to Page. "How many signatures do you need?"

"Only ten. I have six already." She gave the petition to Sarah who signed neatly and passed it to Lincoln.

Lincoln read it. "I don't know. How much would we need to ante up?"

"We thought we might sweet-talk him into one-and-a-half million." Page fluttered her dark eyelashes at Joe.

Joe guffawed. "Sweet-talk Ness? You gotta be shittin'!" He whacked her pink-clad arm with his folded-up *Island Enquirer.* "You've seen his logo, haven't you? A sea serpent circling the globe. That's him. He'd strangle his grandmother for her land."

"He's not so bad," Sarah said. "Go on and sign, Lincoln. All that petition means is that the selectmen have to put it on the warrant. You don't have to vote for it."

"You talk to anyone in town hall about this?" Lincoln pointed down at the petition he was holding.

"Park and Rec voted unanimously," Page said.

"A bunch of ninnies." Lincoln passed the petition, unsigned, back to Page.

"I'm the chairperson of Park and Rec." Page turned on him, eyes brimming.

Joe snorted. " 'Ninnies.' Haven't heard that for some time. More refined than 'assholes.' "

Page flushed and snatched the petition.

"Don't let them get your goat, kid," Donald called out as Page trotted to the parking lot, hair bouncing on her pink hood.

"Don't let the animal rights people catch you wearing that fur coat!" Joe shouted to her back.

"You don't need to be so nasty, Joe." Sarah passed him the cellophane bag of Oreos. "Anyway, it's fake fur. Have a cookie."

CHAPTER 12

The delegation of five doctors, Erickson and Jeffers from the Island, and Gibbs, Sawicki, and Billings from off-Island, invited Harry Ness to lunch at Goose Neck Golf Club, entirely appropriate and nicely casual. It was the day after Josiah had spoken without success to Ness.

Doc Jeffers and Dr. Gibbs were already seated. Jeffers had left his helmet with his motorcycle and had unzipped his black leather jacket, exposing a blue scrub shirt. Dr. Gibbs brushed her hair away from her forehead.

Doc Jeffers was saying to Dr. Gibbs, "I've put my boat in the water. Next nice day, I'll give you a sailing lesson."

Dr. Gibbs turned her elegant head away from him. Her eyes were as black and glossy as her hair with its white wings. "I know how to sail, thank you." She moved her cashmere cardigan from the chair next to her as Dr. Billings approached the table. Jeffers rose, and the older man shook hands with him, leaning over the table to do so, his liver-spotted hand holding his tie against his blue and white striped shirt.

"You a sailor?" Doc Jeffers sat again with a clank.

"No." Dr. Billings's jowls quivered. "I get seasick."

Dr. Gibbs looked at her watch.

Doc Jeffers turned to her. "When I made my rounds this morning your guy looked pretty good. When are you discharging him?"

Dr. Gibbs stared at him as if he were a not-too-bright patient. "Not for a week at least," she said finally. "He hasn't recovered his short-term memory yet. He doesn't recall what

145

he was doing when the tree came down on him."

"How's his thorax?" Dr. Billings asked.

"Recovering surprisingly well. His right lung had collapsed. We've re-inflated it and it's holding. The ribs seem to be healing as well as can be expected."

"Nice bit of work there." Doc Jeffers bared his teeth.

Dr. Gibbs ignored the look. "He's not a smoker and he's in good physical condition. Both in his favor."

Doc Erickson arrived at the table with Dr. Sawicki. Erickson was wearing his usual rumpled linen jacket over his madras shirt and Sawicki was natty in a sports coat, obviously tailor-made to minimize his girth.

"Before Mr. Ness gets here I should say, once again, that I don't want to be involved in a public golf course." Dr. Gibbs brushed her hair away from her forehead with the back of her hand. "I don't object to elitism."

"I feel the same way." Dr. Billings patted Dr. Gibbs's arm in an avuncular manner.

"First things first," said Doc Erickson. "We don't know whether Ness will sell to us or not. I asked the rep from DufferPro to join us today, but he had another commitment."

"More important than a ten-million-dollar golf course complex on Martha's Vineyard?" Dr. Sawicki pursed his small mouth and puffed out his cheeks.

"We are simply exploring possibilities," said Doc Erickson. "None of us has taken a step yet that we can't back out of."

"Here he is now," said Doc Jeffers, who was facing the door.

Doc Erickson stood and signaled Ness with two raised fingers. Ness was wearing a navy blue blazer, tan trousers, and boating shoes with no socks. They introduced themselves all around and Ness sat between Dr. Billings and Doc Erickson.

"Care for a drink?" Doc Erickson asked Ness as the waiter approached.

"Poland Spring, thanks."

The conversation touched on the weather, on Goose Neck, on Doc Jeffers's Harley-Davidson that Ness had admired. They spoke of the yellow custom paint job on Ness's Porsche, of Doc Jeffers's sailboat. Ness said he had a 65-foot motor sailer tied up at the dock that he could see from his kitchen window. He invited all of them to drop in sometime, and they said they would love to. The two Island doctors spoke of Dr. Sawicki's orthopedic practice and told Ness how much the Island needed Sawicki. Sawicki blushed.

Doc Jeffers nodded at Dr. Gibbs. "Our friend here is quite a surgeon. If she hadn't been on-Island the other day, the patient, Kirschmeyer, would never have made it."

Dr. Gibbs said coldly, "Please, Doctor. Patient confidentiality."

"Really?" Ness looked up. "Kirschmeyer."

"You know him?" Doc Jeffers asked.

"How is he doing?" Ness asked Dr. Gibbs without answering Doc Jeffers.

"We don't discuss patients. Or their cases, Mr. Ness."

Ness nodded.

"You know him?" Doc Jeffers asked Ness again.

"Name's familiar."

Lunch arrived and they chatted civilly about Island politics, off-Island politics, international politics.

And then it was time to get down to business.

Ness brought it up. "I assume you've asked me to lunch to discuss Sachem's Rock. I take it you want to make me an offer."

Four of the five doctors exchanged glances. Dr. Gibbs looked down at her salad plate with its shrimp tails and tufts of parsley.

"I'm not sure we've got that far in our thinking," Doc Erickson said. "We're exploring possibilities."

"I see," said Ness. "Such as?"

"We hoped to build a golf course complex, clubhouse,

country inn. We've talked about a system of public trails, but we haven't agreed on that yet." Doc Erickson reached down for his briefcase. "I'll show you some of the sketches, if you'd like."

"I don't believe I need to see them. What sort of offer were you thinking of making?"

They looked at one another, then at Doc Erickson.

"We can go as high as two-point-five million."

"You know the appraisal on the property?" said Ness.

"I know it's higher than that," Doc Erickson said.

"Ten million." Ness looked around the table with a frown. No one met his gaze. "Ten million dollars."

"We can probably go to three million."

"Gentlemen—and Dr. Gibbs," Ness nodded at her, "thank you for a delightful lunch." He pushed his chair away from the table and stood. "I must be going."

"The investors haven't discussed this yet," Doc Erickson said quickly, "but I'm sure we might come to some agreement about making you one of the partners in the project."

"I think a golf course would be more ecologically acceptable to the Island than a housing development," Dr. Billings said.

"Hardly a 'housing development,' " Ness said. "Three-million-dollar homes. Besides, some environmentalists question how desirable a golf course is, in the grand scheme of things." He wadded up the napkin he had been holding and tossed it on the table. "I must be going. I'm hoping to bag a few oysters while they're still in season. Thank you all." He nodded to them. "My invitation stands. Drop in anytime. My door's always open."

The five doctors were silent while Ness left the restaurant.

Doc Jeffers was the first to speak. "Prick," he said. "I'll bet dollars to donuts he's the one who hired Kirschmeyer."

"You have to hand it to him," Dr. Billings said. "He's not the biggest developer on the East Coast for nothing."

"I'd like to see his place sometime," Dr. Sawicki said. "Understand it's quite a spread."

Dr. Billings straightened his tie. "Maybe we could include a small hospital in the golf complex, the Ness Memorial Hospital. Might appeal to his vanity."

"We have enough problems with one hospital on this Island," said Doc Jeffers. "Don't get me started on that."

Dr. Gibbs lifted the cuff of her silk shirt and looked at her watch. "I can make the two-forty-five boat if we're all through. How would you like to settle up?"

"I'll take care of it," Doc Erickson said.

"Can I give you a ride to the ferry on my bike?" Doc Jeffers asked.

"No thank you."

"I'll call you about that sailing lesson."

"Don't bother." Dr. Gibbs put on her cashmere cardigan. Doc Erickson got her coat from the checkroom. She slipped on her gloves, picked up her slim leather attaché case, and left.

"What's with her and sailing?" Doc Jeffers said to the men at the table. "Most women like my lessons."

Dr. Sawicki shook his head and his cheeks wobbled. "Wrong woman, Jeffers."

"You haven't done your homework." Dr. Billings patted his tie with a blue-veined hand. "I gather you didn't know she won the single-handed Newport to Bermuda race two years ago in a thirty-two-foot Hinckley."

"Her own boat," said Dr. Sawicki.

"Oh," said Doc Jeffers.

Before he changed into his long johns and wool pants and bundled up in his plaid shirt to go oystering on the Great Pond, Harry Ness stood at the windows of his bedroom and looked down at the boats passing below the bluff on which his house stood. Not many yet. It was still early in the season.

He could see Crystal jogging on the beach toward the yacht club, her two wolfhounds prancing beside her as if they were on tiptoe. When she moved away from him like this, he liked the way her tight ass was an extension of her long legs. Even now, years after they'd been married, he got a hot feeling of lust when he saw her like this, running with her dogs.

He left to get a sweater, then returned to the window.

He couldn't understand men who went for younger women. What could you talk about? Music? What book they'd last read? The life they'd lived? Part of the fun was talking about things you had in common. How could you talk with a kid who'd never protested the Vietnam War? Kids who knew the Beatles only as classical music?

He thought about the surgeon, Dr. Gibbs, as he slipped the sweater over his head. She was close to his age, and what a woman: bright, cool, as gorgeous as any movie star with that white skin, black eyes, and black hair with its wings of white. The way she surgically handled that oafish Jeffers.

He got knee-length wool socks from his bureau and sat on the window seat to pull them on while he watched Crystal run out of sight beneath a dock, then appear again on the other side.

Minerva Peabody was another woman who made him feel all man. That outdoorsy look really turned him on, that sun-bleached salt-sea-smelling hair, the freckles on her turned-up nose. The preppy clothes, sleekly muscled tan arms and legs. What could she ever have seen in Mausz? Crystal, he was sure, didn't suspect anything was going on between him and Minerva. He and Minerva had gone to extreme lengths to keep their relationship quiet, which was part of the thrill. On this Island, you had to be careful. Rumors spread from Edgartown to Aquinnah faster than the wind traveled. Her husband had been an ass, an inept attorney, but Ness had kept him on retainer because of Minerva. With Mausz gone, certain problems were beginning to crop up. She was getting possessive. Moving in on him. He'd thought about that, and decided he'd better ease himself out of the affair, and soon. This afternoon, maybe. He was going to have to tell her it was all over. Nothing he couldn't handle. It wasn't the first time. She had her own money, so he wouldn't be able to buy her off. He'd have to think about it, the best way out. That was usually the worst part of these things, easing out of them without its turning nasty.

On the beach below, Crystal stopped to talk with someone, a bulky older woman bundled up in a sweater and a kerchief worn like a peasant's. He saw Crystal throw her head back and laugh at something the woman said. God, she was such a nice person. He loved that about her. He took a deep breath. Women really did make the world a better place.

Crystal moved on, and Ness wondered how he could approach the surgeon. With that thought he felt a glorious new surge in his gut. It would be different from any game he'd played before. He would have to do a juggling act to keep all three women separate, all three balls in the air. He laughed at the thought. It made sense to re-evaluate his relationship with Minerva.

Ten minutes later Ness clumped down his marble stairway, waders slung over his shoulder. He stopped abruptly when he saw a short, stocky, bearded man waiting at the foot of the steps.

"Who the hell are you? And how did you get in here?"

The man looked up at Ness with intense, almost luminous eyes. "My name is Tom More," he said. "A woman with two dogs let me in. Your wife, I take it."

Ness said, "I'm just leaving."

"I see." More waited.

Ness paused on the last step and looked down on the man. "Why don't you call for an appointment? Stop by for," he paused, "a cup of tea."

More continued to look up at him with those luminous

151

eyes. "May I ride with you to the gate? I left my truck up there." He nodded toward the entrance.

"I suppose so." Ness went to his four-wheel-drive wagon, opened the tailgate, checked for his wire basket and clam fork, and tossed in his waders. He slammed the back shut and stepped up into the driver's seat.

"Hop in," he said to More.

"I'd like to explain why I need to meet with you."

"I can guess." Ness backed into the paved turnaround. "You're offering to buy the Sachem's Rock property for your commune." He shifted into gear and headed slowly up the long driveway.

"We don't think of it as a commune."

"Whatever," Ness said. "I don't have anything to say to you. Everybody on this Island wants that piece of land to do their thing. Golf course. Playground. Campsite. Country Inn. Nature preserve. Casino. Commune. Haven't heard from the people who want to create a zoo, yet." He grinned. The chestnut horses lifted their heads from the velvet grass as they drove past.

"Very funny," More said. "I'm prepared to offer you whatever it takes to buy that property from you."

"You don't have enough money to buy that land from me."

"I have a backer who's interested in my project, enough to put in quite a bit of her money."

"Oh? 'Her?' Who might that be?"

"I'm not at liberty to say," More said.

They were within sight now of the long white picket fence that divided Ness's property from the road. Ahead of them was the iron gate between granite gateposts.

"How much are you talking about?" Ness said.

"Two-and-a-half million," said More.

Ness laughed. "The doctors offered me three and threw in a partnership."

152

"I might be able to match that."

"Look, buddy, I'm not interested. My project will provide housing for sixty families."

"In three-million-dollar houses."

"That's right. Just because a person can afford to pay three million dollars for a house doesn't mean he shouldn't have a place to live."

"You're exploiting that old woman you bought it from, the Island, the land itself, and the people who'll buy your houses."

"I don't think so," said Ness. "It all depends on your perspective. How much are you charging your homeowners? Three hundred thousand? And you have, how many, fifty of them? If I'm figuring right that comes to fifteen million. Costs you, what, twenty thousand to put up those cracker boxes with their composting toilets and solar panels?"

More stared straight ahead. "Forty thousand," he said.

Ness went on as if he hadn't heard. "So fifty times twenty-thousand dollars plus, let's say I sell you the land for three million, comes to what? I don't have my calculator. Roughly fifteen million less, let's say, five million expenses. Leaves you with a tidy ten million net, all for yourself. Not bad."

"Let's multiply out the same thing for you," More said.

"No, no. I'm in the catbird seat. You want to buy into it. Don't give me any of that for-the-betterment-of-mankind shit."

Ness slowed the vehicle before the gate, which slid open automatically, drove through, and stopped next to More's pickup. He thumped his chest with his open hand. "I'm at least honest enough to tell myself my business is for the betterment of Loch Ness." He waited for More to open the door. "Next time you're in the neighborhood, give me a call first. Be glad to show you around. Maybe you can give me some advice on some of the small construction jobs I've got around the place."

"I need to talk with you for ten minutes, fifteen at the most," More said, without moving. "What about later this afternoon?"

"Sorry. It's getting late and I want to get out on the Great Pond, get my supper. Oyster stew tonight. New recipe."

"What about tomorrow?" More asked.

"I believe we've about exhausted the subject. I don't intend to sell, you can't come up with the money that would induce me to sell, your housing plan sounds one hell of a lot less acceptable to the town and the Island than mine, and will bring in one hell of a lot fewer taxes than mine. Can you get that door open? It tends to stick."

More gave the door a shove and climbed out.

"Give me a call sometime," Ness said. "I'd love to show you the place."

More slammed the door shut and walked to his pickup.

While Tom More was attempting to meet with Loch Ness, Victoria gathered up her cloth bag and her lilac-wood stick, and went around to the front of her house. When she heard a vehicle coming from the direction of Edgartown, she stuck out her thumb. The vehicle, one of the Arujo Brothers septic system pumpout trucks, stopped, and took her to the West Tisbury School, which was just letting out.

Robin was racing around the side of the building, his jacket flapping, his shirt untucked. It looked as though he was about to whack one of his classmates with his book bag, Victoria couldn't see who. She called to him.

"How'd you get here?" he asked when he reached her, out of breath, shoes untied, glasses down his nose.

"I got a ride," Victoria said vaguely. "Tie your shoelaces and tuck in your shirt."

Robin put his book bag down and bent over his sneakers. Victoria looked around to see if there was anyone she knew. Ira Bodman was waiting in his red pickup for his daughter.

"Are you going up North Road?" she asked when he rolled down the window.

"Sure, Miz Trumbull. Can I give you a lift?"

"Do you have room for two of us?"

Ira looked through the dusty back window into the bed of the truck, where his black Lab was beating its tail joyfully against the metal sides. "You and Robin?"

Victoria nodded.

"The kids can ride in back with Douggie."

His daughter Tiffany skipped up to the truck and Robin skulked over.

Tiffany whined, "Not him, Daddy! He's disgusting."

"I'll walk." Robin pushed his glasses back onto his nose.

"Both of you get in, and shut up!" Ira started up the truck with a roar. The kids scrambled into the back and Ira took off. "Not riding with the chief today, Miz Trumbull?"

"She has other business." Victoria changed the subject. "Isn't it a lovely day."

"Nice day for a walk," Ira agreed. "I see you and Robin been up there to the rock quite a few times lately. Trying to get in a last walk or two before Ness locks it up?"

"Something like that." Victoria smiled. "Is Phoebe still in her house?"

Ira made a wry face. "Ness is giving her six months before she has to leave. Generous bastard."

"She must be sorry she sold out."

"If it was me, I'd for sure rather have the house and land than the money," Ira said.

They passed the split oak on the corner, and farther on, passed the entrance to Seven Gates. A flock of crows flew up from the big meadow, then settled again. The trees on the far side of the meadow shimmered green.

Ira jerked his thumb at the entrance. "Everybody there in the duchy wants their gardens tilled right now, this minute. You'd think I was the only guy on the Island with a tiller."

"They probably think you're best."

"Probably so," said Ira with a tight smile.

When he dropped them off at the trailhead, Tiffany and Robin climbed over the back of the truck and dropped to the ground. She stuck her tongue out at him and he swung his book bag at her. She climbed into the passenger seat and her father drove off.

"Must you do that?" Victoria said to Robin.

"She started it."

Victoria grunted. "Your shoelaces are untied again. I'll show you how to tie them properly, if you don't know."

"I know how." Robin bent over to tie them.

While they were retracing their path to the orchid sites, Victoria told Robin about meeting the underground man.

Robin bounded up the trail and back again. "No kidding! Maybe he'll let us go into his cave. I wonder if it's dark in there? Do you suppose he's got electricity? A generator? Maybe he uses candles. I wonder how he cooks. Do you suppose he has windows somewhere so he can tell what the weather's like outside? How does he go to the bathroom?" Robin blushed suddenly.

"He said no one had ever been in his house. Don't get your hopes up."

When they stopped so Victoria could rest they heard leaves rustling. Ulysses stepped out of the undergrowth onto the path.

Robin stood still and stared. Ulysses stared back. He wore a tan and green and brown camouflage suit that blended into the spring woods.

Victoria broke the silence. "I hoped we'd see you this afternoon. This is Robin."

Ulysses nodded at the boy, who continued to stare at him.

"You're the underground man, aren't you?" Robin sounded awed.

"Did you tell anyone you were coming here?" Ulysses asked Victoria without answering Robin.

She shook her head. Then she had a sudden horrible thought. For all she knew, Ulysses might be the killer, the person who had murdered Mausz. No one but she knew Ulysses was here, not even his mother. Victoria was the only person who had seen him. No one except Ira Bodman knew she and Robin were coming here today. If they disappeared, no one would know what had happened to them. She recalled her first encounter with the dog, how alarmed she'd been when it attacked her. What did she know about Ulysses? Nothing to make her feel comfortable. He was Phoebe's son. His name was James Eldredge, he lived in a cellar hole, and he was a bit different. She was willing to take risks herself, but she had no right to risk Robin's life.

"I think we need to go home again, Robin," she said abruptly. "I just remembered something."

"Do we have to? We just got here." Robin dug the tip of his sneaker into the soft sand of the path.

Ulysses stared from her to the boy and said nothing.

"Your parents don't know we're here. Neither does my granddaughter. We need to go home now."

"But I want to see his cave."

"Come along. Right now." Victoria turned her back on Ulysses and started back down the path.

"You said you'd let me see his cave." Robin didn't move. "You promised."

"I've changed my mind. Besides he didn't agree to let us see it."

Ulysses snorted, and when Victoria looked back, he was grinning.

"Victoria Trumbull, afraid?"

"Of course not." She turned. "Come along, Robin."

"Why can't we leave after we see his cave?"

"He hasn't invited us. Come along. Right now."

Ulysses whistled, *bob white! bob white!* then muttered, "I'm the one who should be afraid, not you." Within seconds his dog bounded out of the brush, Robin's cap in his mouth, tail wagging.

"Hey, Mrs. Trumbull. Look! He's brought my hat." Robin kneeled down and put his arms around the dog's neck. "Thanks, dog." The dog dropped the cap. Robin picked it up, brushed it off, and set it on his head.

"Can we see your cave? Can we?"

Ulysses gazed at Victoria with his deep eyes.

Robin had put his arms around the dog's neck again. Ulysses stood with his feet apart blocking the path. He nodded slightly to Victoria.

Victoria gave in. "We can't stay long." She trailed behind Ulysses while Robin and the dog bounded down the slope. Ulysses waited for her where the ground leveled, then waited for her to rest. When she indicated she was ready to go on, he followed a deer path a few feet, then bent and tugged at a small pine stump on the slope. A square of ground, four by four feet, lifted up, and Victoria looked into a black hole with a ladder leading down into darkness.

Chapter 13

Tom More drove from Loch Ness's gate to Minerva Peabody's on North Water Street. Montgomery Mausz's widow ushered him into a solarium that overlooked the harbor and indicated a chair at a glass-topped table. Even though it was still early spring, Minerva glowed with a healthy tan. Her blond hair was streaked with what looked like the effects of sun. Her beige slacks exactly matched her sweater.

"Harry Ness has his weaknesses, Tommy. I know most of them. More tea?" Minerva poised the teapot over the china mug in front of Tom.

"Please." He blotted his mouth with a small linen napkin and nodded. "Nice tea. Good color."

Minerva smiled. "I made it myself with rose hips."

Tom picked up the mug. "How are you holding up since, um, your husband was found?" Tom shook his head.

"You don't need to pretend, Tommy. Whatever Mickey and I had between us at one time was long gone. I'm sorry Victoria Trumbull was the one to find him, and so long after he died."

"Strange, where she found him. Very strange."

"Yes, it is," Minerva agreed.

"At any rate, it's not something you'd wish on an elderly lady."

Minerva poured more tea for herself. "I knew, of course, that Mickey was having an affair. It wasn't his first. Quite frankly I didn't care who the woman was as long as they were discreet. But that's not why I asked you here, Tommy."

"I'm at your service. You know that."

Minerva laughed. The freckles on her turned-up nose crinkled. "Money talks, doesn't it? There's almost nothing you can't buy if you have enough money. Isn't that right, Tommy?"

Tom flushed. "That's hardly the case between us."

"Tommy, I don't care that your discretion can be bought." Minerva picked up her mug. "I've looked at this as an investment, backing your utopia."

Tom was silent. Finally he said, "I met with Ness briefly this afternoon."

"Oh?" Minerva put her cup down. "What was his reaction?"

"He wouldn't talk to me. He was leaving to go oystering on the Great Pond." Tom avoided Minerva's eyes.

"Did you have a chance to tell him you have a backer ready to buy that land?"

"Yes. I got that much in before he cut me off."

"You didn't tell him who that backer was, did you?"

"Of course not, Minerva."

"He told you he was going oystering," she murmured. "I wonder who else he told?"

Tom glanced at her. "What did you say?"

"Nothing, Tommy." Minerva stared at him over the rim of her mug. "Let's get down to business, shall we? And the reason I asked you here."

Tom moved his chair slightly away from the table so he faced her more directly, settled into the chair again, gazed at her intently, and waited.

Minerva laughed. "Come off it, Tommy. You can manipulate your flock all you want with your soulful eyes, but don't try it with me. And don't look so pained."

Tom took off his glasses and brushed his hand across his eyes. "Jesus, Minerva."

Minerva continued. "I'm willing to pay whatever is necessary, Tommy. Three million, four million, eight million. Ten million. I don't care. I'll pay whatever it takes. However, I want my name on the deed, is that clear? You can build your housing complex on it, we can work out a long-term lease. But I will be the owner. I hope that's acceptable."

Tom thought for a few moments. "Yes. We'll need to work out details, but I think that would answer my needs."

"I'll stay in the background, Tommy. You can be assured of that."

Tom More stood and dropped his napkin on the table. "I believe this arrangement will benefit not only us, but all the investors in Cranberry Fields."

Minerva tapped her manicured fingernail on the glass tabletop. "I hope I can count on your total discretion, Tommy."

Tommy bowed his head to her and left.

Casey had already turned out the lights in the police station and was at the door when the phone rang.

It was a woman's voice. "Chief O'Neill?"

"This is Chief O'Neill. Can I help you?"

"My name is Crystal Ness?" The voice went up in a question.

"Yes, Mrs. Ness."

"My husband hasn't come home yet. He was supposed to be here two hours ago. I'm worried about him."

"You're in Edgartown, aren't you? Have you spoken to the police there?"

"He's not in Edgartown. He's in West Tisbury. On the Pond. He went oystering this afternoon. By himself. This isn't like him at all."

Casey sighed and turned the lights back on. "Perhaps he lost track of time. Ran out of gas. A couple of hours isn't long on this Island."

"He always calls me if he's going to be late. On his cell

phone. He always calls. Always." Crystal's voice had a trace of hysteria. "He was going out in the boat he keeps at the gunning camp."

"Camp?" asked Casey.

"That's what he calls his cabin."

"It's probably something simple, Mrs. Ness, but I'll drive down there and check. I'll phone you in an hour or so."

"This isn't like him, honestly it isn't. . . ."

After Casey hung up she called Bill Burnes, the marine conservation officer, who said he'd launch his boat at the landing in three-quarters of an hour and would motor over to the gunning camp.

"Probably nothing," Bill said. "A guy gets out on the Pond and forgets what time it is."

"Not once it gets dark, he doesn't," Casey mumbled.

She phoned Victoria next. "Where have you been?" she said when Victoria answered. "I've been trying to reach you all afternoon. I even came by the house."

"I have things of my own to attend to."

"Where have you been?"

"Out."

"Okay, okay." From where she stood Casey could see one of the swans on the millpond, picked out by moonlight. "Okay, Victoria. I hope you know where the Ness gunning cabin is."

"We Vineyarders don't call them 'cabins,' we call them 'camps.' The gunning camp was part of Freeman Athearn's farm," Victoria told her. "Freeman sold the land with the buildings to Harry Ness seven or eight years ago. The old-timers used the camp for duck hunting. Why do you ask?"

"Mrs. Ness called. Her husband hasn't come home."

"I'll be ready when you get here." Victoria cut off the phone connection with a decisive click.

"What was that all about?" Elizabeth had come into the cookroom while Victoria and Casey were talking.

"She means well, but I'm tired of people minding my business."

Elizabeth laughed. McCavity had wrapped himself around her leg and she bent down to ruffle his fur. "So where are you off to now, Gram, you and the police chief?"

"Harry Ness is missing."

Elizabeth stood upright. "No kidding!"

Victoria held out her coat and Elizabeth helped her into it as vehicle lights jounced into the driveway.

"Take care," Elizabeth called after her grandmother.

The road to the gunning camp was overhung with oak trees that became more and more stunted as Casey and Victoria neared the Great Pond and the sea beyond. The half moon dodged in and out of scudding clouds, casting enough light so shadows of branches formed a dark network on the light-colored road. As they neared the Pond, trees became stunted brush and the brush ended at a grassy clearing. A low shingled building stood at the edge of the woods, pale in the moonlight.

Casey parked beside the building. The grass around them was cropped short and littered with small dry turds.

"Sheep?" Casey pointed her flashlight at a pile of droppings.

Victoria looked down. "Freeman Athearn has a deal worked out with Mr. Ness. Freeman's sheep mow the grass and Ness buys a couple of lambs every year. Freeman butchers the lambs and packages the meat for the Ness's freezer."

Casey could see a line of surf, phosphorescent white in the shifting moonlight, and could hear its distant mutter on the other side of the bar. The wind had picked up, and small breaking waves covered the surface of the Pond and lapped along the shore.

Casey was thinking about ghosts when Victoria whispered, as if someone might be listening, "He probably keeps his boat in the boathouse on the other side of the point. As

163

I recall, there are webbings or ropes that hang from the rafters. They go under the boat and you turn a crank to lift it out of the water."

Casey strode along the sandy track that Victoria told her led toward the point, Victoria next to her. The wind was southerly, directly in their faces, hissing in Casey's ears, blowing her hair back from her face. The moon disappeared behind a ragged black cloud and shadows raced in front of them. Casey could feel the world spinning through dark space. She glanced at Victoria as the moon sailed out from behind the cloud casting a shadow of Victoria's great nose across her cheek. Her head was high, her back was straight, she was smiling.

They came quite suddenly to the boathouse, half hidden by a fringe of prickly gooseberry and wild rose. Racing shadows danced across the roof, blinked across the whitecaps on the Great Pond. Everything seemed to be moving, the surface of the Pond, the boathouse, the land itself. For a moment, Casey felt dizzy, whirled around in space on a hurtling planet. She felt as if she needed to hold onto something to keep from flying off.

Victoria broke the silence. "It's been this way forever. It makes you feel insignificant, doesn't it? The moon and the clouds, the Pond and the sea, the wind. The boathouse was built before I was born and will probably outlast both of us."

Casey pushed through the bushes, wiped her hand across a window to clear away the salt spray, and beamed her light inside. "I can't see anything in there. No boat, certainly."

"Perhaps he leaves it on the shore now that winter's over." Victoria stepped carefully down the small bluff onto the beach, bracing her hand against the shingled side of the building.

They looked for the boat or marks of its keel, following the shoreline of the cove. The sheltered cove was eerily silent.

164

When cattails and marsh grass blocked their way they retraced their steps back around the point, where the wind hit them again. Victoria balanced herself as she walked along the stony beach, stick in one hand, the other arm out to one side like a tightrope walker. There was no sign of a boat, no keel mark, not even any footprints in the sand. Only theirs.

"I hope that's Ness now." Casey cupped her hands around her ears to block the wind so she could hear an outboard motor.

"It's Bill," Victoria said as the boat came into sight.

Bill's boat slid onto the beach, scraping on sand and stone. He lifted the motor into the stern. The trailing wake caught up with a slosh that skewed the boat around. "Kind of a wild night." His life jacket, pale and bulky against his dark uniform and dark skin, made him look huge. "No sign of his boat?"

Casey shook her head. "Guess we need to go out there and take a look." She waved a hand at the breaking whitecaps.

Bill looked down at them. "It's chilly on the water. You going to be warm enough?"

"I'll get a couple of windbreakers," Casey said. "Looks as though we might get wet."

When she returned, Bill had pulled life jackets out from under the stern seat, and Casey and Victoria buckled them over their windbreakers.

Victoria sat on the middle seat, Casey sat in the bow facing her. When they were settled, Bill shoved the boat off the beach, started the motor, and headed out into the wind. The bow slapped the breaking waves, sending a spray of water across Casey's back.

Victoria spoke above the sound of wind and the motor. "Oysters would be in shallow water, right along the shore, no more than three or four feet deep."

"And he probably worked in the lee of the shore to keep

out of the wind," Bill called back. "His engine may have quit on him. He may be broken down someplace."

"His wife said he has a cell phone." Casey's voice was broken up by the pounding of the boat on the waves.

"Cell phones don't always work this far away from the transmitting tower," Bill said.

The moon ducked behind a cloud. For a few minutes Casey could see Victoria and Bill only as shadowy forms until the moon sailed out again. Victoria's face was wet with spray. She blinked as another wave splashed her. Casey was watching her when Victoria raised her hand and pointed.

"There it is."

The boat was drifting off the next point about a hundred yards offshore, sheltered from the wind. Bill steered toward it, and as he did Casey turned suddenly. The boat heeled and shipped water. Victoria leaned to the other side and the boat leveled.

"You don't want to move too fast in a boat, Chief, not that I want to tell you what to do," Bill said.

"I'm sorry, guys. I'm not cut out for this seagoing stuff."

They came alongside the drifting boat, an aluminum dinghy with its motor lifted into the stern.

"Is it his?" Casey asked.

"Looks like it," Bill said.

"I wonder where he is?" Victoria held a hand on each gunwale. "Could he have fallen overboard?"

Bill looked toward land. "If he did, he could have walked to shore from here. It's not deep, not over his head, certainly."

Casey unsnapped her hand-held radio and called Junior, who was in his cabin on the opposite shore of the Pond. "Come on over. We need your help."

They circled the boat, and Casey shined her flashlight into the murky water, its beam a lance of green light.

"Can't see a thing," she said.

Bill pulled an oar out from under Victoria's seat and thrust it down into the water. "Four feet. Too deep to get out and wade. I'll tow it to shallower water."

He looped a line through a ring in the bow, knotted it, and tied the other end around a cleat. He started slowly toward the boathouse. The wind was at their backs now.

They hadn't gone more than a few feet when Bill stopped the motor. "It's not towing right." Ness's boat wallowed sluggishly behind them.

"It acts as though it's full of water," Victoria said. "Or anchored."

"No water in her. I didn't notice an anchor line, but you're right, Mrs. Trumbull. It feels as if she's dragging an anchor."

He tugged on the line connecting the two boats and they came together again.

"There's a line running off the stern." Victoria pointed. "It's there, under the motor."

"Hold his boat, Chief," Bill said. "The line may be fouled. Maybe he set an anchor. Odd to pay out so much anchor line, though."

Casey and Victoria gripped the side of Ness's boat while Bill hauled in the line. "Heavy," he muttered. "One big anchor," he was saying when a large, bulky shape, entangled in the anchor line, surfaced at the stern of the two boats.

Casey let go of the gunwale. "Guess we found Ness."

Victoria held the flashlight while Bill hauled in the line. As the object surfaced, they could see first a pale face, then a sodden wool jacket. Bill grabbed hold of the back of the jacket.

Casey paused while she decided how best to relay information to the hospital without alerting everybody else on the Island. She turned to Victoria. "Does his gunning camp have a phone, Victoria? I don't want to use the radio."

Victoria shook her head. "I don't think so. Is his cell phone still in his boat?"

"Right," Casey said. "Good thought."

"I'll look." Bill stood carefully. "You sit still, Chief." He stepped from his boat into Ness's, and in a few moments handed a small cell phone to Casey, who called the hospital. Doc Erickson was on duty, and she told him what they'd found. Doc Erickson said he'd alert the state cops and Toby, the undertaker.

"We'll have to get the body to shore," Bill said.

Casey put the cell phone in her windbreaker pocket and slumped down in her seat. "First Mickey Mausz, now Ness," she mumbled.

Bill cleated the line to Ness's boat, and started up again. No one spoke as Bill maneuvered both boats back to the boathouse.

"Don't want to disturb things more than I have to," Bill said finally. "Can't tell what happened to him until someone examines the body."

The two boats rocked in the chop, occasionally bumping together with a thunk. Casey heard dipping oars and flashed her light at the boat approaching them. Junior, whose back was to them, turned his head and nodded. He pulled up alongside Bill's boat, shipped his oars, and held on.

"Any idea what happened?" Junior asked.

"Nope," Bill said.

"Crystal Ness said she had a bad feeling." Casey shook her head. "I don't look forward to telling her she was right."

CHAPTER 14

It was after midnight when Casey drove Victoria home.

"How about a cup of coffee?" Victoria asked.

"That would hit the spot." Casey locked the Bronco. "I don't think anything will keep me awake after this evening."

"Crystal and he had no children," Victoria said as she measured out the coffee. "They were devoted to each other. Now she has no one."

Casey seated herself at the table in the cookroom. "She was brave about identifying the body. No hysterics or anything."

"Wonder if this is the end of it," Victoria said. "First Montgomery Mausz and now Harry Ness."

Casey shrugged. "Mr. Ness's drowning could have been accidental. Out alone in a boat with nobody to help if he got in trouble. Not real smart."

Victoria paused while she poured the coffee. "I'm willing to bet Harry Ness's death was no accident."

Casey stirred two spoonsful of sugar into her coffee.

"Too much is happening around that piece of property," Victoria mused.

"Sachem's Rock?" asked Casey.

Victoria nodded. "I can't help but believe those two deaths are connected in some way."

"It's pretty strange, all right." Casey shrugged. "But that's life, Victoria. Accidents happen a lot more often than murder."

Victoria went on. "I wonder how Spencer Kirschmeyer fits into the picture. Why was he listening to Zack and me?" She smoothed the tablecloth in front of her. "How is he, by the way? Mr. Kirschmeyer, that is."

"He's conscious, eating solid food and bitching like crazy. He still doesn't remember why he was here on the Island or what he was doing bugging your place." Casey sipped her coffee.

Victoria shook her head. "Strange." She glanced at her reflection in the night-dark window and saw herself peering back through the steam.

"I wonder who Mausz's mystery woman was," said Casey. "The one he was supposed to be going to Aruba with."

"It will come out eventually. You can't keep secrets on this Island. In the past that's what made children behave themselves and kept adults from straying."

"Speaking of secrets, Victoria, are you going to tell me where you were all day, or not?" Casey set her mug on the table.

"I think I've got some cookies. Do you like ginger snaps?" Victoria pushed herself away from the table.

"You're not answering me, Victoria."

Victoria shook some cookies onto a plate and put the gingersnap box back on the shelf over the stove.

"Well?" said Casey. And when Victoria still said nothing, "I suppose you went back to Sachem's Rock. Did you go with Robin?"

Victoria nodded.

"And?"

Victoria sat down again and looked into her mug.

"You know, Victoria, cops have to level with each other."

Victoria smiled at that. "Yes. We did go back there. Elizabeth drove us."

"I suppose you were looking for that tunnel where Robin got stuck. And the underground house."

Victoria held her coffee mug in both hands and sipped.

Casey sighed. "Victoria, you're exasperating."

"I promised not to tell anyone," Victoria said. "Don't lean back in that chair."

"Ah! I understand." Casey set the chair back on all four legs. "You found the underground house and you found the underground man or woman who lives there."

"Man." Victoria swirled the coffee in her mug.

"You know how dangerous that was, to go hunting for some lunatic all by yourself . . . ?"

Victoria refused to meet Casey's eyes. "Robin was with me."

"Worse still. Putting Robin in danger when there's a killer loose and nobody knew where you were all day."

Victoria looked up. "You don't need to berate me."

"Damn!" Casey slapped her hand on the table. "Okay, what was the place like, Victoria. You can tell me that much."

Victoria settled back into her chair. "The underground man pulled a stump handle that opened a hatch. A ladder went down into a dark hole."

"And you climbed down?"

Victoria nodded. "It was like a boat. You know the way you go down a ladder into the cabin?"

"No. I don't know."

Victoria thought a moment. "You face the wall and go down backwards, holding a railing. There were about twelve steps."

"Was it dark? Are there any windows?"

"He has a glass prism in the roof, like a sailboat. The only visible part outside is flat glass about two inches wide and six inches long. It widens inside like an upside-down funnel and lets in a surprisingly large amount of light." Victoria thought back to this afternoon's excursion. It seemed a long time ago. "The house is on the side of the hill."

"Where we found you and Robin climbing up to the path?"

Victoria nodded. "The house has a window on the hillside

where you would never see it if you didn't know where to look."

"So it wasn't a pitch-black cave?"

"It was cozy," Victoria said.

"Was it an old cellar hole, like we were discussing?"

"Yes, roofed over with heavy beams and boards. He must have put tarpaper or plastic on top of the boards to keep them from rotting, then piled the dirt on top of the plastic. You would never know from the outside that the ground was hollow."

"What's it like inside?" Casey asked.

"It's divided into three rooms." Victoria sketched a rough plan on the back of an envelope. "A living-dining room, kitchen, and a bedroom with a portable toilet in one corner. The floors are brick. Probably the original flooring in the old cellar. The walls are rough-cut boards. Really very comfortable."

"What about heat? And cooking?" Casey leaned over to examine the drawing.

Victoria continued to sketch. "He said he doesn't need much heat because even in the winter when it's cold outside, the temperature below ground is in the fifties. He has a tiny stove set on top of concrete blocks that he uses for heating and cooking. It's like a boat. Everything is built-in and tidy." Victoria wondered if she was giving away too much of Ulysses's secret, and decided it didn't hurt to describe the inside of his house. "He has a kerosene lamp so he can read in bed."

"He likes books?" Casey asked.

"Apparently. He built bookcases into the walls in the living room next to a sofa and easy chair he picked up at the dump. He's hung paintings on the walls."

"That brick floor must be chilly."

"He's got rugs on the floor. He'd picked up everything at the dump, the rugs, the books, the wood. His place is warm and, once he lighted a lamp, quite light."

"What does he do for water?"

"He had a dozen or so plastic jugs. He must fill them at the spring. I guess they were full of water."

"Who is he, Victoria?"

Victoria's mouth set stubbornly. "I think I've told you all you need to know."

Casey got to her feet. "This has been a long day. Get some sleep, Victoria. Who knows what tomorrow will bring."

At the hospital the next morning, Spencer Kirschmeyer called for the nurse who immediately paged Doc Erickson.

"Our boy says it's all coming back, Doc," she told him outside Kirschmeyer's door. "Want me to stick around?"

"Please," Doc Erickson said. "Won't hurt to have you hear what he has to say."

Kirschmeyer was sitting up. His head was no longer bandaged and his hair, which had been shorn, was a gray fuzz with lines of railroad-track stitching running across it.

"How are we doing today?" Doc Erickson asked briskly as he examined the chart at the foot of Kirschmeyer's bed.

The nurse was folding the blood pressure sleeve. "Blood pressure and temperature are normal."

"Been up and about?" the doctor asked.

Kirschmeyer grunted. "What about that steak you promised?"

Doc Erickson smiled slightly. "How do you want it?"

"This side of purple."

"Lucy tells me your memory's coming back."

"Spotty." Kirschmeyer winced. "I remember standing under the old lady's tree in the rain."

"Anything before that?"

"Yeah. Rented a car at the airport, drove around some, got a hotel room somewhere."

"The Harbor View," Doc Erickson said.

"Yeah. I remember sticking a transmitter on the old lady's

window. I was holding a tape recorder. It was a fierce thunderstorm. Pouring rain."

"Do you recall what you were listening for?"

Kirschmeyer grimaced. "That's confidential."

"I understand," Doc Erickson said. "I suppose the name of the person who hired you is, too. Without giving me names, do you recall the details of who it was and what you were doing?"

"Yeah." Kirschmeyer nodded and winced.

"Take it easy," Doc Erickson said. "You're still tender. I want you up and walking around. Not too much, now." He turned to the nurse. "Let him have steak for supper. Rare. Salad."

"Right," the nurse said, writing on her clipboard.

"You're doing better than anyone expected, Kirschmeyer. You'll be almost as good as new in a few weeks." Doc Erickson headed for the door.

"Hey Doc."

Doc Erickson turned. "Yes?"

"Will my memory recover completely?"

"Your memory will come back. Probably be back to normal in a week or so." The doctor paused at the door. "I don't know whether or not this means anything to you, but Harry Ness, the developer, drowned last night." He watched his patient's expression.

Kirschmeyer's face paled. "What do you mean?"

Doc Erickson shook his head. "The West Tisbury police chief and Mrs. Trumbull, your old lady friend, found him. Drowned—with an anchor line wrapped around him."

"Shit," Kirschmeyer said, and lay back on the pillows.

Doc Erickson nodded. "I thought so." He closed the door softly between himself and his patient and padded down the corridor.

By noon that day, well before the weekly *Island Enquirer* had a chance to cover Ness's drowning, the news was all over the Island.

Minerva Peabody was at the Net Result buying lobster meat when she overheard Dolly Browne tell another customer that a man had drowned on the Great Pond the previous night. He'd been fishing for oysters, Dolly said. When Minerva opened her wallet to pay for the lobster, her hands shook so badly she dropped a twenty on the floor. She bent down and picked it up. Dolly was saying to the other customer that the man had got himself tangled in his anchor line. Dolly's brother-in-law had told her about the drowning, she said, and he'd heard about it in the Thrift Shop where he volunteered. Mr. Norton, behind the counter, said, "You'd think a man would know better than to go out alone in his boat. Asking for trouble."

When Minerva got home, she put the lobster meat in the refrigerator and called Tom More, who was there within fifteen minutes.

By the time Tom had seated himself across from her at the glass-topped table in the solarium, she could speak almost normally.

"Harry's dead, Tommy. They found his body."

Tom had been watching the small ferry make its run across the harbor to Chappaquiddick. "That's what I heard," he said, not looking at her.

Minerva tapped her fingernails on the glass top of the table. "I don't suppose you know anything about it, do you, Tommy?"

Tom swiveled abruptly. "I hope to hell you're not implying what I think you are."

"Whatever I'm implying," Minerva kept her voice under control, "the situation has changed now, Tommy. I'm sure you understand."

"What are you talking about?"

"The property. Sachem's Rock."

"Minerva . . ." he started to say.

She interrupted. "Listen to me, Tommy. Harry's dead. That means I no longer need to buy that property. That should have been obvious to you the minute you heard."

Tom folded his arms over his chest and crossed his legs.

"I no longer want to buy it, Tommy," Minerva repeated. "What happens to that property now is no longer a concern of mine."

Tom sat motionless. "Who gets it?"

"Crystal, probably."

Tom paused several moments before he said, "Or possibly you, Minerva?"

She laughed. "No. I don't think so, Tommy. You can forget that."

"You and Ness had a thing going, right?"

"You know we did."

Tom shrugged. "Well, isn't it possible that he wanted to thank you for the good times?"

Minerva laughed again. "You've got it all wrong." She looked past him out the tall windows to the harbor. "I wonder how much Crystal knows."

Tom said nothing.

"I don't suppose it matters now," Minerva said. She watched as an osprey swooped out of the sky, dived at the water, and rose with a struggling fish in its talons. "You do understand what I'm saying, don't you?"

Tom said nothing.

Minerva continued. "I assume you plan to go ahead with the Cranberry Fields development?"

"I have to," he said in a low voice.

Minerva laughed softly. "Yes indeed. You've collected all that deposit money from your communal-living people, and now you've spent it."

Tom stood suddenly. "What makes you think that?"

"Come off it, Tommy. I don't just think that, I *know* it."

Tom sat down again.

"It would be embarrassing, to put it mildly, if they started asking for their deposits back, wouldn't it? How much time do you have, Tommy, before that happens?"

Tom rested his elbows on the chair arms. "Six months, roughly."

"I won't ask what you spent it for."

"I invested it."

Minerva laughed again. "High tech computer stock? A sure thing? I suppose you bought on margin when it was going through the roof?"

Tom said nothing.

"You couldn't wait, could you?" Minerva went on before Tom could respond. "For your own sake, you'd do well to find out—and soon—who owns that property. When the new owner's name becomes public, which it will soon, the whole world will be lusting after that land."

"What about our agreement?"

"What about it?" Minerva tapped her fingernails again. "Surely you recall the agreement was that you would keep quiet about Harry and me." She gazed out at the harbor and then turned again to him. "Harry's dead. You do understand, don't you—Harry's dead. Since you 'invested' your people's money, you have nothing with which to buy the land even if it becomes available, isn't that right?"

Tom said quietly, "I'd need your help, Minerva."

She snorted. "Why should I help you? That pathetic 'poor me' act doesn't work. Haven't you learned that by now?" Minerva continued to tap her fingernails on the tabletop. Tom turned away.

"If I don't finance your scheme, bail you out, where will that leave you—back in hiding for another five years?"

Tom swiveled back to her. "What are you talking about?"

"The statute of limitations hasn't run out on that embezzlement from the architectural firm in New Hampshire, has it?"

Tom stared at her.

"Don't be cute, Tommy. As you well know, there are ways to find out things people don't want uncovered. We could turn this blackmail scheme of yours right around, couldn't we? Except I no longer have anything to hide, and you've got nothing I want. Right?"

Tom stood up suddenly and headed for the door. "I don't want to listen to any more of this, Minerva. Where are you getting this baloney?"

"You knew it was Harry who hired Kirschmeyer, didn't you?"

Tom stopped, his hand on the doorknob. "The investigator. I suspected as much. Is that where you got that piece of information?"

Minerva smiled. "Harry prided himself on his thoroughness. He checked up on everybody with any interest in Sachem's Rock."

"Who else did he tell?" Tom spoke so softly Minerva almost missed it.

She didn't answer the question. "Kirschmeyer is likely to be discharged from the hospital within the next couple of days," she said. "It might not hurt you to talk to him. He undoubtedly collected information on your competitors, too."

Tom held out his hands, palms up.

"That broke?" Minerva laughed. "I feel sorry for you. Have him send the bill to my post office box. I'll do that much for you. No name, please. Leave me alone now, Tommy. I have things I need to do."

Tom More had counted on Minerva for financial backing. He had been so confident that he had taken a flyer in the stock market with his investors' money. It had been a sure thing. Tom bought on margin. And that was when the slump came. It would be a temporary slump, he was sure, but it brought on the margin call and he was wiped out. That was it.

At first, he was not worried. He felt sure he could count on Minerva's support. After he'd found out about her and Ness last fall, he had invited her to invest in his Cranberry Fields project. He told himself it wasn't blackmail. He was simply offering her an opportunity with a return on her investment.

When he found out about Minerva and Loch Ness, Tom had been out in his boat oystering on the Great Pond. It was only a fluke that he had seen them the first time. They were in view for only a few seconds when he spotted them slipping into Ness's gunning camp. Ness had looked around as he opened the door presumably to make sure they hadn't been seen. At that moment, Tom had glanced up from raking up a cluster of oysters. Tom's boat had been drifting, motor off, partly hidden from view by a plum bush on the point.

He had let the boat drift around the point before he started the motor again. While he drifted he thought about Minerva and Loch Ness. If they wanted to keep a secret so badly, perhaps she would be willing to help him buy that property? It was a thought. He'd seen them twice since then, once right after Victoria Trumbull had found Mausz's body.

It never occurred to Tom that Minerva might change her mind about backing Cranberry Fields once Ness was dead.

"It's that tart's doing," Phoebe said to Victoria that afternoon as they sipped tea in Phoebe's parlor. Phoebe was in her rocking chair, Victoria was on the couch. Elizabeth had driven her grandmother to the homestead at Sachem's Rock and had left her there, promising to come back after she'd done errands.

Phoebe rocked vigorously. "I'd rather have a hundred

houses here than let her have this property. Her and her druggie friends. Tattoos. Nose rings. Crinkly hair. You should have seen her. Like a Fiji Islander."

Victoria balanced her teacup and saucer in her lap. "Did you know that Mr. Ness planned to force you out of your house?"

Phoebe paused for a long time, then shook her head. "I suppose I should have read the fine print. That'll teach me." She laughed shortly, a forced laugh. "Some lesson. I listened to that snake-in-the-grass lawyer, Montgomery Mausz. Well, he got what he deserved, I'd say." She touched her napkin to the corner of her eye.

"And then some."

Phoebe leaned forward in her rocker and held out a plate of vanilla cookies to Victoria. "Want another?"

"No, thank you. You heard what happened to Harry Ness last night?"

"I don't listen to the radio."

"He drowned. In Tisbury Great Pond."

"Last night? You don't say!" Phoebe's pale eyes widened.

"The police chief and I found him."

"How'd it happen, do you know?"

"He was fishing for oysters and evidently got caught in the anchor line."

"Can't say as I'm grief-stricken. I suppose that changes things. About my land, that is."

"I'm not sure how, though." Victoria moistened a finger and picked up a cookie crumb from her saucer. "I suppose it depends on whether the land is in his company's name or his own."

"His own," Phoebe said. "That much I do know. He bought it outright in his own name."

"Then I suppose his wife will inherit it."

Phoebe leered. "Never can tell."

Victoria looked up at Phoebe's tone. "What do you mean by that?"

"I understand he had an interest, shall we say, on the side."

"Another woman?" Victoria was surprised. "I thought he was devoted to Crystal."

"Maybe he was devoted to his wife, but he was a man, wasn't he?"

"Where on earth did you hear that?"

"I may not have a radio or TV, but I'm not completely cut off from the world." Phoebe closed her mouth with a self-satisfied smirk.

"He certainly wouldn't leave something that valuable to a mistress," Victoria said.

Phoebe continued to rock. "Never can tell," she said. "You find what you and that boy were looking for?"

Victoria flushed. "I should have asked your permission."

"Pooh!" said Phoebe. "You've never needed to ask my permission to walk my place. Besides, it's not my place anymore. Who's the boy?"

"Robin White."

"Is that Audrey's son?"

"Her grandson. Jessie's son."

"Got my generations mixed up. Didn't think Audrey was old enough to have a grandson."

"She's in her sixties."

Phoebe rocked. "So. Did you find what you were looking for?"

Victoria settled back on the hard sofa, balancing her cup as she did. "Josiah Coffin . . ."

"I know the boy," Phoebe interrupted. "Works for that conservation group. Go on."

"Josiah was hoping we could find something that would halt Mr. Ness's development plans."

"I take it you found something?" Phoebe's eyes glistened. "I don't know as it's going to make a difference, now. I've got my money and my marching orders." She wiped the back of her hand across her eyes. "What a stupid old woman I was to trust those people."

"Where do you plan to go, Phoebe?" Victoria said gently.

"I've no idea. I've never lived anyplace else. Never wanted to. Never been anyplace else, either. Never wanted to go to Florida with the old folks. I figured on dying right here, in my own bed. Even after that man bought me out, I figured I'd live out my days here. After I'm gone, I don't suppose it matters." Phoebe rocked. "I've washed my hands of my son and daughter. And that granddaughter, too." She rocked faster. "Wasn't she mad, though, when she heard how the lawyer told me everything."

"Montgomery Mausz, you mean?"

"No other. She called him up from California hoping he'd spy on me. On me! I guess he turned the tables on her. She flew here as soon as she heard I might sell the land. All lovey dovey. Butter wouldn't melt in her mouth. I knew what she wanted. Her father's daughter, all right."

Victoria thought about Phoebe's son, who lived in a hole in the ground at the foot of Phoebe's hill.

Phoebe went on, rocking vigorously, her face flushed. "That girl was so mad, it wouldn't surprise me if she hadn't killed him out of sheer meanness."

Victoria set her cup and saucer on the floor. "Surely you don't mean that, Phoebe."

"He was killed right around the time she was here. That cold snap back in February."

"Don't even think like that, Phoebe. She's your own flesh and blood even if you don't approve of her lifestyle."

"Humpf." Phoebe got out of her rocking chair and went to the window. She looked down at the ice pond in the distance. "I've always liked that view. Summer, fall, winter. Always changing. Better than watching TV." She turned back to Victoria. "Change your mind about more tea?"

"I guess I will," Victoria said, holding out her cup for Phoebe to pour. "Maybe Ness's death will buy you some time."

Phoebe brushed her hand across her eyes again.

Victoria thought for a few moments. Should she say anything about Ulysses? Phoebe's son James?

"What say?" Phoebe glanced at her, and Victoria realized she must have said something out loud.

"I was thinking about your son. When did you see him last?"

Phoebe paused before answering. "It was before the war. Vietnam, you know." She turned back to the window, set both hands on the sill, and spoke as if to herself. "He enlisted against my wishes. Lied about his age. Never did get along, James and me. Too much like me, I suppose."

"Was there an actual break between you and James?"

Phoebe came back to her rocker and sat again. "After the war he went crazy. Dope, it was. He nearly killed that wife of his, not that she's much of anything. It was dope, all right."

"Vietnam damaged a lot of people who fought in it, men and women both. We called it shellshock after the First World War." Victoria added, "Have you tried to get in touch with your son?"

"How?" said Phoebe, rocking again. "Supposing I wanted to—and I don't much—where would I start? He knows where I am. If he wants to come to me, I'm here. At least for a few more months."

Victoria watched Phoebe over the rim of her teacup. "It might be nice to have a man around."

"No thank you. I'm too used to doing for myself. I don't want some crackpot underfoot, me waiting on him, cleaning up messes after him. No thank you."

"Wouldn't it be nice to have him on the Island, at least? He wouldn't have to live under the same roof," Victoria said.

"I suppose the Island is big enough for the both of us." Phoebe crumbled the cookie she was holding without seeming aware of it. Crumbs dropped into her lap. "I don't know where I'll end up, though. On the Island or in some old age place in Florida. Consorting with a bunch of old people who think they've found the Fountain of Youth. They're not there to die, oh no. Face lifts and tummy tucks and dyed hair . . ."

Victoria interrupted Phoebe, who was getting quite animated, two pink dots on her cheekbones. "With Ness gone, Phoebe, perhaps things will be different." She saw a movement outside and stood up. "Here's Elizabeth now."

"Never did tell me what you found," Phoebe said.

"It was nothing." Victoria avoided Phoebe's bright eyes. "Showing Robin the ancient ways."

"You expect me to believe that, I suppose. Well, come again. Don't see many people these days."

Elizabeth knocked on the door and entered. "Am I too early?"

"We were just finishing up," Victoria said, shrugging into her coat.

Phoebe waited at the front door until Victoria had seated herself in the car. "You're so interested in that good-for-nothing son of mine," she called out. "You happen to see him, tell him the least he can do is give me a call." Victoria lifted her hand in acknowledgment.

"What was that all about, Gram?" Elizabeth asked once they were on their way home.

"Phoebe knows more than she's letting on," Victoria replied.

When Doc Erickson made his rounds that same afternoon, he stopped in at Kirschmeyer's room. He peered over his half glasses at Kirschmeyer, who was sitting on the edge of the bed in a backless hospital gown.

"I see you've gotten your way," Doc Erickson said brusquely. "They're discharging you tomorrow afternoon." He frowned as he wrote something on his clipboard. "If I had *my* way, we'd keep you here another couple of days at least. Here, sign this." He passed the clipboard to Kirschmeyer, who scrawled his name on the form and handed the clipboard back. "You were pretty badly beat up, and it's only been a week."

"Yeah, Doc, I know. Thanks for all you guys did." He slid off the bed and flinched as his feet touched the floor. He was broad and muscular and several inches taller than Doc Erickson.

Doc Erickson stepped back. "You've got to take it easy for a couple of months," he warned, looking up at Kirschmeyer. "I'm serious. Go lie in the sun on some tropical beach and ogle the scenery."

Kirschmeyer limped over to the washroom, opened the door, splashed water on his face, and rubbed it vigorously with a towel. "I've got some unfinished business," he mumbled.

"Came close to never finishing it. That was a damned near thing. If it weren't for Dr. Gibbs . . ."

"The lady surgeon," said Kirschmeyer.

"The *surgeon*," Doc Erickson corrected. "If it weren't for Dr. Gibbs, they'd be shipping your remains off-Island to your next-of-kin."

Kirschmeyer limped back to the bed and eased himself onto it again. "Tell her thanks for me, Doc."

Doc Erickson tucked his clipboard under his arm to free his right hand and shook Kirschmeyer's much larger one. "Good luck," he said. "Take care of yourself. Don't get into any more trouble."

CHAPTER 15

The next morning Casey parked the police Bronco in Victoria's drive and went into the kitchen. Victoria was in the dining room, searching through a stack of papers on a chair next to the table.

Casey looked at her watch. "Are you almost ready?"

"I'm looking for a book I wanted to read from."

"Are you reading your own poems?"

"I thought I'd read a story for a change. I hope I can hold their attention that long."

"I suppose they fall asleep."

"That or they wheel their chairs out of the room when they've had enough." Victoria continued to sort through the pile, stacking papers and magazines on the table in some kind of order.

"I think you're a hero to read at the nursing home every week the way you do. I know they love having you come."

"They like any kind of distraction." Victoria held up a small battered book. "Here's what I was looking for."

"*Winnie-the-Pooh*?" Casey asked, surprised. "Christopher Robin?"

Victoria nodded, and moved the sorted papers back onto the chair. "That's no kind of life. The nurses take good care of them, the food is good, the setting is pleasant. But . . ."

"But it's not like home with kids and grandkids and people dropping in and all the confusion of normal life."

"I'll read the story about Pooh floating into the sky holding onto a balloon and pretending he's a small black rain cloud."

Casey laughed.

They drove to the hospital the back way, past the airport and the blinker and down Barnes Road. Casey parked near the Emergency Room entrance and waited until Victoria slid out.

"Got everything? Your books? Will you be warm enough?"

"Heavens, yes. They keep it like a hothouse."

As Victoria walked away from the Bronco, Casey rolled down her window and leaned out. "I'll see you in about an hour. I have some business with the Oak Bluffs chief. I may be late."

"I'll wait inside." Victoria looked through her cloth bag. "I've got my crossword puzzle. I may drop in to see that man who was under my tree."

"Spencer Kirschmeyer. That would be a nice thing to do."

"I have his glasses." Victoria held them up, wrapped in a paper napkin. "I hope he didn't need them."

"His glasses were probably the least of his worries. Okay, then. I'll be seeing you." Casey rolled her window back up and drove away.

Victoria tugged open the Emergency Room door and went into the admitting area. Doc Jeffers was on duty. Victoria could see his motorcycle helmet on the floor behind him. "Morning, Mrs. Trumbull. Found any more bodies?"

Victoria smiled, waved airily and kept going without replying. She turned right at the entrance to the operating room just as the door opened. A tall woman in a blue hospital scrub suit almost bumped into her. "I'm so sorry," the woman said, then stopped. "You're Mrs. Trumbull, aren't you?"

Victoria nodded and examined the woman. "And you must be Dr. Gibbs. The surgeon who saved the man under my tree. Everyone says you performed a miracle."

"The patient had a lot of luck, including the fact that I was on-Island that day."

187

Victoria's face was sober. "If only I'd . . ."

Dr. Gibbs wagged a slim finger at her. "Don't think like that, Mrs. Trumbull. He's going to be fine. In fact, we're discharging him this afternoon."

Victoria set her bag on the floor. "Would it be all right if I stopped by to see him when I finish reading to the elderly?"

"Certainly. I would think he'd like to meet you in person." Dr. Gibbs pulled off her protective cap and shook out her hair.

Victoria looked at her watch, picked up her bag, and moved on. She went up the ramp that connected the hospital to the nursing home, turned down a corridor that smelled of new carpeting, and walked into a sunny room where a half-dozen people waited for her, all of them younger than Victoria, most of them in wheelchairs.

She shook hands with each one. She did that every week. Limp hands, strong hands, gnarled hands. Hands that once had held onto important lives and now were plucking at the cloth of gift robes or hospital gowns. It was immeasurably depressing to Victoria, who was not easily depressed.

Once she'd asked about their grandchildren, about the afghan one of the women was crocheting, and listened sympathetically to complaints about its being too cold (or too hot), she sat in the armchair next to a wooden table where she would have enough light to read.

Her listeners were restless. Victoria hadn't even reached the part where Pooh fell into the gorse bush, when she heard snores and saw that one of them was fast asleep. A second swiveled his chair around and left.

"Perhaps this isn't what they want to hear," Victoria said to the nurse's aide who was sitting to one side of the room.

"They enjoy it, Mrs. Trumbull. But you know the way it is. It's not you."

Victoria finished early and retraced her steps through the maze of corridors. She never felt old until she came here to read. Then every one of her ninety-two years seemed to weigh her down. The long corridor seemed endless. She was sorry she hadn't brought her walking stick. Silly that she was so vain about using it. Elizabeth understood, and had given her the stick. She had sawed off a branch of the old lilac tree for her to use when she was hiking. People of all ages used hiking sticks, Elizabeth had told her.

Victoria rested on a bench under one of the windows.

"Hi, Aunt Vic. Bet you've come to see Mr. Kirschmeyer."

Victoria, who had been staring at the watermarks on the carpet where the windows had leaked, looked up to see her great-grandniece Hope, a nurse at the hospital.

When Victoria nodded, Hope held out her arm. "I'm going that way. I'll walk with you."

Victoria took Hope's arm, raised herself from the bench, and together they went to Kirschmeyer's room. Hope peered around the curtain that hung from a track on the ceiling between two beds.

"Visitor, Mr. K. Are you decent?" she said brightly.

Victoria heard a mumble that sounded like, "Who in hell would visit me?" before Hope pushed the curtain aside.

Victoria's impression was of a huge man who took up most of the narrow hospital bed. Not fat, large. His hair was gray fuzz, obviously just growing back in. He had thick eyebrows that met over the top of his nose like a gray bottlebrush, thick lips, and heavy wobbling jowls. He was lying on top of the covers in his hospital gown. He quickly pulled a blanket over him, but not before Victoria saw his muscular hairy legs.

"Who are you . . ." he started to say. Victoria saw his expression change from puzzlement to embarrassment to concern. Then, "You're Mrs. Trumbull. Victoria Trumbull."

Hope grinned at her great-grandaunt. "I'll leave you two," she said, wiggling her fingers. "Bye!"

Victoria held out the napkin-wrapped glasses. "I brought these to you. At least, I think they're yours."

Kirschmeyer unfolded the napkin. "Yeah. They're mine. Where did you find them?"

"Where the tree fell. I thought you might need them."

"Yeah. I do. Thanks," he said gruffly. "You want a seat?" He indicated a chair by the window.

Victoria sat, out of breath from the walk down the corridor. "I hear you're being discharged today."

"That's what they tell me."

"Are you all right? Are you fully recovered?"

"Enough to get by, I guess. I gotta get out of this place." He gestured around the room with a large hand.

"I know what you mean," said Victoria. "It's a lovely hospital, but it's a hospital. Will you go home from here?"

He looked out of the window onto the small garden between two wings of the building before he replied. "I got business I have to take care of."

"You were working for Harry Ness, weren't you?"

Kirschmeyer grunted. "No secrets around this place, are there?" he mumbled. "What I was doing was confidential. Between him and me."

"It's common knowledge," Victoria said. "If it's not being too nosy, did he pay you before he drowned?"

Kirschmeyer paused for such a long time, Victoria thought she might have offended him. Finally he said, "Ness gave me an advance plus expenses. The advance ran out. He owed me."

"I'm sure his estate will cover it."

Kirschmeyer shook his head, and winced as he did. "I doubt it. I got nothing in writing. He didn't want people to know I was doing work for him."

"I guess you figured he wasn't likely to die before he paid his bill."

"That's for sure."

Victoria had a fleeting idea. "Where will you stay? I assume the Harbor View is out of your budget range?"

"Right." He indicated a newspaper that was on the table next to his bed and held up a pair of drugstore glasses. "The hospital loaned me these. I've been looking at want ads. Not a lot available in my price range."

Victoria took a deep breath. "I occasionally rent rooms."

"Yeah?" he stared at her.

Victoria spoke with what she felt was the right degree of assurance, "Would you like to strike a deal?"

CHAPTER 16

"Lady, I don't know a thing about plants." Kirschmeyer sounded appalled when he heard Victoria's proposal. "You want a scientist, not a PI." He straightened the pillows behind his back and sat up.

" 'PI'?"

"Private Investigator. Detective. That's what I do for a living." Kirschmeyer opened the top drawer of the bedside table and lifted out his wallet. He flipped it open to his license, which Victoria examined.

"Divorces," he said. "Background checks. Get the goods on people doing stuff they shouldn't."

Victoria handed the wallet back to him. "That's exactly what I have in mind."

"You want me to go hiking around in the bushes looking at some goddamn plant? Same place that lawyer was killed? No thanks." He shook his head.

Victoria settled back in the chair. "You won't need to do that," she said. "I already have."

Kirschmeyer groaned.

Victoria continued. "In exchange for doing some investigation for me, you may stay in my downstairs room until you finish your own business. I don't know what your rates are, but we can work something out between us."

"Let me get this straight, lady. You found some rare plant." Kirschmeyer leaned back on his pillows.

"A cranefly orchid. Several, in fact." Victoria looked at him with concern. "You're not really recovered yet, are you? Perhaps you should stay an extra few days."

"I been here long enough. Too long." Kirschmeyer closed his eyes briefly, then opened them again. "So you found this rare orchid. You go back the next day and it's gone. Dug up."

"That's right," Victoria agreed.

"Then you go there the next day and the plant's back in the ground where it was in the first place."

"Only it's a different plant."

"Yeah? I don't get it. So what?" Kirschmeyer flinched as he breathed out.

Victoria averted her gaze. "It's a different subspecies or variety, I'm not sure which."

"But it's a cranebill orchid, right?"

"Cranefly," she said.

"And then you find that somebody planted the first orchids where someone else wants to build a house?"

"Exactly right."

"And you want me to find out who's digging them up and who's planting them again?" He raised his eyebrows.

"Yes."

Kirschmeyer ran his hand over his bristly hair. "This is the craziest thing I've ever heard of."

"Whoever's been moving the orchids around is causing a great deal of trouble," Victoria said.

"So what?"

Victoria was losing patience. "It's one-hundred-eighty-million-dollars worth of trouble, that's what. Someone cares enough to go around murdering people." She glared at him. "Are you interested in my proposal or not?"

"I heard Loch Ness's death was an accident, not murder."

"You heard wrong. Somebody killed him. I thought detectives didn't take murders for granted." Victoria sat forward in the chair.

"Look, lady, I'm not Sherlock Holmes. I'm a garden variety catch-your-husband-sleeping-with-another-woman kind of detective."

"I see I'm wasting my time." She got up to leave.

"Wait a minute, I'm still thinking."

"Take your time." Victoria sat down again and looked at her watch. "I'm supposed to meet someone in five minutes."

Kirschmeyer sighed. "Okay, lady. I'm not agreeing to the deal, but I'll look at the room." He added, "I know where your house is at."

"I guess you do. I've got to go now."

As they were driving back to West Tisbury Victoria told Casey about the deal with Kirschmeyer. Casey sounded aghast. "You don't know anything about the guy, Victoria. A private eye from Bridgeport creeping around your house spying on you? Are you nuts?"

Casey waited for a car to pass before she turned onto the Edgartown Road.

"I often rent rooms to people I haven't done a background check on," Victoria said stiffly. "He's coming to see me directly from the hospital."

"I'll stick around. Ask him a few questions."

Victoria looked straight ahead. "I'm capable of taking care of my own affairs, thank you."

They dipped into the small valley that marked the beginning of Victoria's property. Casey turned left into the drive.

Victoria held onto the door handle to steady herself. "I've got to have something done about this driveway."

"Better than speed bumps, that's for sure," Casey said. "Okay, Victoria. Give me a call if you need me. And take care, will you?"

Victoria waved and disappeared into the house.

An hour later, Kirschmeyer showed up at the west door. When Victoria answered his knock, he was facing out, examining the uprooted stump of the great silver poplar.

"It's a wonder it didn't kill you," Victoria said as he swiveled around to face her. "You know, don't you, that you're not supposed to stand under tall trees in a thunderstorm?"

Kirschmeyer muttered, "Thanks a lot."

"Where's your car?"

"I left it on the mainland."

"You came from the hospital by cab?"

Kirschmeyer nodded.

"Cabs are an extravagance. How are you planning to get around? Surely not by cab? I ride with the police chief."

Kirschmeyer snorted. "Cops and I aren't on the same wavelength. I'll find a used car. Something cheap."

Victoria showed him the downstairs room and how to find the bathroom. They sat at the table in the cookroom with cups of tea and negotiated.

"The room's not too bad," Kirschmeyer said, and when Victoria scowled he added quickly, "It's pretty nice, actually." He leaned back, tipping his chair.

"Don't do that," Victoria said sharply, and he set the chair down. She went on. "We don't know what the person who dug up those plants was trying to accomplish. If he's hoping to stop development by planting an endangered orchid in the middle of a house lot, that's not the way it works. All he's doing is damaging the rare plants that he's dug up. On the other hand, he might have been working for Mr. Ness."

"Yeah?" said Kirschmeyer.

Victoria sipped her tea. "Someone working for Mr. Ness might have been trying to get the plants *off* the property."

"So it wouldn't be the same person who's planting them again," said Kirschmeyer.

"Probably not."

"You say the new plants didn't come from the Island?"

Victoria shook her head. "The state botanist says they probably came from someplace south of New Jersey."

"That helps me a lot."

"Probably North or South Carolina or Georgia."

Kirschmeyer shifted in his chair and winced. "So that's my assignment."

Victoria regarded him. "You really are not fully recovered, are you?"

"I'm getting there," he said.

"You're going to bed. Right now," she ordered. "I'll heat up some chicken soup and you can have that with a mug of hot lemonade and whiskey."

Kirschmeyer got carefully to his feet. "Okay, lady."

"My name is Victoria Trumbull."

"Okay, Mrs. T. I'll start tomorrow. No guarantees."

"About a car," Victoria said when he was at the door.

He turned. "What about it?"

"You'll need some wheels to get around tomorrow."

"Yeah." He started toward his room again.

Victoria called after him. "You may borrow mine."

He asked, "You got a car?"

"Why are you acting so surprised?" Victoria turned back to the table, her nose lifted.

"No reason. No reason at all." He waited.

Victoria nodded toward the Norway maple at the end of the drive. "It's that green Chevrolet."

"The Citation? That's an antique."

She turned and stared at him. "Of course it's not. It's only a few years old."

"More like twenty. Does it run?" Kirschmeyer leaned against the kitchen counter.

"It did until recently."

"How recent?" he said suspiciously.

Victoria paused a moment before she answered. "Until I had to give up my license."

"Yeah? What for?"

Victoria paused again. "I'd rather not discuss it."

"Okay, okay." Kirschmeyer shrugged. "Is it registered? Tags and all?"

"You may have to do something about that. I believe the registration is a bit out of date."

"Well thanks, I guess. I'll see if it runs, and if it does, I'll take care of the paperwork tomorrow."

After Victoria settled Kirschmeyer into his room with his soup and spiked lemonade, she gathered up her hat and coat, her lilac-wood stick, and a paper bag of stale bread and walked to the police station. Casey was on the phone.

"That was the state forensics people," Casey said when she hung up. She looked puzzled.

Victoria unbuttoned her coat. "Oh?"

"Montgomery Mausz was not killed where you found him, Victoria."

Victoria fanned herself with her coat. "How on earth do they know that?"

"They went over every inch of the ground. Took samples. Measured stuff. Found old footprints, I guess. Drag marks. The forensics people can do magic tricks with stuff you and I can't even see." She indicated Victoria's brown paper bag. "What do you have there, lunch?"

"Bread."

"As if those geese and swans don't get enough to eat," Casey grumbled. "Anyhow, the forensics people think he was killed somewhere near where Robin disappeared."

Victoria stopped fanning herself. "Oh?"

"I guess they measured the direction of the drag marks or footprints or whatever. Who knows?"

"The weather hadn't destroyed the evidence?"

Casey shook her head. "It's amazing what they can figure out." She studied Victoria, who was staring at her through hooded eyes. "What's the matter?"

"Nothing."

"You thinking about the underground man?"

"I've got to go." Victoria started to lift herself out of the chair.

"You just arrived. You're thinking it might have been the underground man, aren't you?"

Victoria said nothing. She buttoned her coat again and started for the door.

"Who is he, Victoria? Are you going to tell me, or not?"

"I gave him my word."

"We might be dealing with a killer, Victoria. You've been taking crazy risks. Did it occur to you that the guy probably *is* the killer?"

"He's not a killer," Victoria said stubbornly.

"Yeah, sure. They said that about Son of Sam." Casey got up and stood between Victoria and the door. "Come on back, Victoria, and sit down. We've got to talk."

Kirschmeyer was up early the next morning, working on Victoria's green Citation. After a couple of hours, Victoria heard the engine start up with a ragged roar, and when she looked out she could see the car wobbling down the drive, a cloud of black smoke belching out of its tailpipe.

Kirschmeyer returned around noon. "I see you got it running," Victoria said.

"Yeah. New battery, new plugs, new license plates, new registration, new insurance." Kirschmeyer stamped his boots on the grass mat outside the kitchen door, dislodging a small pile of sand.

"Would you like some lunch?" Victoria offered. "Toasted cheese sandwiches. And you may have half of my beer."

Kirschmeyer's eyes brightened. "I could go for that." He sat in the captain's chair by the door with a sigh.

Victoria buttered the outsides of the cheese sandwiches and slapped them into the black cast iron pan with a sizzle. "Did you find what you were looking for?" she asked.

"I don't know," Kirschmeyer said. "I went to the airport. I figured if anybody was shipping orchids, they'd air freight them to the Island. The girl at the counter said a shipment got flown in a week or so ago. Marked 'Live Plants, Perishable.' " He sighed again. "She noticed it because there's not much activity this time of year."

Victoria glanced at him. "You'd better lie down after lunch." She flipped both sandwiches and set a lid on top of the pan. "Where was it shipped from?"

"Some place in North Carolina." He closed his eyes.

"Go on," said Victoria.

"That was about it."

Victoria set the sandwiches on plates and Kirschmeyer got up unsteadily and took them from her.

Victoria asked, "Who was it addressed to?"

"It wasn't. Just said, 'To be picked up.' "

Victoria took a bottle of Rolling Rock out of the refrigerator and handed it to Kirschmeyer, who set the plates on the cookroom table and opened the beer.

"I'd like a small glass. You take the rest," Victoria said. "Who picked the package up?"

Kirschmeyer shrugged.

"Was it a man or a woman? Did anyone remember what the person looked like?" After Victoria poured a small amount of beer for herself she slid the bottle toward him.

"Thanks. The girl who was on duty that day is on maternity leave," he said.

Victoria sipped her beer and blotted her lips. "When is her baby due?"

Kirschmeyer had wrapped both of his hands around the sandwich and had just taken a large bite. "It's here already," he said, his mouth full.

"She was working right up until . . . ?" Victoria had cut her sandwich into small squares and was holding one square up to her mouth.

"Yeah. That's the way things are done these days." Kirschmeyer eyed the green bottle appreciatively, tilted his head back, and drank. "Ahh!" he said when he put the bottle down.

"Didn't the person who picked up the plants have to sign anything?" Victoria asked.

"Evidently not."

"Well."

Kirschmeyer finished his sandwich. Victoria had scarcely touched hers. "Here, you can have the rest of mine."

"You sure?" He reached over and slid her sandwich onto his plate. "So I went to the hospital. That niece of yours . . ."

"Hope. My great-grandniece."

"Yeah. Well she's in the baby department. Acted like I was her good ole buddy. Took me to see the new mother."

"That was nice of you," Victoria said. "Was the baby a boy or a girl?"

"To tell the truth, I didn't ask. They all look alike to me. I didn't want to stick around."

"Afraid you'd run into Doc Erickson?"

"Yeah." Kirschmeyer finished off his beer and wiped his hands on the napkin, which he wadded up beside his plate. "He wanted me to stay a few more days."

"This is yours," Victoria said, pushing a wooden napkin ring toward him.

Kirschmeyer looked at her from under his eyebrows, flattened out his napkin, rolled it up, and slipped in into the ring.

"Did she recall anything about the person who picked up the orchids?" Victoria asked.

"Yeah. But I don't know how much help it is." He pried something from between his teeth with a fingernail. "She remembered him because he was strange."

"Strange?"

"His eyes, she said. Like in a skull. A tall skinny guy. Weather-beaten."

"Mustache?" Victoria asked.

"Yeah. Mustache. She said he was, like, spaced-out." He belched and immediately looked sheepish. "Pardon me."

Victoria ignored it. "Ulysses," she said softly. "I wondered . . ."

"What did you say?"

"Nothing," Victoria said.

CHAPTER 17

"If you're heading into Vineyard Haven around three," Victoria said as they were putting away the lunch dishes, "I need a ride to the school."

"Sure, Mrs. T. Anytime," Kirschmeyer replied. "I thought you rode with the lady cop?"

"This doesn't involve her," Victoria said.

"Yeah?" said Kirschmeyer, but Victoria had walked away.

When they arrived at the school later that afternoon, Robin was racing around the side of the school, shirt untucked.

"Who's the kid?" asked Kirschmeyer.

"Robin White," Victoria answered.

Robin looked up with a grin, wrinkled his nose to work his glasses back in place, and darted toward the green car.

"A grandkid or something? Great-grandkid?"

"A friend," Victoria said. "Would you mind dropping us off at the Sachem's Rock trailhead on your way?"

Robin climbed in behind Victoria. "Cool car," he said. "I didn't know it ran."

"Barely," Kirschmeyer muttered. He set both hands on the top of the steering wheel and glanced at Victoria. "What are you gonna do there?"

She stared straight ahead. "I have to see someone."

"Yeah?" Kirschmeyer waited for her to say more, but she continued to avoid his gaze.

"What in hell's going on, Mrs. T?"

"Will you or won't you take us?" Victoria held the door handle, about to get out of the car.

"Sure Mrs. T, sure. But . . . ?"

Robin settled himself into the back seat.

Victoria said, "I have to attend to something."

Kirschmeyer snorted. "And I thought I kept *my* mouth buttoned."

He drove them to the trailhead and waited while they got out. "How are you gonna get back?"

"She hitchhikes," said Robin, jerking a thumb at Victoria.

Kirschmeyer looked away from the road briefly. "You shouldn't hitchhike. It's not safe."

"Mrs. Trumbull knows everybody," said Robin.

"You gonna get yourself killed."

Victoria collected her cloth bag and lilac-wood stick from the front seat of the Citation. "Come, Robin."

Robin had run on ahead when Kirschmeyer called after them. "How long you gonna be?"

Victoria turned. "A couple of hours."

"I'll come back for you at five, then."

She looked at her watch. "About two hours. Thank you. That would be nice."

"Mrs. T, are you sure you know what you're doing? This is the place they found that body."

Robin circled back to the car. "Mrs. Trumbull found him," he said with pride.

"Yeah. And they haven't caught the killer yet. I don't think this is real intelligent, Mrs. T."

"Five o'clock," said Victoria, adjusting her tan hat.

She and Robin followed the familiar route past the now green marsh. Robin stopped suddenly, bent over, and tied his shoelaces. "Do you think he'll be home?" he asked.

"He usually is at this time of day."

"Doesn't he work?"

Victoria stopped to catch her breath and leaned on her stick. "Sometimes, I guess. Mornings, probably."

"Are we going to his cave?"

"He likes his privacy. We'll sit by the path and wait for him."

Robin leaned over and picked up a fallen pinecone. "He probably needs to let his dog go out."

"He probably does."

Robin tossed the pinecone into the air, let it drop on the ground, and kicked it with the side of his foot. "Does that detective think the underground man is the killer?"

"I don't know what Mr. Kirschmeyer thinks. He seems to have something else on his mind."

"Maybe he's the killer," Robin said.

Victoria shook her head. "I doubt it."

They walked again until they reached the spot where Robin had disappeared only a few days ago.

Victoria eased herself onto the log where she'd sat before, using her stick for support. She straightened her coat under her, pursed her lips, and whistled, "Bob white! Bob bob white!"

Robin put his hands over his ears. "Cool!" he said with admiration. "How'd you do it so loud?"

Victoria smiled. "I'll wait here for the underground man. Don't go too far away."

"I hear something," said Robin. He peered through the trees down the slope. "Here comes the dog now. Look at that! You called him and he came."

The black and white dog bounded up the hillside, wagging his tail, tongue hanging out. Behind the dog was Ulysses. His eyes were deepset and sunken, the way the woman at the airport had described them to Kirschmeyer.

"Can we talk here?" Victoria asked.

He nodded.

"Hey, dog!" Robin called, running up the path away from Victoria and Ulysses, looking over his shoulder at the dog. "Come get me!"

The dog barked and started after the boy.

"Is that all right?" Victoria asked.

He nodded. "You wanted to talk."

"The police chief got a call from the forensics lab."

Ulysses was quiet.

"They determined that Mr. Mausz was not killed where I found him. He was carried or dragged there." Victoria gestured down the hill. "From somewhere around here."

Ulysses's hands were still. "Do they know about me?"

"I told them how Robin and I were being followed, and I told them about Robin getting stuck in the dog's tunnel." Victoria stopped. "Casey—the police chief . . . ?"

"I know who she is."

"Casey concluded that I'd visited someone around here, so I had to tell her about your underground house."

Ulysses turned slightly toward the slope that led to his house. He suddenly made a fist of his right hand and smacked it into his left palm, startling Victoria. "It was too good to last," he muttered.

"There's more bad news, I'm afraid," Victoria continued.

He looked down at her.

"After the forensics lab called, Casey decided the killer is—you."

Ulysses shook his head.

"You didn't kill him. Did you?"

"No."

"But you know something about it, don't you?"

Ulysses nodded.

Victoria waited. A beech leaf drifted down. A squirrel chattered. A blackbird caroled from the marsh.

Ulysses hunkered down next to Victoria's log, picked up a handful of leaf litter from the path, and sifted it through his long fingers, from one hand to the other.

"You must feel uncomfortable about trusting me after I gave you away."

"No," Ulysses said. "That's not it." He continued to sift the dirt and pine needles and dried leaves and sand, moving it from one hand to another as he squatted next to Victoria. She waited. She heard a car go by on North Road. Finally he spoke. "I knew they'd find me sooner or later."

Victoria heard Robin playing with the dog in the distance. He must have tossed a stick, because she heard something hit a tree trunk and drop. The dog barked and swished through the underbrush.

Ulysses stood up and dusted off his hands. "It was in February."

Victoria waited.

"There's an old cart track below my house."

"I know where it is."

"No one uses that track. But I heard a car." Ulysses put his hands in his pockets and looked in the direction of the ice pond, which was not visible from the path. "It was a new four-wheel-drive vehicle."

"Do you think they knew anybody lived right there?"

He shook his head. "It didn't seem so." He went on. "There were three people, two men and a woman."

Victoria realized she'd been holding her breath, and let it out softly.

"What did they look like?"

"I couldn't see the woman. She was bundled up in a down parka with the hood up."

Victoria shifted on her log seat. "Was she tall? Short? Slim?"

Ulysses shook his head. "Couldn't tell."

"And the men? What did they look like?" She looked up at him.

"One was shorter than the other. He was bundled up like the woman."

"So you couldn't identify him either, I suppose. The third person—the other man? Was it the one who was killed?"

"Yes," Ulysses said. "Fuzzy gray beard and side hair, bald on top. Glasses. Not dressed for the weather. He was wearing a heavy wool shirt."

"Then what happened?"

"I couldn't see so good. The bearded guy didn't get out of the car right away. The others seemed like they were dressed for a walk."

"It was during that cold spell, wasn't it?"

"It was snowing. They started to squabble. Finally the bearded guy got out of the car, yelling at the woman."

"Were all three arguing?"

Ulysses shook his head. "Him and the woman were having a real set-to. The short man turned his back on them. He stayed by the car. They walked away."

"Could you tell what they were arguing about?"

"No. I only heard voices, hers and his. I had to get back to what I was doing."

"I don't blame you." She looked past him into the woods, which were showing delicate tints of green.

"After a while I heard the car leave."

"Could you see who was in it?"

Ulysses shook his head. "I was gluing a chair. Couldn't leave it. At first I thought it was just a family fight."

"The woman and man seemed to know each other?"

Ulysses shrugged. "I guess. Then I wondered what they were doing here, and figured maybe it had to do with the land. The old lady . . ."

"Phoebe. Your mother."

"Yeah. *My* old lady. She was planning on selling out. You know about her?"

"We're friends." Victoria poked at something on the path with her stick. "That may have been it. The land. What happened next? That wasn't the end, was it?"

Ulysses stood uncertainly. Victoria heard a feeble whistle, "Bob white!" She heard the dog bark. Ulysses didn't seem to notice. He was gazing into space beyond the bare trees.

He focused on her again. "When I went out the next morning, I found the guy." He corrected himself. "The dog found him. Behind my place. Up by the stone wall."

"Dead, I suppose."

"Dead."

"Could you tell what had happened?"

"Looked like he fell against the stone wall. Hit his head."

"Then what? I suppose you carried or dragged him away from your house so people wouldn't come snooping around?"

Ulysses nodded.

"You know you're not supposed to move bodies, don't you?"

Ulysses nodded.

"You're supposed to report that kind of thing to the police."

Ulysses nodded.

"You've got to tell Casey what you saw and did."

"They'll say I killed him."

Victoria thought. "Probably so."

Both of them were silent. Victoria could hear Robin laugh and the dog bark in the distance. Another beech leaf fluttered to the ground.

Finally Victoria said, "They'll come after you if you don't. That would be worse. They know you're here somewhere, and they'll search until they find you."

Ulysses looked around. "I've got to get out of here."

Victoria flicked a small stone with her stick. "You don't want to run again." She looked up at him. "We've got to find the killer, and we've got to find him quickly."

Ulysses took a deep breath and let it out in a long sigh. "All I wanted was to be left alone."

"I know," Victoria said softly. "I know."

She didn't have the heart to ask him about the cranefly orchids.

"I have to go to the lumberyard," Kirschmeyer said to Victoria the next morning. "Talk to someone there."

Victoria glanced up from her bowl of Shredded Wheat. "You look much better. I hope you slept well."

"Slept like a log. Want to go with me for the ride? Nice day."

Her face lighted up. "I'll get my coat while you're having breakfast."

Manter's Lumber Yard was off the Lambert's Cove road, not far from the Conservation Trust office. Kirschmeyer drove past Up-Island Cronigs and the new fire station and turned left onto the narrow winding road. The shrubbery around Uncle Seth's Pond would have new spring leaves in another week. They turned into the lumberyard beyond the pond.

"The man I've got to see rents the shop next to the main building," Kirschmeyer explained as he parked between stacks of vanilla-scented new lumber.

"Who are you going to see?" Victoria asked.

Kirschmeyer looked at her with a smile. "*You* don't tell *me* everything."

"I don't care whether you do or not." Victoria settled back into her seat.

"I don't suppose it hurts to tell. I'm seeing that guy who wants to build a commune at Sachem's Rock."

"Tom More," said Victoria. "I know who he is. What are you seeing him about?"

"Now that *is* my business," Kirschmeyer said, getting out of the car. "I shouldn't be more than ten, fifteen minutes. Are you gonna be okay?"

Victoria held up her crossword puzzle book.

But she found it difficult to concentrate on her puzzle. The image of the desolate look on Ulysses face haunted her. Who were the people who had stopped in front of his cellar hole and argued? Mausz, of course. But the woman. Was she a client? The mysterious woman friend? His wife? Ulysses had intimated that they seemed well acquainted. And who was the other man? She sat up straight. Tom More. That's who the other man was. Tom was short, shorter than Mausz, who had been only average height. That made sense. Tom More wanted the land for his commune. Mausz was the lawyer for Phoebe. And he was also the lawyer for Ness. He was undoubtedly double- or triple-dealing, playing one buyer against another. The killer must be Tom More. He must have killed both Montgomery Mausz and Harry Ness. Victoria remembered how she had seen someone dropping bags of oyster shell cultch overboard the day after she had found Mausz's body. She would call the shellfish warden when they got home to see if More had a boat on the Great Pond. It made perfect sense, she thought. The people at Alley's said Tom More was like a cult leader. She recalled his hypnotic eyes, and shivered.

Why was Kirschmeyer meeting with Tom More now? That didn't make sense. What was taking him so long? She realized with a shock—Kirschmeyer was in danger.

While she waited, Victoria's muscles had stiffened. She opened the car door and carefully set first one foot then the other on the ground, held onto the door frame, and stepped out. She mustn't move too quickly until she limbered up. She reached into the car for her cloth bag, replaced her fuzzy tan hat with her police deputy cap and set the bag on the floor. She retrieved her stick and walked slowly toward the shed. As she approached the building she could hear the sound of a motor and, over the noise of the motor, raised voices. Before she opened the shed door she paused to think. Was it possible, just barely possible, that Spencer Kirschmeyer was the culprit? The timing was wrong. Besides, when Loch Ness died—was killed, she corrected herself—Kirschmeyer was in the hospital, definitely not able to get about. Nobody could fake that injury.

She tugged the shed door open and the sound of the motor was louder. It took her only an instant to realize what was happening. Kirschmeyer was facing her, hands high in the air. She noted, in that instant, that his face was pasty white. His eyes were huge behind his spectacles. His jowls quivered.

The motor cut off suddenly, an air compressor, she realized. The shed was deathly silent.

Tom More was pointing some kind of weapon at Kirschmeyer's stomach, something that looked like an orange death-ray gun. On the side nearest Victoria it had a foot-and-a-half-long metal attachment, a sort of magazine, and a long plastic hose that snaked across the floor in front of her. Kirschmeyer babbled something, over and over, that sounded like, "Don't shoot me. Don't shoot!"

"Put that down, Tom!" Victoria demanded in her best schoolteacher voice.

Tom turned toward her and lowered his weapon. The air compressor kicked on again. He glared at her, his eyes dark, and lifted the weapon in her direction.

Victoria looked around quickly, saw the plastic hose in front of her, leaned down, and tugged it. Tom's weapon jerked toward the ground. There was a loud SNAP!

Tom More screamed.

Kirschmeyer kept his hands in the air. Sweat poured down his pale face. His glasses had steamed up.

"Do something," Victoria said to him. "Take the nail gun away from him before he does any more damage."

Tom stood still, mumbling incoherently.

"You shot yourself in the foot," Victoria said after she had examined him. "It doesn't look terribly serious. They'll probably have to give you a tetanus shot."

Kirschmeyer started to say something, but before he could, Victoria went on. "We'd better leave him nailed to the floor until the police get here." She located the phone. As she picked it up and started to dial she told Kirschmeyer, "Find a chair for him to sit on. He can't be comfortable."

Kirschmeyer took a grayish handkerchief out of his pocket and wiped his glasses and his forehead before he found a stool in the back of the shed and set it behind Tom.

Victoria was speaking into the phone. "We've nailed the killer, Chief," she said to Casey. "You'd better come with the ambulance."

CHAPTER 18

Tom rode to the hospital in the Tri-Town Ambulance, Victoria and Casey followed in the police Bronco, and Kirschmeyer brought up the rear in Victoria's battered green Citation.

The EMTs had pried the nail out of the floor, but had left it in Tom's toe.

Victoria and Kirschmeyer waited outside the Emergency Room. Casey followed the EMTs, who wheeled Tom into one of the examining rooms laid out on a stretcher. "I didn't kill anybody," Victoria heard Tom say. Then "Ouch!" as Hope gave him a tetanus shot.

"When they get you fixed up we'll take you to the station and you can make a statement," Casey told him. "I have to give you the warning, you know. You can have your lawyer there if you want."

"I don't need a lawyer. You don't need to warn me. I didn't do anything. Christ, can't you be more gentle?" The last to Hope, who was pouring antiseptic on his toe.

"We'll have it X-rayed and then Doc Jeffers will want to take a look," Hope said brightly. "He'll probably remove the nail. Doesn't seem all that bad, if you ask me."

"I'm not asking you," Tom grunted. "Jesus! Ouch!"

"Lie down," Hope said. She wheeled the stretcher from the Emergency Room toward Radiology.

"I didn't kill them!" Tom said over his shoulder to Casey, who was following the stretcher.

Casey turned Victoria, who had stood up as the stretcher passed her. "*Them?*" she said.

The five golfing doctors met at the Harbor View Hotel over drinks later that afternoon. Golden light was settling over the harbor. The days were noticeably longer.

Doc Jeffers held up his glass of tonic. "Here's to Crystal Ness and her two hundred acres of prime real estate."

Dr. Sawicki passed a plump hand over his scalp. "Does anybody know what she's decided to do with that land?"

"She's decided against her husband's development, and she's also decided against our golf course," Doc Jeffers replied.

Dr. Sawicki shook his head. "Weird that Ness kept that land in his own name rather than setting up a trust."

Doc Erickson took his pen out of the pocket of his madras shirt and signed the tab the waiter had left on the table. "Ness expected to live forever. Didn't think he needed to hide behind a trust. In addition, he didn't trust lawyers."

Doc Jeffers held up his glass in a kind of salute.

Doc Erickson continued. "He didn't give a damn about taxes or inheritances. He had money to burn. You had to respect him."

Dr. Gibbs flexed her long fingers. "What *does* Mrs. Ness plan to do with it?" she asked. "Do we know?"

"Well," said Doc Jeffers, "besides her husband's trophy houses and our golf course, there's still that community housing project and the conservation group. Were those all?"

"A Native American gambling casino," Dr. Billings said.

"The campground," Dr. Sawicki said, and blushed suddenly.

Dr. Gibbs gazed at him over her pinkish drink. "What do you know about that group?"

"I, er, I had occasion to meet Page Bachwald. The chairperson of Park and Rec."

The other three doctors looked at Sawicki.

Dr. Sawicki swallowed, and loosened his tie slightly.

" 'Occasion'?" Dr. Gibbs said.

"One of her boys broke his arm. I set it."

Dr. Gibbs nodded. "I see."

Doc Jeffers guffawed. "Orthopedic practice on the Island looks better all the time, right, Sawicki?"

"The golf course was a good idea," Doc Erickson said. "But you can't win 'em all. At least we saved ourselves some money."

Dr. Billings lifted his chin and stretched his neck. "I'm afraid I lost interest when I found the club would be open to the public," he said. "I've applied for membership in Goose Neck."

Dr. Gibbs sipped her drink. "Goose Neck coined the word 'exclusive.' You certainly won't have to worry about the un-washed public there."

Dr. Sawicki's face had returned to its usual pallor. He laughed. "I'm surprised they even allowed you to fill out the application forms."

"Not funny, Doctor." Dr. Billings said stiffly. "Besides my professional credentials, which, as you know, are considera-ble, my family has substantial financial assets. Furthermore, my ancestry traces back to, not one, but two passengers on the *Mayflower*."

"That should do it," Doc Erickson said heartily.

Doc Jeffers moved his booted feet with a clank and grinned. "Doesn't all that inbreeding worry you?"

"Goose Neck's got an eight-year waiting list. You planning to live that long?" said Dr. Sawicki.

Dr. Billings rubbed his thumb against his index and mid-dle fingers with a dry sound. "You have to talk to the right people."

"Yes, indeed," Dr. Gibbs said. "Money does talk, doesn't it."

"It doesn't hurt." Dr. Billings changed the subject and turned to Dr. Gibbs. "I understand you discharged your patient, the crushed thorax case."

Dr. Gibbs stirred her drink with the slice of orange impaled on a plastic straw. "He discharged himself, actually," she said. "Dr. Erickson and I both felt he should have stayed in the hospital longer. A week more, at least."

Dr. Sawicki patted the shiny top of his head before he asked, "Have you done any follow-up on him?"

Dr. Gibbs smiled. "In a way. You knew it was Victoria Trumbull's tree that fell on him?"

The others nodded.

Dr. Sawicki added, "I understand he's staying with her. I suppose she feels responsible for him."

Doc Jeffers laughed, showing his great white teeth. "I doubt it. Victoria's probably enlisted him to help her solve the murders."

Dr. Sawicki looked up quickly. "Murders? Plural?"

"She claims Loch Ness was murdered," Doc Erickson put in.

Dr. Billings straightened his tie again. "Surely not. Who examined the body?"

"I did," said Doc Jeffers. "He drowned. Bump on his head consistent with his stumbling against something on board his boat then falling overboard. Happens all the time."

Dr. Gibbs looked thoughtful. "I suppose someone could have hit him over the head?"

Doc Jeffers leered at her. "Start with the simple explanation. Fisherman goes out alone—what do you expect?"

"Maybe Mrs. Trumbull is right. Perhaps he wasn't alone." Dr. Gibbs said.

"I'll be goddamned," said Josiah. He had slit open a large, brown, registered, return-receipt-requested envelope that

Zack had picked up from the Vineyard Haven Post Office, and was staring at the contents. "I can't believe it." He stood up and went over to the window. "It can't be happening." He peered out at the cranberry bog, bright red in the afternoon sunlight.

Zack unfolded himself from his chair and reached over to the sheaf of papers on Josiah's desk.

He read. He pushed his glasses back into place. He combed his hair out of his eyes with his fingers. "Holy cow!"

Josiah turned to him. "What do you make of it?"

"Is someone playing a joke?"

"Pretty expensive joke. All that legal stuff looks real enough."

Zack laid the papers back on the desk. "What are you going to do?"

"I guess I have to assume it's real," Josiah said slowly.

"And then . . . ?"

"Then, I guess I'd better call on Crystal Ness and thank her." Josiah gazed at Zack for several moments. Then, quite suddenly, he whooped and made an exuberant leap, high enough so he hit his head on the low ceiling. Rubbing the top of his head, he bounded over to Zack, pulled him out of the chair, and threw his arms around him. "The cranefly orchid did it," he shouted. "Get Victoria Trumbull here right away. Get Robin out of school." He raced to his desk. "Dr. Cornelius. Where's Dr. Cornelius's phone number?"

"Holy cow," said Zack, shaking his head. "Holy cow!"

The Cranberry Fields group met in emergency session in the basement of the senior center.

"He was trying to help us, is all," Marguerite said, knitting vigorously. "He wanted to double our money."

"If I wanted to gamble, I'd bet on the horses, not the stock market," said the balding middle-aged man who was sitting in his usual seat at the rear of the group. "What happened to that anonymous donor who was going to put in so much money?"

"After Mr. Ness died, she lost interest, I hear," someone said.

"Where do we go from here?" Sanders said. "I shelled out ten-thousand bucks I couldn't afford, with a promise for an- other twenty."

"Thank the good Lord it was only ten thousand. Could have been worse."

"That represented all our savings," the gaunt forty-ish woman seated in front of Deborah said. "It took us years to accumulate that much."

Deborah disentangled her two-year old from her lap and set him on the floor. "You know, it was, like, kind of stupid for all of us to think about setting up our community on a piece of real estate like that. We could go someplace out west where we could afford to buy land. Where there aren't so many people. Where we can, like, farm and work and raise our kids and have dogs and free-range chickens. And if Mar- guerite wants, she can get away from other people's kids and paint pictures of mountains and cactus like what's-her- name."

"Georgia O'Keefe." Marguerite's face flushed a becoming pink. "Thank you, Deborah."

"I don't care whether I live right here on this particular spot or not," the bald man said. "Out west sounds good to me. Anybody want to look into it?"

Sanders scratched his head. "I'd be glad to, but where do we get the money to start over?"

The long silence was broken by a knock on the wall at the foot of the stairs.

"I hope I'm not interrupting anything." It was Carole, the center's director. "But the Papa Bear delivery man brought this big envelope and said I was to give it to you right away."

She looked around at the somber group. "Is everything okay? No more bad news? I was sorry to hear about Tom More getting arrested . . ."

Sanders took the envelope. "We're okay. Nothing we won't get over."

"I'll leave you then." Carole went back up the stairs.

Marguerite twitched a length of yarn out of her tapestry bag. "What is it?"

"Who's it from?" asked the gaunt woman.

Deborah picked up her two-year-old. "Open it!"

The bald man shook his head. "Probably more bad news."

"Hold on, don't rush me." Sanders fished a knife out of his pocket, opened a blade, and examined the envelope carefully before he slit it open. "Some Boston lawyers' office. No one I ever heard of."

"What does it say?" several people chorused.

The bald man laughed. "Maybe it's a summons to testify against More."

Marguerite knitted furiously. "I wouldn't want to do that."

Sanders took a great sheaf of papers out of the envelope and stared at the one on top.

"What is it?" several people asked at once.

Deborah called out, "Is everything okay?"

Marguerite looked anxiously at Sanders's face, which seemed to have lost most of its color. "Are you all right?"

Sanders dropped the envelope and the papers on the floor and sat down with a thump. Marguerite set her knitting down next to her and got to her feet.

She picked up the papers Sanders had dropped. "Oh my!" She put a hand up to her mouth.

The bald-headed man strode to the front of the room and snatched the papers out of Marguerite's hands. "For God's sake. What a bunch of incompetents." He looked at the papers. "What the hell!"

"What? What?" said the group.

"It's from Mrs. Ness. Loch Ness's widow."

"Yes, yes! Go on!"

Deborah said sourly, "Probably offering us the land, now we can't afford it."

The bald man slapped his hand on the legal papers. "Listen to this. She says, and it's all here, she says her heart is still in Nevada, and if we're interested, and if we're willing to change the name from Cranberry Fields to The Loch Ness Memorial Ranch, she'll deed us a thousand acres of land near Tonopah."

Sanders scratched his head. "Where in hell's Tonopah?"

The bald man looked over the frame of his glasses. "Out west."

"Desert. Cattle. Mining," someone said.

Deborah got to her feet again. "I'll see if Carole has an atlas."

Sanders picked up a gavel from the podium at the front of the room and banged it for attention. "I don't know about the rest of you, but I'd be willing to look into this, see what it's all about."

"I hear her father was a big wheel in the Mormon Church," the bald man said.

Deborah turned on her way to the stairs. "She was a showgirl in Las Vegas. Her father didn't care much for that, I bet."

The bald-headed man said, "Mormons are pretty broadminded—get it? '*broad*-minded'?"

Marguerite turned to him. "Not amusing. Tasteless, in fact."

Someone in the back of the room said, "A thousand acres is a lot more land than two hundred acres."

Comments flew around the group.

"Taxes are lower, too, I bet."

"Good place for kids."

"Not exactly waterfront."

"Neither was Sachem's Rock."

Sanders said, "Maybe the first thing we should do is send a delegation to Mrs. Ness to thank her."

"Why not? Well, why not?"

In the West Tisbury police station, Tom More was a small frightened man, no longer the charismatic leader of a band of zealots. He was still protesting. "I didn't do it! For God's sake, I didn't kill anybody!"

"Sit down," said Casey.

Victoria found a cardboard box and set it in front of him so he could put his foot up. He limped over to the chair, his high-tech cast thumping with every other step, and sat with a plop.

Casey had called the State Police who said they would come to her office, and they told her to hold Tom there.

"You don't have to talk, you know," Casey said again, replacing the phone in its cradle.

"I waive my Miranda rights, or whatever it is. I didn't do it, I tell you." Tom lifted his foot onto the box with both hands and grunted.

"Let's start with what you allegedly did do, namely threaten Mr. Kirschmeyer with the nail gun."

"It wouldn't have hurt him," Tom said.

Casey looked over her desk at his foot.

"It wouldn't have killed him even if I'd aimed it at him."

Casey picked up a pen and tapped her desk with it. "Whether it would have killed him or not, it comes out to assault. Would you care to explain?"

Tom pounded on her desk again. "He's a goddamned blackmailer. An extortionist. A bloodsucker."

"Yeah?" said Casey.

"It has nothing to do with Mausz."

Victoria moved one of the extra chairs next to Casey's desk and sat. "An eyewitness saw you get out of the same car Montgomery Mausz was in just before he was killed."

Tom started to sweat. He took off his glasses and wiped them on a tissue he plucked out of a box on Casey's desk.

Casey continued to tap her pen. "Is that true? What Mrs. Trumbull just said?"

Tom looked around the small station house before he replied. "No. It can't be."

Casey stopped tapping. "Oh?"

He wiped his forehead and continued to hold the wadded-up tissue.

"An eye-witness identified you," Victoria insisted.

"Nobody was around." Tom suddenly seemed to realize what he had just admitted. He shifted uncomfortably in his chair. "Okay. Yeah, I was there. But I didn't kill him."

"Who was the woman?" Casey asked.

"His wife. Minerva Peabody."

Casey asked him, "Mind if I tape this?"

"Yes. I mean no. Go ahead and tape it."

Casey set the tape recorder on her desk and turned it on. "Go ahead, Victoria. You were in on this part of it."

Victoria faced Tom. "Mr. and Mrs. Mausz argued, isn't that so?"

"It had nothing to do with me. They got into a squabble about his girlfriend."

Victoria's hooded eyes were fixed on Tom. "Was that all they argued about?"

"I didn't want to get involved in a family spat."

"Was that all they argued about?" Victoria repeated.

"I walked away from them. It wasn't my fight."

Victoria asked for a third time, "Was that all they argued about?"

Tom sighed. "They went from fighting about his girlfriend to fighting about the land."

"Go on."

"She told him it was illegal or unethical for him to represent both buyers and sellers, and said she was reporting him to the Bar of Board Overseers."

"You mean the Board of Bar Overseers."

"Whatever. He said they wouldn't listen to her, and she said she'd filed for divorce and he'd be getting the papers when he got back to his office. She told him to move out of her house." Tom paused. Outside, a car door slammed. "It had nothing to do with me."

The station house door opened, and two state troopers entered. Casey stood. "We're taking his statement. One of you can have a seat at Junior's desk."

One of the troopers was heavy-set and white, the other was short, wiry, and black. The black cop sat on the edge of Junior's desk. The other pulled out the chair behind Junior's desk and sat. "Don't let us interrupt," the black trooper said.

Victoria looked over at them briefly, then went back to her questioning. "Go on."

Tom shifted his injured foot with his hands. "Mausz said he had tickets to Aruba and he didn't plan to stay in that mausoleum for the rest of his life anyway. It went on and on like that."

Victoria stared fixedly at him. "The land. What did they say about the land?"

Tom looked down at his hands, which were clenched in his lap. "Minerva told him she wanted that land. She told him if he knew what was good for him, he'd make sure Ness didn't get it."

"Did she say why she wanted it so badly?" Casey asked.

Tom shifted uncomfortably. "The argument was going round in circles. You know the way it goes. His girlfriend, the land, divorce. They walked away from the car up that hillside beside the stone wall."

Both of the state cops had folded their arms. The one sitting on the edge of the desk crossed one foot over the other.

The one sitting behind Junior's desk looked out the window at the pond.

Victoria continued with her questioning. "Then what happened?"

"Minerva came back alone. 'So who won?' I said. 'I did, naturally,' she said. 'What a fool he is,' she said." More, who had been avoiding Victoria's eyes, looked directly at her. "Actually, she called him an asshole. Her quote, not mine."

Victoria's expression didn't change. "Go on."

"Then she said, 'Let's go.' I said, 'Hadn't we better wait for him?' She said, 'He can find his own way to Aruba from here.' I said, 'He's not exactly dressed for a long hike.' She said, 'It won't kill him.' " Tom looked from Victoria to Casey to the two state troopers. "Those were her exact words: 'It won't kill him.' "

"So you left him there? Did Minerva tell you what had happened on the hillside?"

"She said he swung at her, but she's taken courses in defend-yourself-against-rapists, so she deflected his arm and knocked him down and left him."

Casey stood up. "Get yourself a lawyer. You need one, whether you want one or not."

CHAPTER 19

When Casey drove Victoria home, Kirschmeyer was waiting for her at the kitchen door with three stalks of chrysanthemums done up in clear plastic. "I gotta thank you, Mrs. T. That was some quick thinking."

Victoria took the flowers with a smile, cut the stalks to fit the green glass vase, and filled the vase with water. "I need to ask you something, Mr. Kirschmeyer."

"Call me Studs," he said, placing both hands on his chest. "Ask me anything you want."

McCavity appeared in the kitchen from some hiding place and wrapped himself around Victoria's legs.

Victoria set the vase in the center of the kitchen table. "Tom More mentioned something when we were at the hospital." She bent down to pat McCavity, avoiding Kirschmeyer's eyes. "Blackmail and extortion. Was that why you went to see him?" She glanced up at him.

Kirschmeyer coughed and looked behind him nervously.

Victoria went on, "I know Harry Ness didn't get around to paying you for the investigation you did for him. Was there something you found out about Tom More that you thought he might pay you to hush up?"

"Look, Mrs. T., I owe you. But . . ."

"No one else needs to know." Victoria took the chrysanthemums out of the vase, broke off an inch more of stem, and put them back in the water. She tilted her head critically. "I'll feed the cat and make tea."

Kirschmeyer was silent while the water heated. He stood by the west door, staring at the stump of the fallen tree, hands clasped behind his back. McCavity made soft noises while Victoria opened a can of cat food, dished some into his bowl, and put it on the floor.

When the tea was brewed, Kirschmeyer carried it into the cookroom. Victoria shook gingersnaps onto a plate. Neither had said a word during the tea-making ceremony.

Finally Kirschmeyer spoke. "I wouldn't have called it blackmail or extortion. But I guess maybe he could have seen it that way."

"You asked him to pay you for the information you'd found for Harry Ness, was that how you put it?"

Kirschmeyer stirred sugar into his tea. "Yeah. That was about what it amounted to."

Victoria held her mug in both hands and looked at him through the steam. "Can you tell me what it was?"

He let out a great sigh and set his mug on the table. "I guess I can trust you."

Victoria said with some asperity, "I should think so."

McCavity sprang into Victoria's lap and turned, eyes half-closed, to face Kirschmeyer.

"I traced him back to when he first came to the Island, about ten years ago. No one seemed to know where he'd come from before that. He just appeared one day, started working as a carpenter, and the first thing anybody knew, he had his own business and was building eco-homes."

Victoria stroked McCavity. " 'Eco-homes'?" she asked.

"You know, solar energy, floors made out of recycled tires, composting toilets, the whole nine yards."

"Of course. I recall now. There've been articles about his houses in the *Island Enquirer*."

"I couldn't find out anything about him before then. It was like he got born ten years ago. Just showed up on the Island full-grown."

"That seems odd."

"Damn right it was odd. I said to myself, 'What's he hiding?' I figured it must've been something serious."

"What did you do then?"

"Well, you know, if I'd have been able to check back, found he'd served time, no big deal. He would've paid his debt to society, as they say. So the guy deserves a break. But when I found nothing—not one damn clue—it made me think he was hiding something big. A lot worse than serving time." Kirschmeyer popped a gingersnap into his mouth and chomped down on it with a crunch.

"And you found something."

"Yeah. I figured he comes from New England—you know, the way he talks, and all."

"Yes," Victoria nodded. "I know what you mean."

"Then I figured he had to of been in the business for a while. He knows a lot about building houses."

McCavity kneaded Victoria's thighs. She disengaged his sharp claws. "That was clever."

"So I called around."

"What a huge undertaking."

"You said it, Mrs. T. Here on the Island, this little tiny place, there's about a dozen home building companies, plus a bunch of architects and engineers. You just multiply that out."

"How did you ever do it?"

"As I say, I got buddies. I figured the guy probably changed his name and his appearance. He's got that big beard. But he couldn't hardly change those eyes of his or how tall he is. You've seen how he wears those high-heeled boots?"

"I noticed," Victoria agreed.

McCavity, still in Victoria's lap, licked his paw and started to scrub behind his ears.

"I asked about a short guy with bright eyes. Couple of my contacts said a guy of that description had worked for them twenty or more years ago. Stayed a year, two years, then moved on. He'd changed his name, all right."

"What was his name before?" Victoria asked.

"Ted Moskovitz." Kirschmeyer passed the plate of ginger-snaps to Victoria, who shook her head. He helped himself to another.

"Same initials," Victoria mused.

"That's what people usually do. A new name with the same initials. In case they've got something with initials on it, they won't have to change it."

Victoria thought for a moment. "It was Sir Thomas More who wrote about Utopia."

"Yeah? He live around here?"

Victoria laughed. McCavity, startled, jumped off her lap and walked away. "He lived in England around the time of Shakespeare, in the 1500s. He wrote about an imaginary is-land called Utopia where everything was perfect."

"Yeah?"

"That's what our Tom More had in mind with his Cran-berry Fields, I suppose. A new Utopia. His idea must have gotten out of hand. I can't imagine why he felt he had to kill anybody." Victoria shook her head. "What did you find out about Ted Moskovitz?"

"One of the companies he'd worked for told me where he'd gone to, an architectural company in New Hampshire that specializes in environmental homes. Where he got his ideas, I guess. I called them, and—Bingo!"

"Oh?"

"He worked for this company, Green Architects Limited for five or six years. They promoted him to supervisor, then a couple years later to handling contracts and money. Then, Bam!" Kirschmeyer slammed his fist on the table, and one of the gingersnaps bounced off the plate onto the table. "One day he disappeared. And so did a pile of money, like around two-hundred-thousand."

Victoria brushed cat hairs off her lap. "Dollars?"

Kirschmeyer nodded. "Green Architects tried to track him, but he'd vanished clean off the face of the earth."

Victoria smoothed the tablecloth in front of her. "Strange," she said. "It's not that easy to vanish."

"That's for sure. I figured, if I was going to disappear, where would I go? And I figured I'd leave the country, go someplace in Central America, like Costa Rica. They love Americans down there, and I hear it's a nice place to stay."

McCavity scratched at the kitchen door. Victoria got up stiffly and let him out. "Is that what happened? He left the country?" she said when she returned.

"Right. I know this girl works for an airline, so I had her check for More or Moskovitz around the time he disappeared. It wasn't all that easy because the records were in some back storage. That's why I'm so bullshit about Ness getting himself killed without paying me."

"That *was* unfortunate. His death."

"This girl found the records. He'd used his own name, Moskovitz, his own passport, and sure enough, he'd gone down to Costa Rica. Lived there for about five years, then came back here on a new passport with the name Tom More."

"Interesting," Victoria murmured.

She sipped her tea. "What happened at the lumberyard when you confronted him today?"

"I was up front. I told him about Ness hiring me, about me not getting the money, about how I'd shelled out a lot from my own pocket, and asked how's about him reimbursing me."

"I suppose you told him what you'd learned?"

"Yeah, of course." Kirschmeyer pushed his chair back from the table and crossed his legs.

"Then what?"

"He says, 'That's ridiculous,' or something like that. I says, 'I've got proof.' He says he doesn't have any money. I

229

laughed in his face. 'You mean,' I says, 'You're developing two-hundred acres of prime real estate on Martha's Vineyard and you've got all these investors and you don't have any money?' He got red in the face. 'Come on, come on,' I says." Kirschmeyer gestured with both hands. "That's when he picked up that death-ray gun."

"It was a nail gun," Victoria said.

"I never seen one before. How am I supposed to know what it was?"

"It looks pretty lethal," Victoria admitted. "I suppose it could kill you if it was aimed exactly right." She sniffed. "It's not the weapon *I'd* choose, though."

Kirschmeyer shrugged. "So that's where we're at."

Victoria thought. She glanced up at the baskets hanging from the whitewashed rafters. Finally she said, "Why don't you write out your report and give it to Crystal Ness with your bill. I'm sure she'll honor it."

Kirschmeyer wiped crumbs from his mouth with a paper napkin, wadded up the napkin and dropped it on the table. "Ness didn't want anybody to know I was working for him."

"The situation has changed. Decidedly. I'd go to her, if I were you, Mr. Kirschmeyer . . ."

"Studs."

Victoria coughed delicately. "Yes. Well. I'd also give a copy of the report to Chief O'Neill. She'll know how to handle this."

Kirschmeyer shook his head. "I don't like the idea of cops getting involved. Especially a lady cop."

Victoria fixed him with her deepset eyes. "You realize you're in danger, don't you? I don't know how long they can hold Tom More, but the minute they release him, he'll obviously try to silence you. The safest thing for you to do is to notify the police. Right now."

Kirschmeyer lifted his shoulders.

"I mean it." Victoria slapped her hand on the table. "Tom More has nothing to lose. You do. Go to Chief O'Neill, right away."

Joe stepped up onto the porch at Alley's. "You heard about Tom More shooting himself in the foot?"

Lincoln laughed. "What you call 'toe nailing,' right?"

"It's not funny," said Sarah, who was sitting on the bench next to Donald. She stirred her coffee. "You know how much it hurts when you stub your toe. Imagine getting a nail in it." She shuddered.

Joe laughed.

Donald leaned forward, his elbows on his resin-splotched jeans. "I hear Miz Trumbull rescued the detective."

"She knew more about nail guns than he did." Joe chortled. "He thought it was a death ray."

"How long are they keeping More in jail, anybody know?" Lincoln asked from his spot next to the door.

They looked at each other questioningly.

Donald said finally, "I hear Miz Trumbull thinks he killed Mickey Mausz."

"No way to prove it," Lincoln said. "Some guy who's camping out there moved the body."

"Yeah?" Joe rocked from his heels onto his toes. He put his hands in his pockets. "Where'd you hear that?"

"It was probably on the scanner," Sarah put in.

Joe continued to rock. "Tom More's got a pretty good deal, being locked up in that country club."

Donald leaned back against the wall behind the bench. "You heard about the quee-zine at the jail?"

"It was in the *Enquirer*," Sarah said.

"What about it?" Joe stopped rocking.

Lincoln rubbed his back against the door frame. "They got a French chef serving time for doing drugs."

"Yeah? That what they eat, French quee-zine?"

Sarah finished her coffee and folded the paper cup. "Makes you think, doesn't it?"

"So all they can hold Tom More for is the threatened assault on the private eye?" Lincoln looked around at the others.

"I guess." Sarah shrugged. "I don't think they can keep him there forever, eating French cuisine at taxpayers' expense."

"Somebody told me the private eye isn't pressing charges," Donald said.

Joe looked up with interest. "Yeah? How come?"

Just then, a white VW convertible pulled up in front of the store and Elizabeth went around the car from the driver's side and onto the porch. She greeted the four, and went inside. Victoria rolled down her window and waved. "Nice day," she said.

Joe straightened up. "Yes, ma'am."

"Where are you off to, Mrs. Trumbull?" Sarah called.

"An outing," Victoria replied. "What my grandfather called 'a cruise.' "

Elizabeth came out of the store with a stack of mail. "What a waste of paper." She held up a half-dozen catalogs. "Stuff we'd never buy."

"Someone does," Sarah said.

Elizabeth flipped open one of the catalogs to an ad for a Potty Putter. "Want to play golf while you sit on the john?"

Sarah laughed. "So where *are* you and your grandmother going?" she asked. "Back up to Sachem's Rock, now she's nabbed the killer?"

"I'm taking her there, but I have to get back to work. I wish Robin was with her."

"I suppose she'll hitch a ride home again?"

Elizabeth said quietly, "I worry about my grandmother

sometimes, but honestly, she's impossible. There's nothing I can do to stop her."

From the porch they could see Victoria's owl-like profile, her beaky nose and hooded eyes. She seemed to be writing something. She looked up from whatever she was writing. Her chin jutted out stubbornly.

"I see what you mean," said Sarah with admiration.

Elizabeth handed the mail through the window to Victoria, got back in the car, made a U-turn in the middle of the road, and drove off down Brandy Brow.

After a few minutes' silence, Joe said, "What do you suppose the old lady's up to now?"

Victoria stopped by the log where she'd summoned Ulysses before and sat. She was tired and felt, for the first time, that perhaps she'd bitten off more than she could chew. Robin was in school, and she missed him. But she needed to talk to Ulysses alone. When she caught her breath, she pursed her lips and whistled, "Bob white! Bob bob white!" remembering how Robin had been awed by her loud whistle. She smiled.

Soon the dog bounded up the hillside followed by Ulysses.

"We caught the killer," Victoria called out as soon as she saw him.

Ulysses smiled grimly. "Yes, ma'am. I heard."

"You don't need to worry about being accused of murdering Mr. Mausz now. But you have to talk to the police chief about moving his body. You're not supposed to do that, you know."

Ulysses squatted beside Victoria, picked up a handful of leaf litter from the ground.

Victoria watched him for a few moments. "I don't know for a certainty, but I don't think they'll do any more than give you a lecture."

The black and white dog lay down on the path in front of Victoria. He put his head on his paws and looked up at Ulysses through sad eyes.

"He misses the boy," Ulysses said abruptly.

"He's in school. I wanted to talk to you alone."

"About giving myself up."

"That, but something else, too." Victoria poked the ground between her and the dog with her stick, inscribing small circles. The dog lifted his head and dropped it back on his paws.

Ulysses waited.

Finally Victoria said, "Why did you dig up the cranefly orchids?"

Ulysses stood suddenly, dropped his handful of dirt, and dusted off his hands. He said angrily, "I didn't dig them up."

"Someone air-shipped live plants to you."

"Maybe they did. But I didn't dig up anything."

"I suppose those were cranefly orchids in the shipment?" Victoria continued to draw circles in the dirt.

Ulysses nodded.

"Will you tell me what that was all about?"

Ulysses hunkered down again beside Victoria.

"I followed you and the boy, from the first time you came here together."

"I knew someone was."

"I wasn't the only one following you," Ulysses said.

Victoria raised her eyebrows. "Oh?"

"Somebody else was. You heard them. Not me."

"Who was it?"

"I could never get close enough to see."

"Could you tell if it was the caretaker?"

"It wasn't him. He makes the rounds of the main trails twice a day with his dog, regular as clockwork. Then he leaves."

Victoria thought over this new information. "Then who dug up the plants?"

"Whoever was stalking you."

"But you definitely didn't?" Victoria looked at him.

Ulysses stood up and paced back and forth for several minutes. Then he said, "Someone finds some rare plant or animal on this land, developers would back off. Why should I dig up something that might save my family land? Used to be my family land."

"That's true," Victoria conceded. "Who could the other person be, I wonder. Someone working for Harry Ness?"

Ulysses said nothing.

Victoria asked, "How do you happen to know so much about cranefly orchids?"

"I looked them up on the library computer after I heard you and the boy talking about them," Ulysses said.

Victoria stopped drawing circles with her stick. "The new orchids—why have them flown in? And where on earth did you get them?"

Ulysses didn't answer directly. "I heard when you and the boy found them. He made enough fuss."

Victoria put her stick aside. She shifted so she could reach a napkin in her trousers pocket and wiped her nose with it. "I was afraid Robin would trample them."

"That other person must have heard the boy too. I went back later to see what you'd found, and the plants were already gone."

Victoria whistled softly. "Someone worked fast."

"I read all about those orchids. They aren't rare in the south. There's plenty of them in North Carolina and Georgia." Ulysses walked a short distance up the path and back again. He continued, "I have an Army buddy who works in the Smokey Mountains. North Carolina. I asked him to find me some plants and send them to me."

"You don't have a phone, do you?"

Ulysses grinned. "I faxed him from the drug store."

"I see," Victoria said. "You know the orchids your friend sent are different from the ones that were dug up? The ones that grow here naturally?"

Ulysses shrugged. "It was the best I could think of."

"I suppose you re-planted the original orchid plants on the house sites?"

Ulysses shuffled his feet in the dry litter. "Yes, ma'am."

"Why?" Victoria asked.

"I didn't find the original plants until after I got the new ones from the Smokies. I thought that whoever dug them up would have gotten rid of them fast. They probably wouldn't dump them on the ground or bury them. For fear they'd grow back, you know?"

Victoria nodded.

"I decided somebody must have come by car, but didn't park near where you and the boy always start walking."

Victoria put the napkin back in her pocket. "I'd have seen them, if so. I wonder how they knew when Robin and I would be here?"

"You weren't exactly sneaky," Ulysses said, and smiled.

"Hmmm," Victoria murmured.

"A couple of other roads lead in here. One is the old road that goes by my place. The other is off Tea Lane."

"The way I go to Phoebe's—your mother's."

"Yes, ma'am. The Tea Lane road seemed like where they'd most likely park. There's an old trash barrel there. Nobody ever empties it, but whoever wanted to get rid of the orchids probably wouldn't know that."

"It must be full of rubbish if it's never emptied."

Ulysses shook his head. "It's not public property. Nobody goes there. The barrel had a couple bottles, a lot of leaves, some soggy paper. I thought I'd find the orchids there, and that's where I did. In the rubbish."

"So you planted them where Ness was planning to build the houses."

"Yes, ma'am. Didn't see any point in putting them back where they were, what with the new plants growing okay."

Victoria sighed. "That explains a lot."

"I heard the fellow from the state . . ."

"Dr. Cornelius?"

"Yes, ma'am. I heard him say it was the wrong habitat, the house sites."

"They probably won't survive there," Victoria agreed.

"I'll move them back to where you found them."

Victoria laughed. "That will confound Josiah and Zack." She paused for a few moments. "Ulysses?"

"Ma'am?"

"Your mother would like to see you."

He turned his back on her. "I haven't seen her for twenty years."

The dog sat up and laid his muzzle on Victoria's knee. She patted his head. "It's time you went to see her, Ulysses."

"I got nothing to say to her." Ulysses turned back to Victoria.

"I don't think she has anything to say to you, either," Victoria said. "But you should go see her anyway."

"She sold the land. It's not hers anymore. She'll be moving off one of these days."

"Things have changed," Victoria said. "You know Crystal Ness gave Sachem's Rock to the Conservation Trust?"

"I'd heard so. They'll be moving me off, too, I imagine."

"I don't think so," Victoria said. "Josiah Coffin told me he needs a caretaker for the property. I recommended you. I think he plans to work out something so your mother can stay in her house."

"Does she know?"

Victoria shook her head. "That might be a good excuse to talk to her."

"I don't know," Ulysses said, turning away again.

"She doesn't want you living with her and taking care of her. She'd hate that." Victoria patted the dog, who moved closer to her. "She wants her place to herself. Just like you. But it would be nice for her to know her son's around somewhere."

Ulysses wiped his hands on his trousers. "I guess I better talk to the police chief."

CHAPTER 20

Casey hung up the phone and sighed. "Let's go, Victoria. Mr. Ferro's lost his car again. He's sure it's been stolen."

Victoria was sitting in the wooden armchair in front of Casey's desk, her blue coat flung over its back. "This must be the third or fourth time."

Casey stood and buckled on her belt. "More like the fifth. Last time he forgot he left it at Up-Island Cronigs, and came home by shuttle bus." She led the way down the station house steps to the parking area. Victoria took her usual seat in the Bronco.

As she started up the vehicle and backed out onto the Edgartown Road, Casey muttered, "Things were never like this in Brockton. We had proper crime there."

"Don't murders count as crime?"

"Victoria, honestly! There's no proof—no indication, even—that either Mausz or Ness was murdered. The only crime that was committed was your underground friend moving the body. Nothing else."

Victoria pulled down the visor to check the angle of her cap in the small mirror before she responded. "You can't deny that Tom More attempted to kill Mr. Kirschmeyer."

"For a murder attempt, that was pretty feeble. Kirschmeyer didn't even press charges."

"Which leaves Tom More free to kill again."

"Be careful who you say that to, Victoria. That could be libelous." Casey looked in the rear view mirror and turned onto Old County Road. "Ness's death appears to be an accident, pure and simple, even though I know you'd like it to be murder. And Mausz's death—well, it could have happened the way Tom More said. Mausz and his wife argued, she left him to go off to Aruba with his girlfriend, and he fell and hit his head on the stone wall. There's no way we can prove otherwise."

"That's what Tom More wants us to believe," Victoria said stubbornly, and changed the subject. "I suppose we have to respond to Mr. Ferro's stolen car complaint as if the car really has been stolen, don't we?"

"If I were to ignore the complaint and tell him his car will show up where he left it, that'll be the one time somebody does steal it. He really shouldn't be driving still."

"Humpf," said Victoria.

"You wouldn't be riding with me if you hadn't given up your license, Victoria."

Victoria rolled down her window and looked out.

"You know, don't you, they're releasing Tom More today?"

Victoria turned. "How can they possibly?"

"I told you—Kirschmeyer won't press charges," Casey said. "You can't lock up somebody just because you think he's a killer."

"He *is* a killer."

"Victoria, I swear, one of these days I'm going to ask the selectmen to send you to police school."

"When?" asked Victoria.

Casey turned onto the dirt road where Mr. Ferro lived. "I'd tell you to go find the proof, but you probably would."

"It's outrageous," Victoria said. "With Tom More out of jail, Kirschmeyer is now in danger. Kirschmeyer can't defend himself. He should be in bed still." Victoria studied Casey. "He did go to you with what he found out about Tom More, didn't he?"

Casey shook her head.

"I told him to."

"Well, he didn't."

"I suppose I should let him tell you." Victoria thought for a moment. "Tom More's real name is Ted Moskovitz. Kirschmeyer traced him back more than twenty years and found he'd absconded with two-hundred-thousand dollars he took from an architectural firm in New Hampshire."

"Yeah?"

Victoria told Casey what she'd learned from Kirschmeyer. When she finished she said, "I wonder why Kirschmeyer's not pressing charges against him?"

"Who knows?" Casey responded. "You were the only witness to the nail gun incident. Do you have any idea who made the first move? Did Kirschmeyer threaten More with something? What he'd found out about him maybe?"

"Ahhh!" said Victoria.

Casey slowed to go around some deep ruts in the road. "Sounds as if he did. Blackmail, maybe?"

"Something like that," Victoria said.

They bounced along for another quarter-mile before they came to Mr. Ferro's house, a shingled one-story Cape with plastic deer in front of the door.

"I wouldn't think he'd need the statues," Victoria said. "There are plenty of real deer about."

"If it were anybody but Mr. Ferro, I'd think he was using these as decoys. He wouldn't be the only one planning on a venison stew," Casey said.

Mr. Ferro, a slight, dark man with wispy white hair, was waiting for them at the end of his driveway. He was wearing a sagging yellow cardigan and worn leather bedroom slippers.

"They must have come while I was taking a nap," Mr. Ferro said when Casey got out of the Bronco with her clipboard.

"When did you last use the car, Mr. Ferro?" Casey asked.

"This morning. I went to Alley's to pick up the paper."

"Did you drive it home, sir?"

"I'm sure I did."

"Did you meet anyone at the store you knew, sir?" Casey asked.

"Yes, that woman who works at tribal headquarters in Gay Head."

"You mean Aquinnah," Casey said.

"Sarah something."

"Right," said Casey. "Did you leave the keys in the car, sir?"

"Of course," he said indignantly. "I was only in the store a few minutes."

Casey sighed. "Why don't you come with me, sir. We'll take a look around before I report it stolen."

Mr. Ferro shoved his hands deep into the pockets of his sweater. "Time is of the essence."

"Yes, sir," said Casey.

"You haven't left something on the stove, have you?" Victoria called out from the front seat.

"Yes. Thanks for reminding me." He held up a finger. "I'm heating up a cup of coffee. I'll be right out."

"You'd better change your shoes, while you're at it."

While Mr. Ferro was shuffling back to his house, Casey said, "What do you bet Sarah brought him home, and his car's in Alley's parking lot? With the key in the ignition."

"No bet," said Victoria.

Kirschmeyer was getting ready to leave when Victoria came home later that afternoon. He was wearing his leather jacket and was jingling the keys to the Citation.

"They're letting Tom More out of jail today," Victoria said. "You've got to watch out for him."

"Thanks to you, he can't get around too good, himself, Mrs. T," Kirschmeyer responded.

Victoria took off her coat and laid it over the back of a kitchen chair. "He's probably planning to make you victim number four."

"I'm not worried," Kirschmeyer said, moving toward the door. "I'm off to see Mickey Mausz's widow now. You need anything at the Edgartown A&P while I'm in town?"

"No thank you," said Victoria. "What are you seeing Minerva about?"

"Tying up some loose ends," Kirschmeyer said vaguely.

Victoria sat down heavily. "Surely you're not trying to sell information to her, are you?"

"Who, me?" Kirschmeyer slapped his hand on his chest, and coughed.

"You're still not back to normal," Victoria said. "You've got to take it easy."

"I'm only visiting that nice refined widow. I don't expect any gymnastics, Mrs. T." He leered. "I'm sure she'll behave herself."

"That's not what I meant," Victoria said.

After Kirschmeyer left, Victoria puttered about the kitchen. She emptied the dishwasher and put the cups away. She kept thinking about Kirschmeyer. He was not as strong as he pretended to be. If only she were still driving she could follow him to Minerva's, or wherever he was going, make sure he was all right.

She thought, too, about Tom More being released from jail this afternoon. The jail was in Edgartown, only two streets from Minerva's. It was quite likely that Tom More and Kirschmeyer would run into each other. Victoria thought some more. She had seen Minerva's car near the senior center during one of Tom's Cranberry Fields meetings. Suppose Tom should decide to visit her when he was released from jail. Suppose he should run into Kirschmeyer.

Victoria dropped the dishtowel she had been holding on

the countertop and called Casey. "Do you remember telling me—when you took my license away—that you'd drive me wherever I wanted to go if I asked?"

Casey said, "Yeah?" with more than a touch of suspicion.

"I need to go to Edgartown," Victoria said. "To see Minerva Peabody. Will you take me?"

Casey hesitated.

"If not, I can always hitchhike," Victoria said.

"Okay, Victoria. Give me about ten minutes to finish up here, and I'll be by."

Victoria paced the kitchen. Should she take a weapon of some kind to defend Kirschmeyer against Tom More? Her lilac-wood walking stick would do. It was tough. And not likely to look suspicious.

When Casey came to the door, Victoria was ready.

"How long do you expect to be?" Casey asked.

"I don't know," Victoria replied. "Do you have your handcuffs and gun with you?"

"For crying out loud, Victoria. I suppose you're planning on having me arrest Tom More, aren't you?"

"Yes," said Victoria.

The road to Edgartown had been an Indian trail originally. It ran in a straight east-west line from Edgartown to West Tisbury, across the glacial outwash plain, dipping into sudden valleys that hid oncoming cars. When Victoria was a girl, she had gone with her grandparents and aunt in the horse and wagon to pick blueberries on the great plains. The road ended at Main Street. The white clapboard building that faced them was the jail. Between the jail's front door and the brick sidewalk was a white picket fence, festooned with neatly pruned climbing roses, almost in leaf in the mild spring weather.

Casey slowed before she turned onto Main Street. "There's your car, Victoria. In front of the courthouse."

Victoria stared at it. "Anyone leaving jail will see it."

"It's distinctive, that's for sure." Casey glanced at Victoria. "All those dings and dents."

"Mr. Kirschmeyer must be at Minerva's already. What time was Tom More going to be released?"

Casey looked at her watch. "About three-quarters of an hour ago."

Victoria straightened her cap. "We've got to hurry."

"I agreed to drive you here, Victoria, but not in an official capacity. If you need help from the police, I'll call the Edgartown cops for you. This isn't my jurisdiction."

Victoria ignored her. "We'll need to be surreptitious. I'll go in the front door, you go around to the back."

"No way. Absolutely not. As a police officer, I can't simply walk into somebody's house without an invitation. Or probable cause."

"There's plenty of probable cause," Victoria said. "If you won't do it, I will. You wait in the car."

Casey sighed. "I'm calling the Edgartown chief to let him know what you're doing. And take off your cap. This is *not* official police business."

Victoria twitched off her baseball cap and flung it onto the seat. Her hair stood up in white feathery tufts where the cap had been. She slammed the door of the Bronco, and marched down the driveway to the right of the house, swinging her lilac stick in front of her.

"Hey, Victoria," Casey called softly. "Where are you going?"

Victoria called back, "This is no longer your business." In a few moments she heard Casey's voice on the radio, and smiled to herself.

Victoria knew Minerva's house well. One of Victoria's sisters had owned it years ago, long before Minerva had bought it. Minerva had modernized the house and had added a solarium that overlooked the harbor. Victoria marched up the back steps and opened the door that led into what used to

245

be her sister's kitchen. The kitchen no longer had her sister's comfortable clutter. It was as immaculate as an operating room, and looked like something out of a fashion magazine, dazzling white with stainless steel appliances on spotless counters. She shook her head and went slowly toward the dining room that opened off the kitchen.

After the bright kitchen, the dining room was dark. Victoria heard raised voices coming from the front of the house, but the door between the dining room and the parlor was closed and she couldn't distinguish words. She could tell only that a man's voice was shouting angrily and a woman's was responding softly. Victoria tiptoed uncomfortably, her arched-up toe rubbing painfully against her shoe, until she realized the two people were so intent on their argument, they would never notice her footsteps. She needed to size up the situation, and she needed to conserve energy for whatever was going to happen next. She grasped her walking stick firmly and edged around the dining room table, sliding one foot after the other. Her eyes had not adjusted to the gloom. To give herself support, she trailed her hand along the backs of the chairs drawn up to the table. As she got closer to the parlor she could make out distinct words. Not enough to understand what was being said, but enough to give the impression of fear and anger. Victoria could smell fear around her, a rusty metallic scent that permeated the dining room. The woman sounded like Minerva, the man like Kirschmeyer. If so, where was Tom More? Perhaps she was mistaken. Perhaps he had not come here after all. Casey was calling in the Edgartown police, and this might be a false alarm. However, the voices sounded nasty enough.

Victoria paused, her hand on the last side chair. She had to make a decision, and make it quickly. She could see a crack of light showing around the edges of the closed parlor door. The scent of fear was strong, as if it were here, in the dining room.

She slid one foot forward, then another. Suddenly, her foot rammed into something soft and bulky on the floor, and, startled, she cried out. She put her hand up to her mouth, too late to muffle the sound. The voices in the other room stopped. Victoria stood still, her heart pounding.

"What was that?" the woman said.

Victoria couldn't hear the response.

Then Kirschmeyer shouted, clearly, "What in hell are you doing, lady? Put that down!"

Victoria skirted the mound on the floor, barely registering the fact that it was the size and shape of a person. She hustled to the parlor door and wrenched it open. The sudden light was so brilliant it made the parlor seem like a stage. Kirschmeyer had both arms over his head.

"Hey, cut it out! Put it down!" he shouted.

Minerva turned when Victoria burst through the door and faced her. She was holding a large polished brass candlestick by its stem. Minerva's face was white, despite her tan. Victoria noticed in that brief second how her freckles contrasted with her pallor.

"Leave her alone, Mr. Kirschmeyer!" Victoria ordered.

Minerva laughed.

"She's trying to kill me," Kirschmeyer blurted out.

Victoria turned to Minerva. "Put the candlestick down. You're safe, now."

"Safe!" shouted Kirschmeyer. "*She's* safe?"

Minerva laughed again.

Victoria, leaning heavily on her stick, walked quickly between the two into the front hall and flung open the front door. "Police!" she called out loudly. "Police!"

"I hear you, Victoria." Casey was standing on the brick sidewalk in front of the house. "The Edgartown cops are here." A police car had stopped in the middle of South Water Street, its blue lights rotating.

Victoria reached into her pocket for a napkin and wiped

her forehead. "I believe we may be too late," she told Casey.

Casey turned to the two patrolmen, one a tall, lanky blond, the other a much shorter black woman. "It's your turf, fellows." She hitched up her belt and followed the two into the house.

Minerva had collapsed into a chair. She was still holding the candlestick, which dangled from one hand. Her left elbow was on the chair arm, her forehead rested on the back of her wrist.

Kirschmeyer stood where Victoria had first seen him. He was sweating profusely, and his breath came out in a wheeze.

Casey looked from Kirschmeyer to Minerva to Victoria. "Okay, Victoria. What's up?"

Victoria leaned on her stick. "I believe you'll find Tom More in the dining room," she said.

CHAPTER 21

"There's a body in there," Victoria said, pointing to the closed door. The three police officers fanned out, Casey circled behind Kirschmeyer, the female Edgartown officer behind Minerva, and the blond officer stood to one side of the dining room door and flung it open. He came out immediately.

"Barbara," he said to the woman officer, "I want you here in the parlor. Chief O'Neill, come in here."

Casey glanced around at the four in the parlor before she followed. Minerva still held the candlestick. Kirschmeyer stood in the center of the room, sweating profusely, and Victoria stood between them, her back to Kirschmeyer. Barbara stood to one side, watching all three, her right hand touching the gun at her belt.

Victoria glanced behind her at Kirschmeyer, who was having a coughing fit. He pointed to the candlestick Minerva was holding. "She clobbered him with that. She must have. She was about to clobber me, too."

Victoria looked back at Minerva. "Was he threatening you?" she asked.

Minerva laughed.

"Jesus! She was threatening me," Kirschmeyer said, and coughed again. "You got here in the nick of time again Mrs. T." He coughed.

Victoria stared at him for a moment, then said, "You'd better sit down, er, Studs."

Minerva laughed again. "Really, this whole thing is just

249

too ridiculous. I can imagine what the neighbors are thinking."

"I suppose Tom More pushed you too far, didn't he, Minerva," Victoria said. "How sad."

Minerva began to talk. "I must say, Mrs. Trumbull, you're the only person on this entire Island who seems to have any concept of reality." Minerva leaned her back against the chair and closed her eyes. "None of them would be dead today if it weren't for their own behavior. In every case, it was their own fault." She looked up at Victoria, who was leaning on her lilac-wood stick. "I certainly didn't plan to kill any of them."

At that, Victoria glanced around at Kirschmeyer, who had collapsed onto a footstool, his head down, holding his hands between his knees.

The dining room door opened, and Casey looked in.

"I think we need Officer Barbara to take Minerva's statement," Victoria said. "I don't believe I'm qualified." She smoothed her hair, tousled where she usually wore her blue cap.

"No, no, I insist on talking to you, Mrs. Trumbull," Minerva said. "I refuse to talk to a policeman. You are more my sort of person."

The Edgartown police officer, who was standing behind Casey, stepped forward. "You have a right to have your attorney present, Mrs. Mausz," he said formally.

Minerva turned to Victoria. "Tell him it's Peabody. Minerva Peabody. I don't go by Mausz."

The police officer said, "Yes, ma'am."

Minerva waved dismissively. "I'm fully aware of my rights, Mrs. Trumbull. My husband was a lawyer, after all. The officer has my permission to take notes, if she must, but I don't intend to speak to anyone but you."

Minerva was still holding the candlestick. The square base

was blotched with a gummy substance. Tom More's blood, Victoria thought.

The blond officer spoke to his partner. "Put the candlestick in an evidence bag, Barbara, and label it."

"Of course, certainly," said Minerva, holding the candlestick out to Victoria, who backed away with her hands behind her. "Evidence. Sorry about that."

The officer, Barbara, tugged a plastic bag out of an inside pocket of her uniform jacket and slipped on surgical gloves.

Barbara's boss moved back into the dining room and shut the door quietly.

Minerva started to say something but interrupted herself. "I'm forgetting my manners, Mrs. Trumbull. Won't you sit down?" She half rose, then sat again with a sigh.

Victoria turned to see what Barbara was doing. The officer was standing between the two front windows, writing in a small notebook. Victoria moved a parlor chair closer to Minerva and sat down, holding her stick in front of her.

Minerva sighed again and leaned back. "Actually, they made me kill them. All three of them." She paused for several moments. Victoria waited. "Mickey was playing one person against another. He was utterly amoral. On the land transaction alone, he was acting for Mrs. Eldredge the seller, for Harry Ness the purchaser, and for Tom More, who hoped to obtain it somehow from Harry. I believe he was working for the doctors on their golf course plan as well."

She stopped to take a breath. In the distance a song sparrow sang, the first Victoria had heard this spring. A car passed in front of the house.

Victoria swallowed. Her eyes felt raw and scratchy. She asked Minerva, "Why did you kill your husband?"

"It was entirely fortuitous, Mrs. Trumbull. I didn't intend to kill him on the Sachem's Rock property. I'd been asking him repeatedly for a divorce and he refused."

Victoria was not sure how to respond. She nodded, and looked down at her toe, which protruded from the cut-out in her shoe. Her toe throbbed.

Minerva paused. "I suppose that's not entirely right. He didn't refuse. He demanded that I settle a rather large amount of money on him before he would agree to a divorce." She gazed at Victoria, who had looked up, her eyes hooded. "I suppose you know Mickey had no money. The money's mine. I was *damned*"—for the first time Minerva was animated—"I was *damned*," she repeated, "if I was going to settle *my* money on *him*. A womanizer, that's all he was. And not terribly successful at womanizing, either." Minerva's face flushed.

Victoria looked away again.

Minerva went on. "So for some time I had been thinking how to get rid of him. I didn't really intend to kill him at first. And it never occurred to me that Sachem's Rock might be the ideal place. Ironic, isn't it?" Minerva smiled. "Mickey, Tom, and I drove to the property. Once we got there, one thing led to another. I told Mickey what I thought about his ethics. Rather, his lack of ethics. With respect to legal matters, that is. I said I intended to inform the Board of Bar Overseers—not that I expected that to do any good." Minerva gave a slight shrug. Victoria listened without interrupting. She could hear Barbara writing. "That got to him. Not the threat of divorce, but his exposure to his legal colleagues. He got quite belligerent."

Victoria tried to shift to a more comfortable position in the lumpy parlor chair. "I can imagine how upsetting that must have been. Did he threaten you?"

"He was verbally abusive," Minerva replied. "He called me some ungentlemanly names. He was quite beside himself about the ethics question." She looked toward the front windows. The sunlight had lighted up the tree in front of her house. "He denied he was acting unethically. At that point I

252

told him not to bother to come home." She indicated the wide, painted floorboards. "Here, that is. I own the house. I bought it, but it was his home as well."

Victoria heard the scratch of the police officer's pen on her notebook. She could hear movement behind the door to the dining room. "What did your husband say to that?"

"He laughed. He said he wasn't planning on coming home anyway—he said 'home' with a kind of sneer. That was when he told me he was going to Aruba. With the woman he'd been seeing."

"I don't blame you for feeling humiliated. Had you known about this other woman?" Victoria asked.

The sunlight had moved to Minerva's face, and she shifted slightly. "Mickey was never what you'd call faithful. I accepted that, as long as he was discreet about his affairs. I had my own life, after all, and my life involved less and less of Montgomery Mausz."

Victoria tried again to get comfortable in her chair. "This must be difficult for you to talk about."

"Not any longer, Mrs. Trumbull."

Victoria waited. Behind her Kirschmeyer blew his nose.

Minerva continued. "Then, I'm sorry to say, I raised my voice and we got into a shoving match. I knocked him down, stunned him." She seemed to think Victoria needed an explanation. "I've studied defensive maneuvers at the women's support group."

Victoria nodded. "Is that when you left him?"

"No, I'm afraid not. He'd fallen near a stone wall, and I picked up a large rock and smashed him on the side of his head. I was angry. As I'm sure you can see, I was justifiably angry."

Victoria felt her stomach rumble. She held her stick tightly. "Did you go back to the car then?"

"Yes." Minerva moistened her finger and rubbed at a spot on her tan slacks. "Originally I had planned to drive there with Tom, who wanted to look over the property for his Cranberry Fields development. It was he who invited Mickey to come with us, thinking, apparently, that Mickey had agreed to represent him. When Mickey and I started to argue, we walked up the hill to have some privacy, and Tom stayed with the car."

Victoria's mouth was dry. She wanted to be back in the police Bronco pointing out new spring growth to Casey. When Minerva didn't say anything more, Victoria asked, "As I recall, that was during that spell of awfully cold weather, wasn't it?"

"That's right. In fact, it was snowing. I was dressed for the cold, but Mickey wasn't. He was wearing only a heavy wool shirt. He was so intent on arguing, he never noticed the cold or the snow."

"After you hit him with the rock and returned to the car, did you tell Tom what had happened?"

"Well, I wasn't entirely candid with Tom, Mrs. Trumbull. I told him that Mickey had hit his head, which was technically true. I let Tom believe that I was upset at Mickey's womanizing and that I'd decided to let him find his way home alone."

Victoria shifted again in the uncomfortable chair. "Apparently Tom was convinced," she said. She heard voices in the dining room and wondered what Casey and the Edgartown officer were doing with Tom's body. The song sparrow called again. "Was it necessary to kill Harry Ness? Had he done something to you?"

"You knew I killed him, didn't you, Mrs. Trumbull?" Minerva laughed again. "Everyone else was calling that an accident, but you knew. Good old Harry. He told me over and over again, 'If it weren't for Mickey, I'd leave Crystal for you, just like that.' " She snapped her manicured fingers together. "That sweet Mormon showgirl of his. Harry and I had been seeing one another for well over a year."

Victoria looked back at Kirschmeyer, who hadn't moved. He was leaning forward on the footstool, his hands still between his knees.

"Crystal had no idea," Minerva continued. "Harry told me his wife didn't understand him. Crystal hadn't grown with him, he said. He told me over and over how much he appreciated my sensitivity." Minerva's face twisted in a pained expression. "He was so sincere. I believed him. We had our trysts at the gunning camp on the Pond, a place that Harry and I loved."

Victoria nodded. She, too, knew the Pond.

"Crystal didn't care for roughing it, Harry had told me. We would go out in his boat, eat oysters that we fished from the Pond, and spend idyllic hours together. Sometimes I'd have a glass of sherry. Harry didn't drink." Minerva looked down at the floor.

Victoria waited for Minerva to continue, and when she didn't, asked softly, "What happened that day?"

"It never occurred to me that Harry intended to stay with his wife. Never. We had such a wonderful relationship, both physically and intellectually. If it weren't for Mickey . . ." She rubbed at the speck on her lap. "Both Harry and I had discussed what our life would be like if I were free of Mickey."

Victoria ran a gnarled finger across her forehead, lifting her hair away from her scratchy eyes. She had to keep Minerva talking, she told herself. Behind her, the police officer rustled a page in her notebook and then was silent. Victoria swallowed. "Did Harry ever suggest killing Mickey?"

"No, of course not, Mrs. Trumbull." Minerva sounded appalled. "Harry assumed Mickey would eventually go along with the divorce. As did I." Minerva reached for a tissue from a box on the small table next to her and blotted her eyes, which had begun to tear. "But then, once I got rid of Mickey, what do you suppose happened?" She gestured toward herself. "Harry dumped me. That's what he was telling me that last day. We were out on the Pond. It was quite warm for this time of year. There was no wind, and the sky was that brilliant spring blue that artists love. The water was only about three feet deep where we were, so we could reach the oysters from the boat with a rake. I had no idea what he had in mind. Dumping me, that's what it was."

Victoria steadied herself on the chair and waited.

Minerva blotted her eyes again. "After dull years of being married to Mickey, it was exciting to be with Harry Ness. He was so brilliant. So sure of himself."

Victoria nodded.

"We were out in the boat when he told me that it was over. Just like that. He said, and I remember his exact words. 'Minerva, my owl,' " she looked at Victoria. "That's what he called me, his wise owl. You know the owl was Minerva's bird, don't you?"

"Yes."

"He said, 'Minerva, my owl, our fling has been wonderful. Right away I assumed he was telling me he was leaving Crystal for me. I put my arms around him and said, 'It will be marvelous to make it permanent, won't it, darling?' He said, and I will never forget how he looked, 'I'm afraid that's not what I meant. It's over, Minerva.' I felt the blood drain out of my face. 'You'd better sit down, Owl,' he said, looking concerned. 'I didn't mean to shock you. I assumed we both knew this wasn't permanent.' I sat down on the thwart suddenly, and the boat rocked. 'That's not so,' I said. 'You said . . . At that he got quite cross. 'Forget what I said.' He practically snarled at me. 'Things have changed. It's over.' I protested. 'But . . .' I said. 'It's over,' he said again. 'Get that into your head.' He'd never spoken so harshly to me before. I couldn't believe it was my Harry talking. I simply could not believe it." Minerva lifted her hands from the arms of the chair and dropped them again.

Victoria heard the officer behind her scribble. Another car

went by the house. A horn honked somewhere. The Chappaquiddick ferry whistled. Dust motes danced in the sunlight.

Victoria didn't know what to say. Behind her Kirschmeyer coughed and shifted his feet.

Minerva went on. "Then Harry said, 'Let's celebrate the good times we've had together, okay? A fond farewell. I have a bottle of champagne cooling back at the camp. Just for you, Owl.' That seemed like the ultimate insult. I was supposed to drink champagne all by myself to celebrate his dumping me? It was all planned, I realized. He turned his back to me to haul up the anchor, and I snapped. I grabbed a wrench from the toolbox he kept next to the console, and with all my strength I hit him on the left side of his head. Without a sound he slumped over the gunwale. I lifted up his feet and he slid overboard easily. He had been hauling up the anchor, and when he went over, he got tangled in the line as the anchor went down again."

"How did you get home?" Victoria asked softly.

"The boat was on the anchor, but it was a fairly long line. With one of the oars I paddled as close to shore as I could get, the length of the line. Then I waded ashore on Plum Bush Point. The water was only a couple of feet deep. I walked to where I'd left my car, drove home, and changed my clothes."

Victoria felt dizzy and nauseated. "And Tom More? What happened with Tom?" she asked in a thick voice.

"You knew the sort of person he was, didn't you, Mrs. Trumbull?" She glanced at Victoria, who was watching her through half-closed eyes. "He tried to extort money from me before Harry died. Once Harry was dead, he tried again."

Victoria was puzzled. "What was he blackmailing you for?"

"He knew about Harry and me, and was threatening to make a scene about our relationship. With Harry dead, it didn't matter. That's why it was so foolish of him."

Victoria thought for a moment. "Was that why you wanted the land so badly? To give to Tom?"

Minerva nodded. "It was worth it to me at the time in order to keep Harry's and my secret. I could afford the money and I was amused by Tom's project. Tom planned to set me up as an investor, so it wasn't as if I was simply paying blackmail money. I expected a return on my investment."

"So you agreed to help Tom acquire the property from Mr. Ness . . . ?"

"Yes. Harry didn't know I was behind Tom's bid to buy the property from him—and I certainly didn't want him to know."

"When I came in just now, I stumbled over the body in the dining room. It is Tom's, isn't it?"

Minerva nodded.

"Do you want to tell me how that happened?" Victoria asked.

"Tom came here, right from jail, and told me he had proof—I don't think he did—but he said he had proof that I had killed both my husband and Harry. He needed money, he said, to pay off his Cranberry Fields investors, and he wanted enough to leave the area and get a new start somewhere else."

"And then?"

"I laughed at him. I said Harry's wife had given the property to the Conservation Trust, so there was nothing I could do about that even if I wanted to. I asked him why he expected me to bail him out when it was he who stupidly gambled his investors' money away on those internet stocks."

Victoria watched the dust motes dance in the sunlight. "What did he say to that?"

"He said again that he had proof I'd killed both men. I told him that was impossible since, as I'd said, I didn't kill them. He couldn't have had proof. I knew I was safe. The police were calling Harry's death accidental, and they had decided to believe Tom's story about my leaving Mickey to find his own way home. I told Tom he'd made his own bed and . . . you know the rest of the saying."

"Yes," said Victoria. "Then what happened?"

"Tom got quite upset. He was stalking around the room, like the little banty rooster he is, pontificating about how he had enough information to send me to jail for years, if not for life, and it finally got to me."

"Oh?" said Victoria.

"He was pacing back and forth in the dining room like a little Napoleon in those high-heeled boots of his, and I simply lost control. I picked up one of the candlesticks from the table, and whacked him with it on the side of his head."

"You knew by then just where to hit, I suppose," Victoria said dryly.

"Just as he fell on the floor, someone knocked on the front door. I closed the door between the parlor and the dining room and answered."

"And it was Mr. Kirschmeyer."

Victoria looked around. At the sound of his name, Kirschmeyer had looked up.

"Yes. I couldn't believe it. That lowbrow," Minerva gestured toward Kirschmeyer, "had the audacity to ask me for money to cover up his findings about Tom's background and his suspicions about me." Minerva pointed to herself. "Me!" she said.

At this, Kirschmeyer spoke. "It wasn't to cover up nothing," he said. "I knew you and Loch Ness was close. He hadn't paid me. I figured you'd honor his commitments."

Victoria said, "I suppose that's when I appeared after stumbling over the body."

Minerva nodded. Everyone was quiet. Barbara, the police officer, had stopped writing.

The dining room door opened and Casey looked in. "Are

you finished, Victoria?" She and the other Edgartown officer came into the parlor, both wearing surgical gloves.

"The ambulance should be here momentarily," Casey said. "Officer Murray here called for it. The emergency room is standing by. Both Doc Erickson and Doc Jeffers were there."

"Is Tom still alive?" Victoria asked.

Minerva let out a shriek and stood abruptly.

Casey shrugged. "Barely. I'm staying with him until they get here." She started back to the dining room, then turned. "Here's your cap, Victoria." She took the crumpled baseball cap out of her pocket and handed it to Victoria. Victoria smoothed out the wrinkles, and put it on. Sunlight glinted on the gold stitching, "West Tisbury Police, Deputy."